PLAZA
MAYOR

CATEDRAL
NUEVA

HUBER HILL

AND THE

Brotherhood

OF CORONADO

Praise for *Huber Hill and the Brotherhood of Coronado*

"*Brotherhood of Coronado* is a wonderful mix of adventure, mystery, and humor."
—Obert Skye, international bestselling author,
Leven Thumps series

"*Brotherhood of Coronado* is a thrilling adventure."
—Frank Cole, bestselling author, Hashbrown Winters series
& *Guardians of the Hidden Scepter*

HUBER HILL

AND THE
Brotherhood
OF CORONADO

B. K. BOSTICK

Sweetwater Books
An imprint of Cedar Fort, Inc.
Springville, Utah

ISBN 13: 978-1-59955-981-0

Published by Sweetwater Books, an imprint of Cedar Fort, Inc.,
2373 W. 700 S., Springville, UT 84663

Distributed by Cedar Fort, Inc., www.cedarfort.com

LIBRARY OF CONGRESS CATALOGING-IN-PUBLICATION DATA

Bostick, B. K. (Bryan Keith), 1980- author.
Huber Hill and the Brotherhood of Coronado / B. K. Bostick.
    pages cm
Summary: When the Dead Man's Treasure is stolen, Huber and his gang convince their parents they are part of a special study-abroad program and travel to Salamanca, Spain, an old city full of even older secrets, where they are not the only ones looking for the treasure.
ISBN 978-1-59955-981-0
[1. Buried treasure--Fiction. 2. Salamanca (Spain)--Fiction. 3. Brotherhoods--Fiction. 4. Adventure and adventurers--Fiction.] I. Title.

PZ7.B649557Htm 2012
[Fic]--dc23

                                       2012025572

Cover design by Brian Halley
Cover illustration by Mark McKenna
Cover design © 2012 by Lyle Mortimer
Typeset and edited by Melissa J. Caldwell

Printed in the United States of America

10 9 8 7 6 5 4 3 2 1

To my son, Daniel Makana.
How wonderful life is now that you're in the world

PROLOGUE

MALIA STIRRED FROM A restless slumber within her dark, grimy cell. How long had she been in this place? Days? Weeks? Years? There existed no concept of time here. Was it day? Night? She had no way to tell. Squinting her eyes shut, Malia tried to remember her mother and father; her brothers and sisters. She tried to remember the color of sunset splashed across the vast New Mexican sky, the endless reds flowing across the Painted Cliffs of the Zuni mountains, and the amaranthine mesas of the reservation, or *rez* as she had called it. She'd been here so long, that those memories seemed to stem from an alternate reality—a different lifetime. The last thing she remembered from home was that night. As she did so often during the summertime, she'd climbed atop the mesa nearest her home to stargaze. For hours, she'd lain on her back, staring up into the vast

expanse of the universe when she noticed something—
a small, red dot on her arm. Seconds later, a feathered
plume was sticking out of it. She awoke sometime later,
bound in a seat within what had to be a boat of some
kind. She'd screamed for help above the noise of the boat's
engines, but no one had come.

She opened her eyes and saw only the charcoal-col-
ored walls of her cell that'd become her new home. The
sound of her metal chains rattled against the concrete
floor. As she'd done so many times before, she screamed.
"Help me! Somebody! Please!"

She knew it would do no good, but at least she was
doing something. It helped to hear her own voice.

"I'm here," a high-pitched voice whispered from the
darkness. A face suddenly materialized—a gleaming,
metallic face reflecting what little light the torches outside
the cell gave. The metal face wore a melancholy expression, as if it were about to shed tears. It was the same
face she'd first encountered inside the boat after transfer-
ring from the plane. She'd heard others refer to him as
El Rey Susurro. For weeks, she was seasick, confined to
a space no larger than a closet. The voyage overseas had
taken weeks, maybe months. This Susurro was the same
man who'd come to relentlessly torture her mind. The two
times she'd been allowed up on deck, she'd observed the
fancy yacht, full of men—sailors of some kind who wore
strange clothing and metal helmets. Gray-colored mesh
covered their faces. She remembered their whispers and

chuckles upon seeing her disheveled form. In their midst were always the men of her nightmares. Three men who wore silver masks along with the same shiny helmets as the goons. The leader carried an expression that was even and almost affable. The second wore a face that conveyed meanness and brutality. The final man wore the sad, silver mask. Before being returned to her confinement each time, she'd noticed something peculiar stored away in the bulkhead of the yacht: three massive chests brimming with gold. She'd overheard the sad one in the silver mask talking about it. He'd called it the long lost treasure of Coronado's defectors. Tesoro de something.

"Get away from me," she screamed at the man wearing the sad, silver mask.

"You called for help." His voice whispered, as if he were actually concerned for her welfare. "Are you ready to help us? You've been here so long . . . I'm sure you'd do anything to see home again . . . to see your family. All I ask is that you—"

"I'll never help you," she spat.

Susurro had visited her countless times, always trying to convince her to translate the tablet. Each time Malia refused, but she didn't know how much longer she could hold out. She knew the stakes and prayed her will would hold strong enough for the many months, perhaps years, ahead. It had been easier before Halcón escaped. The man had been imprisoned in the cell adjacent to hers. Their long conversations had carried her through difficult months. He'd told her of his plans of escape—and promised to come back for her. How long ago had it been? He was not coming back.

Susurro stood and walked further into the light, his red robe undulating behind him. His crown, or rather, the metallic sheen of his conquistador helmet, glimmered in the firelight from the corridor just outside the cell. He held up an envelope with his grimy fingernails.

"In this envelope, I have an airline ticket to America, to your home," his high, scratchy voice whispered. "The plane departs tomorrow night." He opened the envelope and showed her the ticket. "We have prepared a passport for you as well."

Susurro handed her the passport. The picture was hers, but she wasn't sure how they'd got it.

"Don't you want to see your family? Your father? Mother? Brothers and sisters? I'm sure they are worried for you. Last we checked, they still believe you ran away from home. Your picture is plastered on milk cartons all over the United States, but they will never find you."

Susurro then retrieved a thin, golden tablet from beneath his robe. She'd seen it countless times before. Malia eyed the glyphs and symbols only she could translate.

"Assist the Three Kings of the Brotherhood and you'll go home tomorrow night. You have my word."

"Home?" she said to herself. The concept of home had

seemed nearly implausible at this point. She looked up at Susurro with pleading eyes.

"*Mi amor*... it does no good to resist. You are not the only one able to read this language. There are others within your tribe ... perhaps within your own family who can help us. Tell us what it says and no harm will come to them or you, I promise. Do you really want to stay here any longer?" He pointed at the thick walls. "With or without you, the Brotherhood will prevail and eventually find what your people have concealed for so long—what *your people* hid from Coronado."

"I won't read it," Malia said, her voice wavering. "You're wasting your breath."

Susurro replaced the golden tablet within his cloak. He then bent down and stroked Malia's cheek with his overgrown, yellow fingernail. "*Mi amor.*" He cocked his head at her as if examining a small bug. "How does it make you feel? That your family's demise will be caused by your own stubbornness?"

"Get away from me, monster!" Malia breathed, straining to hold back tears.

Susurro came closer, until his metal mask was just inches from her face. "This will not be over soon, young one. I will come back tomorrow, and the next day, and the next. Now, rest." Susurro put his hand in his pocket and brought it back out clasped in a tight ball. He unclasped it in front of her face, extending his fingers, and revealed a tiny mound of white powder resting within his palm.

"No! Please! Don't make me sleep," she begged.

Through a small slit along the lip line in his metal mask, Susurro gently blew the powdery substance into Malia's face and stepped backward. *"Duérmete, mi amor . . .* sleep."

Chained to the wall, Malia couldn't escape. She held her breath as long as she could, but eventually inhaled some of the cloud that had laced the air. Her lungs burned, and she coughed violently. Seconds later, drowsiness began to overtake her. Knowing what kind of terrible nightmares awaited her after inhaling the powder, she fought the sensation, but her body succumbed. Her eyes closed, and an image appeared in her mind: the silver, blurry face of the lesser of the three kings—*El Rey Susurro* . . . the Sandman King.

1

To: *huberhill47@gmail.com*
From: *yeseniaferrero@gmail.com*
Date: *September 17*
Subject: *Dead Man's Treasure*

Estimado Huber,

You do not know me, but my name is Yesenia Ferrero. I am resourceful and found your email. I am fourteen years old and live in Salamanca, Spain. My grandfather, Carlos Salazar, knew your grandfather, Nicholas Eldredge. Perhaps he told you about him? I know what evil you endured at the hands of his nephew Juan Hernán, and I hope you do not assign his attributes to my grandfather and I simply because we are related. I messaged you because my abuelo claims he knows who stole the treasure from Tesoro de los Muertos *and more important, he claims he can help you get it back and return it to its rightful place.*

Tú amiga estimada,

-Yesenia

To: yeseniaferrero@gmail.com

From: huberhill47@gmail.com

Date: September 18

Subject: Re: Dead Man's Treasure

Yesenia, I normally don't answer email from strangers. But how did you know all that stuff about me? How do you know about Dead Man's Treasure? And if you and your grandfather are who you say you are, then your grandfather should be dead. Juan Hernán Salazar said he killed him. You say your grandfather knows who took the treasure? How? And how can he possibly help get it back? And why would he care?

-Huber

To: huberhill47@gmail.com

From: yeseniaferrero@gmail.com

Date: September 19

Subject: Re:Re: Dead Man's Treasure

You are correct in that Juan Hernán did nearly kill my grandfather. However, he failed in his attempt.

Whether or not my grandfather's claims are valid, I cannot say. However, he is adamant that he does know who is responsible. My grandfather has considerable resources and wants to meet with you in person. In a few days, your Spanish teacher will announce an opportunity of a lifetime—an all expense paid, study abroad program in Salamanca, Spain, for three students from your school. The exchange will be three weeks in duration, more than enough time to find the Dead Man's Treasure. You will be required to write an essay for your application, persuading the ISAP (International Study Abroad Program) why you should be selected. You, your sister, and one other are free to enter this contest. I have a feeling you will all be selected.

Tú amiga estimada,

-*Yesenia*

To: yeseniaferrero@gmail.com
From: huberhill47@gmail.com
Date: September 25
Subject: Study Abroad Program
I talked it over with my sister and friend. We entered the contest.
-Huber

To: huberhill47@gmail.com
From: yeseniaferrero@gmail.com
Date: October 8
Subject: Re: Study Abroad Program
Congratulations! After a long and thorough evaluation of the many entries submitted, you, your sister, and friend have been selected for a prestigious scholarship to study abroad at Salamanca, Spain. Let's hope no one at the school looked too closely at your friend Scott's four-sentence submission. Your airline tickets and travel packets should arrive to the school shortly.
Your study abroad host (y amiga),
-Yesenia

To: yeseniaferrero@gmail.com
From: huberhill47@gmail.com
Date: October 12
Subject: A problem . . .
We received the packets and airline tickets today. Everyone in the school hates us and thinks we cheated (and they're right). But there's a bigger problem—my Spanish teacher, Señor Mendoza. He's insisting, and so are our parents, that he travel with us. He already has a substitute lined up and has paid for the trip out of his own pocket. What should we do?

To: huberhill47@gmail.com
From: yeseniaferrero@gmail.com
Date: October 13
Subject: Re: A problem . . .
My abuelo says we have no choice. We will reveal
the truth to him once he arrives with you. Travel safely,
Huber. I will see you soon.
Tú amiga estimada,
-Yesenia

● ● ●

From 34,000 feet in the air, Huber couldn't take his eyes off the LED screen attached to the back of the seat in front of him. Every few seconds, the graphic of the plane blipped infinitesimally closer toward its destination of Salamanca, Spain. Looking around, most people slept, read, or were calmly chatting. Didn't they know that in a second's notice, they could all plunge to their watery graves? That they'd be eaten by sharks? All it would take is a simple mechanical error or a pilot's mistake. What if a lightning strike tore them apart? He took a few breaths to calm down. Huber had always hated flying. The feeling of being trapped and placing his life in the hands of the pilots had always been too much. They'd been in the air for a total of thirteen hours, but it may as well have been thirteen days. After a brief layover in New York City at 5:00 a.m., Huber, Hannah, and Scott had switched planes.

Now, only six more hours until they reached Salamanca. He wished he'd brought more to do. Already, he'd read through the paperback novel his mom had packed for him. It was about a boy who traveled back in time over and over to stop the assassination of Abraham Lincoln. No matter what the boy did or how many times he tried, he couldn't change the outcome. Hannah, Scott, and Mr. Mendoza had slept most of the time, but Huber's head refused to stop spinning, thinking of what lay ahead.

On the way to New York, they'd all sat together. After switching planes, they'd been reassigned. Huber was now wedged between an old lady returning home to Spain and a college-age-looking guy with long, dreggy hair capped with a Rastafarian hat. His fingernails were almost longer than his hair. The guy reeked like dirty socks soaked in pickle juice. Huber had asked the white-haired lady if she'd switch him seats a few hours ago, but she simply shook her head and muttered something about not speaking English before turning her gaze toward the window. However, Huber had seen her steal a glance at the man sitting next to him and shake her head, disgusted. There was no way she was going to trade him seats. The old woman was now asleep. Her head kept swaying and falling on Huber's shoulder. A small dapple of saliva pooled on his shoulder. He had tried to nudge her toward the window a few times, but her head invariably found its way back to him like a magnet. Strangely, he didn't mind the woman near as much as his other neighbor. The guy's headphones constantly blasted some music that sounded like cows being tortured. Between the noise of the headphones and the pungent body odor radiating into his nostrils, Huber had no way of sleeping, even if he wanted to. The plane was overbooked, so of course Hannah had been bumped to first class. On her way up toward the realm of endless soft drinks, ample leg room, and cushy pillows, she gave her brother a smug look of satisfaction and crinkled her nose as she passed the malodorous man adjacent to the aisle. She mouthed, "Sorry." Inwardly, he knew she'd never been less sorry. He wondered what luxuries she was enjoying. Mr. Mendoza was somewhere far up ahead, out of sight.

Huber shifted upward and craned his neck back. Several rows behind, his eyes beheld Scott, perched between two beautiful, black-haired Spanish girls. They looked to be sixteen or seventeen years old. The girls were giggling and flirting with him, tussling his red hair as if they'd never seen such a thing before. As Huber made eye contact, Scott's eyebrows flittered up and down before he gave Huber a thumbs-up sign. Huber shook his head and sighed in frustration. He mouthed the words, "Trade me." Scott shook his head as if he hadn't understood and ignored him when he repeated the gesture.

"Hey bro, you look kinda young to be traveling by yourself overseas," the disheveled man said, suddenly taking notice of Huber.

Huber slumped back down into his seat and faced

the college guy. "I'm part of a study abroad program with my sister and friend. My Spanish teacher is here with us too." Huber's parents and Mr. McCormick had jumped at the idea of their kids taking part in the program. Their Spanish teacher, Mr. Mendoza, had made the whole school aware of the opportunity. Only three students would be awarded the scholarship for the study abroad program. Their room and board would be provided, paid for by the educational organization ISAP, the International Study Abroad Program. Once they arrived in Spain, an associate of the program would pick them up and take them to their host's home where they'd spend the next three weeks studying the Spanish culture.

Practically everyone taking Spanish applied, but only Huber, Hannah, and Scott had been selected for the trip. Huber swallowed the guilt that gurgled up each time he thought about the crestfallen expressions of those who hadn't been selected. Even more difficult were the constant accusations of cheating. Huber couldn't rightly explain how he, his sister, and friend had been the ones selected. He would've been suspicious too. Mr. Mendoza assumed that Hannah had written everyone's essays and made her promise she hadn't when he received the award letters. Reluctantly, he let the matter go. Strangely, their parents had seemed to harbor no doubts that their kids were the most brilliant in the school and now everyone knew it. The prospect of the trip had become more exciting as the date approached. Huber constantly reminded himself that he wasn't going on vacation—he was going to reclaim Dead Man's Treasure for those who had given their lives to protect it. It was the least he could do.

"Right on." The man nodded. "Always good to broaden your horizons and enhance your perspective," he replied pensively. "So, where you from, little bro?"

"Little town in Colorado."

"No way! I love Colorado. I once camped out in the Rockies for an entire month, man. I'm not kidding you. Lived completely off the land. You ever spent a month just living in nature, bro? Eating grubs and pine gum?"

"Umm, no. Can't say that I have."

"Really? I find that hard to believe. Well, you can't tell me that you've never been camping up there."

A wash of images flooded Huber's mind at the comment. It'd only been the beginning of last summer when he, Scott, and Hannah had found *Tesoro de los Muertos* or Dead Man's Treasure, the legendary repository for a vast Spanish treasure. His Grandpa Nick had left an old gold coin to him and his sister after he died—the same coin that Huber had massaged in his pocket all during the plane ride to help soothe him whenever the vessel shook. Grandpa Nick had also left an old map that directed them to the treasure. How could they have known that they were leading *him* right to it? Juan Hernán Salazar's wicked eyes flashed through his memory along with the image of the man and his brother being stopped in their tracks by Hawk, the guardian of Dead Man's Treasure, and his companions. Of course, it had all been in vain. Months ago, they'd all learned that the mine had been ransacked in the night. By whom, they had no clue. Hawk's dying words had been *"They took the treasure!"* The loss of the treasure coupled with the greater loss of their friend and savior was almost more than they all could bear. Huber still suffered nightmares several times a week.

"Yeah, I've camped up there before," he finally replied.

"Nothing like being one with nature, am I right? To feel the earth's breath flowing freely through your soul. You know what I'm talking about, don't you? I can tell. That's the problem with society—people don't get in touch with nature anymore."

Huber shifted uncomfortably in his seat as the man launched into a diatribe on modern society and all its ills. Huber had no idea what the guy was talking about. He used big words he'd never heard before. He nodded to be polite, but after awhile it was if the man forgot Huber was even there. He was just thrilled to have someone listening to him. Huber stared ahead at the screen. The plane's image seemed to be stuck in the same spot over the ocean.

"You a Deadhead, bro?"

Huber nodded absently as he had for the previous twenty minutes.

"I knew it! Yes!"

Huber now shook his head. "Wait, wait, wait. What'd you say? A what-head?"

The man laughed. "Come on now. Jerry Garcia? The

Grateful Dead? I knew you were a Deadhead the moment I saw you! Don't deny it. Here, listen to this. This is Jerry in his prime!" The man slipped his headphones over Huber's ears. A psychedelic guitar riff rocked his eardrums. Huber tried to peel off the headphones, but the man kept pushing them back on, forcing him to listen.

"Yeah, that's great. What's your name?" asked Huber, yanking off the headphones.

"Me? Oh, my parents named me Will. But I legally changed my name to Will-ow. You know, like a Weeping Willow Tree? 'Cuz I'm constantly weeping for all the ignoramuses within our society," the man answered, looking at Huber intently, waiting for him to acknowledge his depth and brilliance.

"Oh, okay. I'm Huber."

"Huber? What kind of name is that?" His shoulders bounced up and down as if he'd just heard a great joke. He started laughing so hard, a tear trickled down his face. "Well, it doesn't really matter. Names are just artificial labels anyway."

"Yeah, I guess it's not as common of a name as Will-ow."

"You crack me up, Huber! Huber! It just sounds so funny when you say it."

"Well, um, Willow, I think I'm going to get some shut eye for awhile. That way I'll be nice and rested when we land."

"Oh . . . yeah, bro. No worries. I hear you. You want

Jerry to put you to sleep? I always listen to the Grateful
Dead before I take a snooze. Relaxes me big time." The
man tried to slip the headphones over Huber's head again.

"No, no, that's all right." Huber pushed the headphones back. "I'll be fine on my own. Thanks though."

"What's mine is yours, bro. I mean we all share the
same air, the same water—why not the same headphones?"

"That's okay, really. It was nice to meet you." Huber
extended his right hand.

"What's that? A handshake. No man, we're brothers.
We *understand* one another. Brothers don't shake hands,
we hug."

The man wrapped his arms around Huber, forcing
his nose straight into his damp, foul smelling armpit,
the fountain of the man's peculiar funk. The stench was
nauseating. Huber forced himself free of the man's grasp,
rubbed his nose clean of Willow's musk, and edged himself closer to the old, snoring woman. Willow replaced his
headphones and cranked up the Grateful Dead. Huber
reclined his seat as far as it would go and laid his head
back. His eyes fluttered, then shut.

What felt like moments later, a loud *ping* over the
intercom awoke Huber from his fitful *siesta*. The fasten
seat belt sign illuminated overhead. Still half asleep,
Huber buckled himself in. The old lady's head was still
plastered to his shoulder. The seat on the other side of him
was empty. Where was Willow? Maybe he'd decided to
harangue someone else with his nonsensical ramblings.

Then Huber noticed something else across the aisle. Those seats were empty too. He scanned the rows ahead and behind him before a sickening realization hit him. Everyone was gone. The plane was empty. The only passengers were him and the old woman. He tried to undo his seat belt, but it wouldn't budge.

"Hey! Where'd everybody go?" he yelled, fiddling with his restraint. "Hey, my belt's stuck! I can't get it loose. Somebody?"

His voice echoed throughout the dark, empty cabin. The only sound was the gentle whirring of the engines outside. In front of him, the screen on the seat had turned to grey static. The woman next to him snored even louder, not even stirring at Huber's shouts. The blinking lights atop the plane's wings washed the cabin in an eerie red glow every few seconds. Huber's heart pounded in panic.

"Hello? Somebody, please help!"

A disconcerting silence pervaded the aisles. Huber forced himself to take deep breaths. Goose bumps sprouted all over his skin as the air turned frigid. He even wished for a moment that Willow was back. An image suddenly flickered on all of the screens attached to the seats. It was as if he were watching a black and white surveillance video. The scene was the entrance to Dead Man's Treasure—the skull. Loud footsteps sounded through the screen and rattled through his brain. A bell rang thirteen times and the mouth of the skull opened up. A darkened, blurry figure emerged from the skull's mouth and limped toward the screen. Huber wanted to close his eyes, but they refused. The figure moved closer. He wore a wide brimmed hat. Huber knew who it was. The figure looked up and stared into the camera before the blinking graphic of the plane returned. The image of the plane began to spin wildly as turbulence shook the aircraft violently. It felt as if the whole thing would break apart any moment. Oxygen masks dropped from above. Huber turned toward the old woman and shook her shoulders.

"Ma'am, wake up! The plane is breaking apart!"

The white haired head stirred. As it did, her hand shot across the seat and gripped Huber's forearm, holding him in place with unnatural strength. Huber's stomach dropped as a paralyzing fear shot through him. The tattered skin clinging to the bony arm displayed remnants of a snake tattoo wrapped around it. Huber turned and stared straight into Juan Hernán Salazar's necrotic, decomposed face. His good eye was gone, but the scarred blue eye glowed with an ethereal light. Patches of skin and sinew clung to his cheekbones. A deep, unearthly voice gurgled up from within and wheezed, "*Yoo-berrr!*"

Another ping sounded and Huber thrashed awake. The old lady next to him was still asleep like a baby. The small dribble of saliva was now a large puddle.

"Hey bro, you all right?" Willow asked.

Huber struggled to catch his breath. "Yeah . . . yeah, I'm okay."

"You must've been tripping big time, man. You were muttering all sorts of crazy stuff." He chuckled.

The captain's voice sounded overhead. "We will now make our final descent. It is currently 5:00 p.m. in Salamanca, Spain. We should hit the runway in just about ten minutes. I ask at this time that you buckle your safety restraints." Huber looked at the seat belt, hesitated for a moment, but then complied. The old lady awoke from her snooze and smacked her lips together. She smiled amiably at Huber but then realized she'd slobbered all over the poor boy. Her smile turned to mortification, "Oh my! I'm so sorry!"

"I thought you didn't speak English."

The woman shifted in her seat. "Well, I . . . ummm . . ."

"It's okay." Huber looked at Willow, then faced her again. "I understand." He wiped the spittle off his shoulder with a napkin. In the background, he heard Scott and the two Spanish girls laughing loudly at something. If the plane ride were any sign of things to come, this was going to be a long trip. Looking at the old woman, he forced a smile but couldn't contain his sigh. "*No problema.*"

2

"DANG, THAT WAS THE fastest trip of my life,"
Scott remarked to Huber as they disembarked the plane.
Hannah was already waiting for them in the terminal, her
face aglow with exuberance. "How was life in first class?"
Scott asked as they approached. "Think you're too good to
associate with lowly coach folks like us now?"

"Well, I thought that long before I moved up to first
class. But yes, I had a nice time."

"So what'd you do up there?" Huber asked.

"It really wasn't that cool."

"You can be honest."

"Okay . . . it was awesome! The flight attendant
brought me these hot towels to put over my face and as
much to eat and drink as I wanted. I must've had four
lime rickeys and ten packages of M&M's! For dinner, I
had this juicy steak with three jumbo shrimp. For dessert,

he brought me a sundae covered in hot fudge, caramel, and peanuts. Then he brought me a feather pillow and a down blanket while I watched three different movies that are still in the theaters! The seats reclined all the way back, so I fell asleep for the last one though. Slept like a rock! Sorry . . . guess I got a little carried away. How was the trip for you guys? I noticed you having a pretty good time, *Scotty*."

"Yeah, those two girls gave me their emails and told me to look 'em up while I'm here. They think I'm a real cowboy from out west."

Mr. Mendoza snuck up from behind and chuckled. "Nice one, McCormick. You best milk that cowboy bit for all its worth while we're here."

"Thanks, Mr. M. Not that I'm complainin' or nothin', but I still don't see why we need a chaperone on this trip. We ain't babies."

"Well, I know I probably cramp your style, but I'm sure your parents wouldn't like the idea of you all roaming the streets of Spain by yourselves. Besides, you think I would pass up the chance to skip school and come to Spain?"

They continued walking down the terminal toward the baggage claim. An associate of ISAP was supposed to meet them there, holding up a sign with their names.

"Cowboy . . . give me a break," Hannah muttered under her breath.

Shortly after the events of Dead Man's Treasure,

Hannah had told Scott that she thought it best they just be friends. She decided that she didn't want to be tied down or be romantically involved yet. Scott had disagreed, but her decision was final. Since then, Huber walked on eggshells whenever the two were together. At times, there still seemed to be some playful flirting between the two, but most of their interactions were laced with an underlying hostility.

"What? Jealous or somethin'?" Scott asked, raising an eyebrow. "You were the one who dropped me like a bad habit, remember?"

"Jealous?" She laughed. "They can have you all to themselves for all I care, cowboy. Although I wouldn't wish that misery on anyone."

"Can you two stop for five minutes? I've never had such a miserable experience during my whole life as that plane ride. The last thing I wanna hear is you two going at it," Huber said.

"What's the matter, brother? Didn't have a pleasant flight?"

"Yeah, what's the matter, Huber? Looked like you were hittin' it off with that hippie guy sittin' next to ya."

"Funny. Just never ask me for a favor again."

From across the way, they all heard a shout and turned toward the sound. Willow waved his arms wildly while surfing through a crowd of people. Cupping his hands around his mouth, he yelled out, "Hey, Huber! I'll never forget you, bro! Don't forget the wisdom I shared with you!"

Huber gave a haphazard wave back, then turned his face away. Scott and Hannah struggled to contain themselves. Mr. Mendoza laughed heartily.

"Looks like you made a new best friend, Huber," Hannah said.

"Yeah, way to go, *bro*," Scott chimed in. "I'm sorry, but come on, would ya've traded me seats if it were the other way around? Those girls next to me were smokin' hot."

"You're such a chauvinist." Hannah shook her head.

"What's that supposed to mean? A good lookin' guy, I assume. Thanks!"

"I wouldn't expect an illiterate 'cowboy' to know. Look it up."

"Ya think you're so much better than me, just 'cuz ya know what words mean?"

"Enough!" Huber said.

"Hey, she started it."

Minutes later they arrived at the baggage carousel and gathered their belongings. All around them people were speaking rapid Spanish. Exquisite art and tile work lined the walls. It was as if everything was modern but looked old at the same time. They were definitely a long way from Carbondale. Huber was a fish out of water. Scanning the crowd, Hannah sighted a scruffy looking man in a chauffeur hat holding up a sign with their names, *McCormick & Hill*. A young Spanish man and woman, looking to be near their age, stood adjacent to him.

"There's our ride! Let's go. Mr. Mendoza, do you know where we're going?"

"The organization set us up with a host. I'm not sure who it is."

The three trotted over toward the man. "We're McCormick and Hill." Hannah extended her hand. The man in the hat rolled his eyes and turned toward the door leading outside.

"This way."

"I am sorry," the young man apologized in a smooth voice as they bounded out the door and walked alongside a busy road. "Unfortunately, not everyone in *España* treats beautiful women with the manners they deserve. My name is Alejandro Luján and this is my cousin Yesenia Ferrero," he said, pointing to the young woman. "You will be staying with us and our grandfather here in Salamanca." The young man flashed his shiny dark eyes at Hannah. Half of his mouth curled up into a smile, revealing dazzling white teeth. A shock of dark hair fell just below his left eye.

"It's okay," she finally managed. "I'm—"

"Hannah. I know." He kissed one side of her face, then the other. Hannah's face turned scarlet. She raked her long hair behind her ear in an effort to avoid looking like some unkempt bumpkin. Before she could respond, Scott pushed his way between them.

"Name's McCormick, Scott McCormick," he said, trying to sound intimidating.

"Hey, *amigo. ¿Que tál?*"

"Huh?"

"*¿No te hablas español?*" He chuckled.

"Scott doesn't speak Spanish." Hannah pushed him aside. "You see, he's a *cowboy* from way out west and barely speaks English." She turned back to Scott. "He asked how you're doing."

"Oh. *Bueno*, I s'pose."

"*¿Un caballero?* Wow, I've never met a real American cowboy before!" the boy said as if he were meeting a celebrity. He then also kissed Scott on both sides of his face.

"Whoa, whoa, there! Yeah, nice to meetcha too, Rico. We don't do that kinda thing where I come from."

"You are a humorous one, cowboy!" He clapped Scott on the back and kissed both sides of his face again.

Mr. Mendoza introduced himself and repeated the custom with their two new acquaintances.

They all continued walking outside as the girl introduced herself. "I'm Yesenia. We are very excited to have you stay with us," she said never taking her eyes off Huber. He couldn't hold her gaze. Her thick, lustrous hair gleamed in the last rays of the sun's setting and bounced along her shoulders. Her eyes danced with an invigorating depth and playfulness. The smoothness of her olive skin brushed his arm, causing him to lose his breath. So this was the girl who had emailed him. "So, you are Señor Mendoza. And you Hannah, Scott . . . and you must be . . ."

"Puber," Scott said before Huber could answer.

"I do not understand. I thought your name was Huber."

"Shut up, Scott!" Huber elbowed him hard. "Huber. He meant to say *Huber.*"

"Oh, I see . . . Huber." She winked, then whispered, "So nice to finally meet you in person."

"How do ya say your name again?" Scott butted in.

"Jay-sane-ya. However, you may call me Jessie if you like."

"Nice to meet you, Jessie." Huber's voice shook as he extended a clammy hand.

"No, no, we do not shake hands in *España*, Huber." She leaned over and kissed one side of his cheek and then the other. He could feel the blood pumping through his face. He tried to say something but the words dived deep into his gut.

"Cat got your tongue, Huber?"

"No, I, uhh . . ." The words bubbled their way back up. "*Mucho gusto en conocerte,*" he answered in Spanish.

Yesenia's eyes widened in surprise. "*Encantada,*" she replied, brushing his forearm with her hand.

"Nice use of the verbiage, Hill." Mr. Mendoza smiled. "That was B-plus annunciation right there. Perhaps even A-minus material."

"Listen to me when I say it, Mr. Mendoza," Hannah interrupted and looked at Huber jealously. "I've been practicing—*Hola. ¿Como estás? Yo me llamo Hannah. Yo soy de America.*" She beamed proudly.

"Hannah, you're not getting graded on this trip. Don't worry about it."

She looked away disappointedly.

"However, compared to your brother, I'd have to say he's got a leg up on annunciation. That was probably B-minus, best."

Huber's lips parted like curtains in a Broadway theater. Maybe Spain wouldn't be so bad after all. The man led them to a mid-size car.

The driver pointed to Scott. "You, *caballero*, up front with me. The rest in back."

"What? Why me?"

"You are the biggest and take up the most room."

"You mean muscleiest, I assume. Must be the language barrier."

Huber scrunched next to Yesenia, and Hannah was shoulder to shoulder with Alejandro. For both of them, the jet lag was suddenly gone. As they departed the airport and rolled down the ancient streets, Huber felt captivated by his surroundings. He'd never seen such amazing architecture. Everything seemed to be made of orangish-red brick and stone, casting a warm, relaxing ambiance over the city. The last light of day glinted off towering steeples, spires, and cupolas that belonged to old, gigantic cathedrals and buildings. Ornate statuary and artistry decorated every corner.

"What do you think of Salamanca?" Yesenia asked.

"It's amazing," Huber answered. "I've never seen anything like it."

A smile lit up her eyes and she nodded.

Fifteen minutes later, they rolled to a stop along a narrow road just outside the city limits. It was close to dark now. The troupe exited the vehicle and unloaded their suitcases from the trunk and stood before a stone complex that looked hundreds of years old but still in fairly good shape.

"This is where we're staying?" Hannah said excitedly.

"Yes. This is where our grandfather lives," Alejandro replied.

"You didn't mention he was rich."

"*Abuelo* made a lot of money a few years ago."

"How?"

"He was poor almost all of his life with his business. Then things turned around when he sold the store and invested all of his money."

"Wow! What'd he invest it in?"

"Gold," she said flatly. "He did rather well. This estate is over four hundred years old."

"I'll get that." Scott wrenched Hannah's suitcase from Alejandro's hands.

"And since when are you such a gentleman?" Hannah shook her head.

"Well, when in Rome."

"No, no, cowboy, we are in Salamanca," Alejandro reminded him.

"It's a saying," Hannah explained. "It means when you're in Rome, you should do as the Romans do or, in this case, as the Spanish do—it means to adopt the customs of the place you're in. Apparently in America, boys don't possess chivalry like they do here."

"There she goes with them big words again." Scott sighed.

"Oh . . . yes." Alejandro laughed, understanding. "When in Rome."

They all entered the massive building and walked through the lush, verdant courtyard and up a set of stone steps toward a large wooden door. The face of a brass lion served as a knocker. Yesenia gripped the ring and rapped several times. "*¡Abuelo, somos nosotros!* We are here."

Seconds later, the massive door swung open to reveal an old man, dressed in jeans and a loose, long sleeved, white shirt. Wavy mounds of grayish white hair decorated his head along with a finely pointed goatee. Starry eyes greeted them beneath feather duster eyebrows. Holstered to his side was a small green canister attached to a cart that transported oxygen to his nose through a thin plastic tube.

"*Bienvenidos a mi hogar.* Welcome, young ones to my home. I am so happy to finally meet you. I am Carlos Salazar."

CHAPTER
· 3 ·

WITHIN THE WARM, RICHLY furnished apartment of Carlos Salazar, the group, scattered over sofas and chairs, listened transfixed as the old man told his story of the previous spring. At first, Huber wasn't sure of the old man. After all, this was Juan Hernán Salazar's uncle. But the friendliness and gaze of the man gave him the feeling he could be trusted and set Huber at ease. A large array of cuckoo clocks and weaponry adorned the walls. Over the mantel hung two rapiers crisscrossed over a wooden buckler shield. Emblazoned over the shield was the family's coat of arms: a knight's helmet with a feather sticking out of it and a red and white flag beneath it. Alejandro, Hannah, and Scott were seated on a sofa across from Huber. Mr. Mendoza sat in a chair opposite Carlos listening to the unbelievable story, his face impassive. Hannah was in the middle. The old man, Carlos, rested in a wicker rocking chair next to the fireplace.

Mr. Mendoza finally spoke up. "Please, Carlos, hold on for a second and tell me what's going on here," he said. "You all seem to know of one another."

"I'm afraid the study abroad program was a bit of a hoax." Carlos's eyebrows furrowed. "I was the one who sent out the mailers and applications to your school, Master Mendoza. I had hoped to bring Huber, Hannah, and Scott here *without* adult supervision."

"Sorry to ruin your plans," Mr. Mendoza said. "If you thought these kids were going to travel internationally by themselves, you're more naïve than I thought." He then looked at Huber, Scott, and Hannah. "I don't like this. We're going back home tomorrow."

"Please just listen to the story," Huber pleaded. "We can use your help, Mr. Mendoza. If you still want us to go home after you hear the whole story, we will."

"Señor Mendoza, please just hear Carlos out," Hannah pleaded.

They interpreted Mr. Mendoza's silence as indication that he would at least listen.

Yesenia emerged from the kitchen carrying a metal plate with an assortment of bite-size meats and cheeses. "*Tapas?*" She handed the plate to Scott.

"Whatas?"

"*Taw paws.* How do you say in America? Finger food?"

"Oh yeah, thanks," Huber said and sampled a piece

of beef. The juice and flavor burst in his mouth. It was delicious! He pilfered a few more before passing the plate across to Hannah, Scott, and Alejandro. Yesenia squeezed into the love seat next to Huber, their knees just touching. Huber's foot began to tap the floor involuntarily. He tried to focus on Carlos. For the past half hour, the old man had been spouting off the story of how his nephew Juan Hernán had almost killed him the previous spring.

The old man continued. "Luckily for me, the *médicos* arrived just in time. I was sure I was a dead man."

"Your nephew thought you were too," Huber said. "He pretty much told us he had killed you."

"Indeed, maybe he should have," Carlos breathed. "It's no less than I deserve."

Yesenia gasped. "Abuelo! Why would you say such a terrible thing?"

"Because I was the one who unleashed all this evil." He choked up.

"What do ya mean?" Scott asked, his mouth full of smoked cheese.

Carlos drew a long breath. "I was the one who told Juan Hernán where to find the map leading to *Tesoro de los Muertos.*"

An awkward silence fell over the room as the old man continued in a heavy voice. "My nephew, Juan Hernán, was a disturbed man. I took him in when he was just a boy and raised him the best I knew how. He was always obsessed with finding *Tesoro de los Muertos.* One summer,

I departed *España* in search of the place. Alejandro and Yesenia's parents were still young and in school. When I returned home from my quest empty-handed, Juan Hernán was furious. What's more, when he found out that I had given the map away to a stranger I'd met in the mountains, he was even more irate. As my nephew grew and eventually moved out, I did not hear from him for many years. Then last spring he returned and demanded to know who I had given the map to *Tesoro de los Muertos*. I refused to tell him, so he tortured me. At the time, I was ill with pneumonia and bedridden—on the verge of death itself. Still I refused . . . until he threatened the lives of my family." He pointed to Yesenia and Alejandro.

"So you told him about Grandpa Nick and the map?" Hannah said absently.

"To my everlasting shame—yes, I did. I am so sorry, *mi amor*. I did not know what to do. In desperate moments, a person will do anything to protect their loved ones. After I regained consciousness, I contacted your grandfather and warned him of my nephew's coming for the map. He assured me that Juan Hernán would not obtain it. He would keep it safe. As I pled for his forgiveness," Carlos's eyes moistened, "he told me not to blame myself . . . that he held no ill will."

Huber turned toward his sister. "That's why he left it to us."

"It is a regret that I shall carry with me to my grave, I fear. I know my apologies mean nothing."

"Why didn't you call the cops or something?"

"I tried. Believe me I tried. They dismissed my story as just that . . . a story."

"Why didn't they believe you?" Hannah asked.

Alejandro answered before his grandfather could, "At times Abuelo has been known to say and do things that, to others, appear strange."

"Strange?" Scott said. "What do ya mean by that, Rico?"

"Abuelo sometimes forgets who and where he is."

"Oh," Scott said. "He's got Old Timer's."

"It's Alzheimer's." Hannah rolled her eyes. "It's probably just better if you keep your mouth stuffed with food and don't talk the rest of the evening."

Alejandro continued. "Sometimes he puts on his nightgown, attaches his oxygen to his belt, and walks down the streets in the middle of the night fighting demons and dragons with his sword. In his younger days, Abuelo was a master fencer. He is not crazy though."

"Naw, don't sound crazy at all," Scott said, chomping away on an olive wrapped in bacon. "Some old geezer wanderin' down the street swingin' a sword around at demons."

Alejandro glowered at Scott. "Do not speak ill of Abuelo, cowboy," he said, defensive. "He is the smartest and bravest man in all of España. He is *not* crazy!"

"*Calmáte, mi nieto,*" the old man chastised his grandson.

"It's okay . . . I am a little crazy at times." He winked. "It happens as you get old timer's. I do confess that part of the reason you are here is so I can offer my apologies in person. However, as you know there is another reason I have brought you here . . . only the hearts of youth are pure and valorous. I brought you all here because I know something others don't." He eyed Mr. Mendoza suspiciously. "Something that others cannot know. A secret I can only entrust to you . . . I know who took the Dead Man's Treasure."

Huber, Hannah, and Scott all exchanged looks. Huber had been waiting to ask Carlos more questions. "How do you know that?"

"I have my sources."

"Wait a second," Mr. Mendoza said. "Are you all saying that you found the Dead Man's Treasure hidden in the mountains around Carbondale? That's just a local folktale. There's no truth to it."

"We found it over the summer," Huber said a bit too proudly.

Mr. Mendoza looked incredulous. "Forgive me if I'm a bit skeptical, Hill. People have been looking for the Dead Man's Treasure for over a hundred years. You expect me to believe the three of you actually located it?"

Huber took out his grandpa's gold piece from his pocket and handed it to Mr. Mendoza.

He eyed the thing, unable to believe what he was seeing. "Amazing! Where did you get this?" Mr. Mendoza asked, rotating the shiny coin within his fingers. "It has all the marks of eighteenth-century Spain."

"It's a piece from Dead Man's Treasure," Huber answered.

Reluctantly, Mr. Mendoza handed the coin back to Huber. "Honestly, I can't believe this . . . "

"Found it all right," Scott answered. "Only the mortality police over there wouldn't even let us take none of it home. Lotta good it did."

"Morality police," Hannah corrected him, sighing. "Not mortality police."

"What do you mean it didn't do any good?" Mr. Mendoza asked.

"The treasure was recently stolen," Carlos answered.

"Again, how do you know all this?" Hannah asked pointedly.

"It doesn't matter. What does matter is that I know who was behind it. That is why you are here. You must help me find the Dead Man's Treasure and return it back to where it belongs. It is the only way I can make amends for what I've done. Alejandro and Yesenia will aid us in our quest."

Hannah looked at the old man like he'd lost his marbles. "Okay, suppose we believe you are telling the truth. Who took the treasure?"

"You may really think me crazy after I tell you this, but it is true, you must believe me. I've been researching them for many years. Some say they are myth, but they most certainly are not! Members of this secret society are scattered all throughout España and the world for that matter, from businessmen to government."

Scott and Huber exchanged a concerned glance that seemed to ask what they'd gotten themselves into.

"They have one objective." The old man's eyes took on a faraway look. "To locate and retrieve all of Spain's lost fortunes and restore her to her former glory. They call themselves the Brotherhood of Coronado."

● ● ●

Outside in the courtyard, Huber looked at the sky, which was blanketed in stars. Although exhausted, he couldn't resist when Yesenia asked him to accompany her on a walk before they retired for the night. Scott and Alejandro were still inside, competing for Hannah's attention and eating *tapas*. Carlos and Mr. Mendoza had gone to bed shortly after their conversation and told them all to get a good night's rest. Mr. Mendoza had seemed upset but hadn't said whether or not they'd be returning home the next day. Meandering through the yard, off to their right, Yesenia pointed toward a stone bench next to a fountain, which babbled lazily. Verdant ferns and bushes surrounded the once ornate plaza. She followed and sat right next to him, even though there was plenty of space.

"So, Huber, what do you think of our España?"

His mouth was dry. "It's good," he choked. "You guys have . . . nice . . . air."

Yesenia laughed. "Yes, I suppose our air is good. Do you like . . . anything else?" She slid a bit closer.

Huber wavered. "Umm . . . those tapas were really tasty. Did you make those yourself?" His voice cracked.

"I did."

"Yep, very good stuff . . . thanks."

"*De nada. Es un placer.*" Her eyes danced. Huber knew she was enjoying making him squirm. "When I found out you were coming to stay with us, I got very excited. We've never had guests from America before."

"Tell me about your grandpa. Does he really roam the streets with a sword slaying demons?"

Yesenia laughed and slapped his shoulder. "Oh yes! One night, my mother found him in the city square, holding five policemen at bay with his sword while holding a kitten. He was convinced the men were vicious bears trying to devour a small child. You can imagine the reputation he has gained around here."

"So, do you think he's all there?"

"Most of the time he is. He goes in and out. Abuelo is really a genius and kindhearted. He's read thousands of books and sometimes those stories get mixed up with reality. He's just—have you ever read the story of Don Quixote?"

"Yeah, we read it in Spanish this year."

"Tell me. What did you think of the Man of La Mancha?"

"He cracked me up most of the time. Attacking windmills, thinking he's a knight saving beautiful women. I kinda felt sorry for him at times, but his heart was in the right place. He made people happy."

"Exactly! Abuelo is a bit like Don Quixote."

"So this whole thing about the Brotherhood of Coronado . . . do you think it's all just stuff he's read and mixed up?"

"Possibly. But he seems convinced that they are real, even in his most lucid moments."

"You'll have to forgive me if I have my doubts. But I still don't understand how he knows we found the treasure."

"That I do not know. He is secretive about some things. But he was right about that, wasn't he?"

"Yeah . . . he was. So what's the plan for tomorrow?"

"Abuelo says it's a surprise."

"Oh great. I can only imagine."

"Maybe he will take us on a quest to battle windmills." She laughed.

"Or to rescue some poor kid from demonic chickens!"

"Yes, parents must mind their children after dusk. Those evil chickens are very dangerous."

As they laughed, Yesenia placed her hand on Huber's knee. "I'm glad you are here in España, Huber."

Before he could respond, a figure rustled through the bushes behind them. Startled, they jumped to their feet and moved backward. Beneath a long night gown, Carlos was decorated haphazardly in leather armor, staring Huber down as if he were a monster. In his right hand, he brandished one of the swords from above the mantle. In his other, he held the wooden buckler. He brought the tip of the sword to Huber's chest. "You have chosen the wrong castle to attack this night, dragon fiend! How dare you assault this lovely maiden!"

Huber threw up his hands in terror and exclaimed, "I'm not a dragon. It's me! Huber? Remember?"

"Ahh, a clever trick. Just the thing a dragon would say!" Carlos raised the sword above his head.

"Abuelo! It's Yesenia!"

A look of vague familiarity registered within Carlos's eyes. Slowly, he dropped the sword to his side.

"Hand me the sword, Abuelo."

"Yesenia?" Confusion stretched the corners of his face.

"Yes, Abuelo, it's me."

"Huber?"

"Yes, sir." He nodded.

"What in the world are you two doing out here? Don't you know it is time for sleeping?"

"And is it not time for you as well?" Yesenia said stubbornly.

Carlos mumbled something incoherent before reason found its way back into his voice. "To bed. Both of you."

Huber and Yesenia strode past Carlos. As Huber brushed by the old man, Carlos clapped him on the shoulder. "I apologize, Huber. I hope I didn't scare you or say anything . . . strange."

"Not to worry."

Carlos nodded emphatically. "Okay then. We must get inside and get some rest. Tomorrow, we have a big day."

"What happens tomorrow?" Huber asked.

A look of stern resolution crossed Carlos's face and he raised his sword high in the air. "Tomorrow, we embark upon a noble quest," he said, his eyes taking on a starry look. "Many years hence, scholars and poets will likely speak of our deeds upon this adventure. Sonnets shall be written and songs shall be sung in our honor. What happens tomorrow, you ask? The beginning of a quest to right grievous wrongs . . . to execute justice upon the guilty . . . to remove foul abuses . . . to do our duty and obliterate the Brotherhood of Coronado! Are you with me?" He again pointed the sword at Huber.

Wide-eyed, Huber didn't know what to say. He looked at Yesenia who nodded at him. "Yeah, sure thing. See you in the morning." Huber nodded uncomfortably and made his way briskly toward the house with Yesenia. What had he gotten himself into?

THEY'D BEEN ROUSED AWAKE by the clanging
of pots and pans. Carlos had made them an exceptional
breakfast of Spanish omelets composed of fresh eggs,
cheese, and peppers. Shortly thereafter, the old man
whisked them all out the door and into separate taxis, and
soon they were navigating their way through the bustling
urban area of downtown Salamanca. The area was a hive
of activity. Vendors hawked their wares, elderly people
shuffled by with canes, and young adults chatted away
on their phones, oblivious to everyone around them. The
smells of bread and grilled meat hung heavy in the air.
Carlos had told them all they were going to see someone
important.

"Where are you takin' us, old man?" Scott finally
asked.

"Huh?" Carlos yelled over the din behind his shoulder.

"Where are we going?" Huber said more loudly.

"Pincho."

"Where?"

"Not where . . . who."

"Pincho's a person?" Hannah asked.

"Pincho is one of grandfather's friends," Alejandro answered. "It is his nickname. His actual name is Paco, but we call him Pincho."

"What's that mean?" Huber asked.

"Pincho means, how do you say . . . an appetizer in the taverns. He got the nickname because he is always in the bars snacking on them."

"Is he as crazy as your grandpa?" Scott said.

Alejandro's eyes smoldered. He opened his mouth to speak, but Jessie beat him to it. "Pincho is a fraud. *Un ladrón.* We are wasting our time," she said loudly so Carlos could hear.

"Eh?" he yelled. "Ah, here we are!" Carlos pointed to a rundown tavern, rotting away in the otherwise vibrant neighborhood. "Come along."

"You want us to go in there?" Huber asked.

"Yes, yes, it will be fine. Pincho will surely be within. He is the most honorable of men. Virtuous and above reproach!"

"I'm not allowing these kids inside a tavern," Mr. Mendoza said flatly.

"Relax, Master Mendoza," Carlos assured him. "There will be no trouble. We'll be in and out."

Mr. Mendoza hesitated. "Make it quick."

They filed inside the dank, smelly place. The tavern was dark and all but deserted. Even though it was morning, there were a couple of sad-looking men drinking at the bar.

"I don't like being in here. It feels . . . icky," Hannah said, eyeing her surroundings.

"Yes, I feel the same way whenever Abuelo drags me here to see Pincho," Alejandro agreed. "Hopefully this won't take long."

Carlos pointed to a squatty man slumped over a table in the corner. The table vibrated as he snored. "Ah, there he is! My trusted companion and friend." Carlos hastened over to Pincho and shook him. The man let out a few snorts but didn't stir. "Pincho!" Carlos yelled. The table kept vibrating. Carlos brought his fist down hard next to the man's head, rattling the half-drained bottle of beer. Instantly, his head snapped to as he gasped for air. Dried saliva and tomato juice clung to the man's sandpapery stubble. Pincho appeared confused, then suddenly aware.

"Heyyyy, Carlos," he slurred, almost stumbling as he arose from his seat. "My friend!"

"Pincho, my brother in arms. So good to see you again."

"Have you been drinking?" Alejandro asked. "It's ten in the morning."

"Just . . ."—he burped—"a little." Pincho turned to Carlos. "What can I do for my old friend?" He smiled widely, revealing several missing teeth. His body reminded Huber of an oversized water balloon. A wiry mustache ran along his upper lip. The rest of his face and neck were covered in five o'clock shadow. He was completely bald and the oil from his head glistened in the dim light above the table.

"I came to introduce some friends. You know my grandchildren Alejandro and Yesenia. This is Scott, Hannah, Huber, and their teacher, Master Mendoza."

"Ahhh . . . *Americanos*. A long way from home, aren't you? What do you think of"—he burped again—"Salamanca?"

"Very lovely," Hannah answered, disgusted.

"Where are my manners? Would you like a drink?" He hoisted his half full bottle of beer toward Huber, who shook his head emphatically.

"When in Rome." Scott shrugged and went to take the bottle.

Hannah slapped his hand away before he could take it. Pincho shrugged as well and drained the rest of the bottle in one swig. Wiping his mouth with his sleeve, he motioned them all to sit around the table.

"Any news, Pincho?" Carlos asked. "Of the Brotherhood?"

Pincho looked around nervously and motioned them all to move in closer. "Yes . . . there's been a lot of activity of late." He looked around again. "I hear they're getting ready for something big. Word is the treasure they recently found was just moved to their headquarters, the castle Alcazar de Segovia in Seville. There you will find the treasure you are seeking."

"Alcazar de Segovia?" Carlos murmured. "That castle is a fortress."

"Yes, my friend. Virtually impenetrable."

"Hold up a sec," Scott interrupted. "Are you actually listening to this rummie? Look at 'im!"

"I agree, McCormick," Mr. Mendoza said. "I think it's time to go."

"Pincho's information is trustworthy," Carlos replied without hesitation. "His good name and reputation are without equal in Spain. A valorous squire and loyal companion if one ever existed! Pincho, can you tell us where you received this valuable intelligence?"

Huber looked at Yesenia skeptically.

Pincho shook his head. "Thank you, your grace for your kind and honest words . . . rumor is that the treasure you seek is nothing compared to what they're planning next. The treasure is but one cog in a grander scheme."

"We must move quickly to the castle," Carlos said, wide-eyed, eating up Pincho's every word.

"Noooo," Pincho droned. "You cannot simply enter the castle. You would not make it beyond the front gate." He looked around the room once more.

"There's no one here but us," Yesenia said. "You can drop the dramatics."

Pincho looked at the girl annoyed, then continued to whisper. "There is another way. A secret passage, they say."

"Please, Pincho," Carlos pleaded. "We must reach the Brotherhood and regain this treasure. It is imperative and the duty of all righteous knights!"

"Knights," Huber mouthed to Yesenia.

She shook her head and rolled her eyes.

"Tell us where we can locate this passageway!" Carlos pleaded.

"Yes," he said, his eyes squinting. "I understand your need to know. However, I cannot share the source of my information nor how to access the passage just yet. Perhaps with more time and resources, I could . . ."

"¡Ladrón!" Yesenia stood up, her chair sliding backward. "How dare you try to take advantage of Abuelo. Making up stories about the Brotherhood to an old man just to get money."

"I make no stories!" Pincho's face reddened and his lips puckered. "My information is true!"

Alejandro grabbed Pincho's collar. Pincho flailed about like a fish. "You've been filling my grandfather's head with lies for too long."

Carlos gasped and tore Alejandro's hand away from Pincho. "Alejandro! That is no way to treat a squire of Spain!"

"Abuelo," Alejandro blustered. "This man is no squire! He is a drunk! You cannot trust him."

"Release him, *nieto!*" Carlos said, his eyes flashing. "Let him speak!"

Reluctantly, Alejandro released the barfly and he slumped back into his seat. "Make no mistake, friends," Pincho said, looking at each person one by one, "the Brotherhood is dangerous and I advise you all to not involve yourselves in their affairs."

"We must!" Carlos stammered. "To do nothing is to allow evil to triumph!"

Pincho took a breath and rubbed his head. "*Sí, sí,* your grace. You are wise as you are noble. Here is what I know—an associate of the Brotherhood . . . one of the *comandantes* will be at the bullfight tomorrow afternoon at La Glorieta Stadium. He'll be sitting in the VIP box. Follow him and you'll find what you're looking for." Pincho turned to face the others. "Then you will know I only speak the truth." Pincho's face twisted into what seemed to be a look of feigned concern. "I must ask, are you sure you want to make enemies with the Brotherhood of Coronado? Most of those who do don't live to tell about it. They say the three Kings of the Brotherhood are ruthless animals. *El Rey Matón,* or King Crusher is more muscle than man and tortures enemies for fun. *El Rey Susurro,* the Sandman King dives into your mind and drives you mad with his incessant chattering and night-mares. Last, *El Rey Fausto*—or King Fausto the Great, is the leader of all three . . . and the most evil. He designs clever traps and games for his enemies to maneuver while

he watches from his throne in amusement. He designs
the games so you cannot win. You do not want to make
enemies with these men, believe me."

"They made enemies of us first," Carlos said, unafraid.
"Their wicked deeds will not go unpunished nor shall
they skirt the heavy hand of justice when we meet them.
Gracias, Pincho. You are truly a noble squire and I will be
sure to compensate you handsomely for this information."

Pincho bowed. "Gracias, my grace. As always, I am
your humble servant."

"Abuelo," Yesenia said, shaking her head. "This man is
a thief . . . *un rata*. If you feed him a morsel, he will only
beg for more."

Pincho's eyes widened, then narrowed in contempt.
"Just wait, young one. You cross the Brotherhood, it is
you who will be fed to the *ratas*. Now leave me be. I have
things"—he let out a long burp—"to do."

● ● ●

The group of fourteen-year-olds continued their journey down the streets of Salamanca. Scott and Alejandro
walked a few klicks ahead, vying for Hannah's attention.
Carlos said he needed rest and had returned home, encour-
aging his grandkids to show their visitors hospitality and
to give them a splendid tour of the city. Mr. Mendoza
had decided to see the old man home, just in case he got
lost or started hallucinating. He gave them permission to

explore but to return to the house before it turned dark. As they traversed the cobblestone alleys and roads, Huber's senses were overwhelmed with the atmosphere. Buildings a thousand years old stood next to brand-new complexes. It was like the old and modern age collided in a beautiful and striking way. The city itself was a living, breathing museum. So much history on every corner.

"Why does your grandpa listen to that guy?" Huber asked Jessie.

"I do not know," Jessie shook her head sadly. "We cannot convince him that Pincho is not trustworthy. He will continue to fill Abuelo's head with stories to get meals and money out of him. He's been doing it for years. Abuelo always chases these leads that Pincho gives him. Of course, none of them ever pan out. Pincho then convinces Abuelo that the Brotherhood eluded him or he just missed them by chance. Abuelo believes him because Pincho tells him what he wants to hear and pretends to be his friend . . . his squire."

"So, you don't think there's going to be anyone at the bullfight tomorrow?"

Jessie's angry look conveyed her answer.

Up ahead, Huber and Jessie noticed Scott and Alejandro were about to come to blows. They were yelling loudly and pushing each other in the chest. Huber ran in the middle to break them up. "Hey! What's going on?"

"They were arguing about what's better, soccer or football," Hannah said.

"Soccer's for sissies," Scott hissed.

"American football is a game of oafs," Alejandro countered. "It is not difficult to ram into a man and knock him to the ground. Soccer requires real skill."

"Uh-huh. I'm gonna use my skills to knock you to the ground, Spaniard!"

"Come try it, cowboy!"

"C'mon, stop it, Scott!" Huber demanded.

"Alejandro," Jessie chastened her cousin. "This is no way to treat our guest. Apologize."

Alejandro looked stunned but then relented. Taking a deep breath, he glared at Scott. "I am sorry," he said unconvincingly.

Scott appeared pleased. "Yeah, yeah, I'm sorry too . . . that Spaniards can't play real football. Ya'd probably break a nail or something."

Alejandro appeared ready to throw a punch, but Hannah put a hand on his shoulder. "Alejandro, it's okay. It's just the way he is. That's probably the best apology you'll get out of him. For the record," she said, glaring at Scott, "I think soccer beats football any day."

Alejandro's features softened, and he smirked. Hannah slowly removed her hand from his shoulder. "*Gracias*, Hannah." He reached out his hand toward Scott. "Truly, I am sorry."

Scott ignored the gesture and walked forward. "Kinda hungry. What do ya Spaniards got to eat 'round here in these *rest'a'rantes*? Probably weird stuff like sheep guts. Don't s'pose ya have anything good."

Jessie pointed to a nearby *carnicería*. Racks of sausage and cuts of meat hung in the window. "Scott, in España, we have some of the best beef in all the world. That is Javier's Carnicería. Best sausage and steak in all of Salamanca. Would you like to try?"

"Ya had me at beef," he answered.

As they entered the *carnicería*, a reflection in the glass caught Huber's eye. Dozens of passersby ambled down the sidewalk, but amidst the crowd, Huber noticed a solitary figure simply standing and watching them. The man wore a wide-brimmed black hat and had a scar running down his face. Huber gasped and turned around, but Juan Hernán Salazar was nowhere to be seen.

"Hey, brother, you okay?" Hannah shook Huber by the shoulder. "You look like you've seen a ghost or something."

Huber continued to scan the crowd for the man he was sure he'd seen. "Yeah, I'm all right." He shook off the dreadful feeling. "Let's go get something to eat."

THE *SALCHICHA*, **OR** **SAUSAGE,** they'd all consumed was some of the best tasting meat Hannah, Scott, or Huber had ever tasted. Their stomachs full, they'd begun the trip back to Carlos's home. The meal had even seemed to cool down Scott and Alejandro's tempers. As they approached Carlos's home, they noticed the front door was ajar.

"That is strange," Alejandro said. "Abuelo always locks the door when he goes inside."

Trotting closer to the door, it was obvious the door had been locked, but someone had used a crowbar or something to pry it open. "Abuelo!" Jessie cried as she bolted inside.

"Mr. Mendoza?" Huber yelled behind her.

Inside, the house was torn to shreds. Splinters of cuckoo clocks littered the floor. Furniture was overturned. Alejandro and Jessie were yelling for their grandfather.

There was no answer. After searching every nook and cranny of the house, the realization that Carlos and Mr. Mendoza were gone hit home.

Jessie was reeling. "Who did this? Where are they?"

Huber spoke up. "Could it be?"

"So it is true . . ." she whispered.

"Hey, found somethin'," Scott yelled as he emerged from the kitchen. In his hands, he held what looked like a top portion of a human skull with a note slipped through its eye socket. "I can't read it." He untied the note from the skull and handed it to Alejandro.

"Is that real?" Huber asked, going green.

Scott knocked on the head's skull. "Naw, think it's ceramic."

Alejandro read the note. "*Tal es el destino de todos los que impiden la Cofradía.*"

Hannah edged next to his side. "What does that mean?"

"Such is the fate of all who cross the Brotherhood," Jessie answered.

Huber looked at her. "Guess that removes all doubt."

"Abuelo . . ." she trailed off.

"Yes, *mi amor*?" Carlos answered suddenly from the front doorway. Mr. Mendoza stood by his side.

"Abuelo, you're alive!" Jessie shrieked. She and Alejandro ran to their grandfather's side.

"They've made quite a mess of things in here, haven't they? And that poor bird," he said, pointing to a dislodged bird from one of the cuckoo clocks. "One of my favorites."

"Where were you?" Alejandro asked.

"When we arrived home and witnessed this destruc-
tive scene, we immediately reversed course and came to
find you. We were afraid that the Brotherhood would be
seeking you next. It's obvious now they're watching us—
trying to impede our progress. This," he indicated the car-
nage, "was a message meant for me."

"Shouldn't we call the cops?" Huber asked.

Carlos shook his head. "Many of the police are in
league with the Brotherhood or they think I've lost my
marbles. It would do us no good. I've rented us some
rooms downtown next to the La Glorieta stadium. We'll
be safer where there are more people. Tomorrow, we'll go
to the bullfight and find this man Pincho speaks of."

Hannah couldn't take her eyes off the skull. "Do you
think that's a good idea?"

"The Brotherhood has declared war upon us and war
they shall have. Good shall always triumph evil!"

"Hey, wait up a sec!" Scott said. "I didn't come here
really thinkin' we were gonna get mixed up in some kinda
war . . . I thought more than anything, I'd be spending
most of my time just making the acquaintances of some
lovely Spanish young women."

Alejandro sneered. "Well, you are mixed up with it
now whether you like it or not."

"Scott, these are the people who took the treasure,"
Hannah said forcefully. "The same ones responsible for

what happened to Hawk and the others! You don't seem to care very much." She stepped closer to Alejandro.

"Of course I care. You don't think I do? I'm just sayin' if it's true that this Brotherhood is some kinda small army, what's an old man, a Spanish teacher, and the five of us gonna do?"

"I have to agree with McCormick on this one," Mr. Mendoza said. "I can't allow any of you to stay here a minute longer. It's not safe. We're going home."

"Master Mendoza," Carlos said, shaking his head. "That would be most unwise. Once a person is marked by the Brotherhood, there is no refuge from their reach. They will hunt you to the furthest reaches of the earth. The safest thing to do now is go on the offensive. Their operatives are everywhere, including the airports."

Mr. Mendoza shook his head angrily and glared at the old man and then Huber. "What have you gotten us into?"

"He's right," Huber said resolutely. "We'll take back what they stole and expose the Brotherhood to the world. It's the only way we'll be truly safe."

"Are ya James Bond or somethin' now? How do ya plan to do that?" Scott asked.

"Not sure yet, but we'll start at the bullfight."

● ● ●

Huber, Scott, and Alejandro were stuck in one room

of the Helmántico hotel next to La Glorieta Stadium. The
room was small, dark, and shabby. White stucco walls, yel-
lowed with age, hemmed them in all sides. The only light
came from a weak floor lamp in the corner. A window faced
the stadium, while outside a sea of taillights flowed down
the highway surrounding the monumental sight. Hannah
and Jessie were in the room adjacent to theirs and Carlos
and Mr. Mendoza were on the other side of them.

Inside the boys' room, Alejandro and Scott sat across
from the other, engaged in a staring contest. Huber broke
the uneasy silence.

"What's your guys' problem, anyway?"

Scott spoke first, pointing to Alejandro. "Him."

"What did I ever do to you, cowboy?" Alejandro
replied defensively.

"I'm just tellin' ya now to stay away from her."

"Stay away from who?"

"You know who. I've seen the way you've been starin'
at her. She doesn't like ya. I can tell."

"I do not know of what you speak, *Americano Loquito*."

"Don't speak that gibberish to me!"

"Will you guys give it a rest, please? We're on the
hit list of a secret organization, and you're worried about
who my sister likes? If it makes you feel any better, I don't
think she likes either one of you." Huber pulled out a deck
of cards. "How about we play some war or something?"

"War's already started," Scott said, looking at
Alejandro. "Go ahead . . . deal 'em out."

CHAPTER · 6 ·

THE NEXT DAY ARRIVED quickly. After eating breakfast in the hotel lobby, Carlos took the group to La Glorieta stadium to give them a tour of the place. The stadium's plaza was immense and people were already lining up to watch the bullfight. Mr. Mendoza and Carlos went to purchase tickets for the spectacle to take place in the coming hours. All around the stadium hung paintings and pictures of famous matadors. Some photos included them standing victoriously next to the dead bulls.

"I don't understand," Hannah said sadly. "How can people make killing an innocent animal into a sport? What's so heroic about stabbing a bull to death?"

Alejandro seemed put off. "It is a tradition. The people of Salamanca have been bullfighting for hundreds of years. The matadors are brave men. Many of them die in the ring."

"It's their own fault if you ask me. If I went around prodding a big, dangerous animal with a sword, I wouldn't act surprised if it got a little upset."

"Yes, I agree with you Hannah," Jessie commented. "I think the sport is barbaric and should be outlawed. I cannot bear to watch."

"I am not saying I enjoy watching the animal die," Alejandro said, becoming more defensive, "but you do not understand. These bulls are treated like royalty from the time they are calves. They are fed and taken care of better than most people. Would not a bull think a few minutes of pain worth such a life of luxury?"

"I don't know. Why don't you ask him?" Hannah said sternly.

"Hannah," Huber said, "it's their country and their traditions. You should stay out of it."

"Hold on there, Huber. I havta agree with Hannah," Scott said as he stepped next to her. "It's cruel and . . . and . . . bad."

Alejandro glowered at Scott.

"Come off it, Scotty," Hannah said. "I'll bet if I wasn't here, you'd be the first one in line to watch this. You all go enjoy watching an innocent animal die. I'm staying out here."

"Me too," Jessie said, folding her arms.

"I'm gonna go watch," Scott said. "But only so I can give a firsthand account of how uncivilized this sport is when I get back to the good ol' U S of A."

"Huber? What are you going to do?" Hannah asked her brother.

He looked at the two boys and then at the two girls, unsure who to side with. "I'm going to go with the guys. If we're going to find out who's sitting in the VIP box, I have to."

"Fine. Go enjoy your blood sport." The two girls did an about face and tailed away from the boys.

"*Sí! Machistos!*" Jessie spat out.

"Where are y'all goin'?" Scott yelled.

"We'll hang out front—go shopping. You can come find us when it's done."

Carlos and Mr. Mendoza approached the group. "Here are your tickets," Mr. Mendoza said and handed them a stub each while watching Jessie and Hannah walk away. "I assume the girls won't be joining us."

"No, Señor Mendoza," Alejandro said. "They are crazy."

"We purchased seats just above the VIP box," Carlos said. "You will be sitting across the stadium from us at a safe distance. Here, take these." He handed Alejandro a pair of mini binoculars. "Watch the man in the box closely. Try to memorize his face. After the bullfight, we will meet up with the girls and follow him out."

"So we're just supposed to sit there like lumps on a log?" Scott asked.

"That's right, McCormick. You seem pretty good at it

when you're in class," Mr. Mendoza said sternly. "Should be right up your alley."

"What are you two going to do?" Huber asked.

"Just stay at a safe distance," Carlos repeated.

● ● ●

La Glorieta stadium filled to capacity within the next hour. Huber, Scott, and Alejandro found their seats and watched an entertaining preshow of flamenco dancing. Carlos and Mr. Mendoza were sitting directly across the stadium. Huber borrowed the small pair of binoculars from Alejandro to spy on the VIP box. So far, no one had arrived to sit in the shaded, green chairs. Sitting directly above the box, Mr. Mendoza and Carlos waited patiently. Mr. Mendoza noticed Huber watching and gave a thumbs-up sign. Huber returned the gesture and scanned the crowd around the box. His eyes blurred past someone wearing all black. His heart suddenly stopped. *It couldn't be.* Huber whipped the binoculars back and focused on the person. As he came into focus, Juan Hernán Salazar stared straight back with a menacing grimace. Huber's heart stopped and his breathing became labored and shallow. The man-in-black's grimace turned to a wry grin. Gasping for breath, Huber dropped the binoculars and started to hyperventilate.

"What's the matter, dude?" Scott asked.

Huber shoved the binoculars into Scott's hands.

"Look! Over there!" He pointed with a shaky finger. "He's here . . ." He gasped between words. "Salazar's here! Juan Hernán Salazar! Look!"

"Huber, I think you've gone plumb nuts or somethin'." Scott shook his head and brought the binoculars to his eyes and looked where Huber had been focused. He started to chuckle.

"What?" Huber said angrily.

"Take another look."

Huber yanked the binoculars from Scott's hands and peered through the lenses. A slender woman, dressed in a black dress and sun hat came into view. Scott couldn't resist bursting into laughter. "Unless Salamander's somehow turned into a rich old lady, I think you're safe."

Huber sighed and went red. "I swear it was him . . ." he trailed off.

"Aww, don't worry about it." Scott turned to Alejandro. "Looks like the VIP box is still empty. Maybe this Pincho guy had it all wrong."

"Let's hope not," Alejandro replied.

Loud, booming music suddenly blared over the speakers. "*Señores y Señoras, bienvendios a la Corrida de Toros!*" The crowd let out a whoop.

"What's he sayin'?" Scott yelled to Alejandro.

"Welcome to the bullfight," Alejandro yelled back, annoyed.

A man, glittering in green, gold, and black sequins exited a stone archway, wearing what Huber thought looked like a Mickey Mouse hat. As he stepped out onto the red dirt in the ring, the crowd came uncorked, showering the matador with cheers. The sound was deafening. The matador yanked a gold cape from his back and waved it in the wind before doing a small jingle with his feet. The crowd ate it up. From another archway on the other side of the stadium, two of the matador's assistants emerged into the ring, carrying barbed swords that looked like shish kebab skewers. Colorful cloth adorned the blades. Several less decorated assistants on horseback with lances emerged as well. A bugle sounded and a door opened at the far end of the stadium. A massive black bull rumbled out into the open. Boos and cheers emanated from the crowd. The animal seemed nervous and confused as it took in its surroundings. Huber's stomach started to churn.

"I don't know if I can watch this," he said uneasily to Scott.

"C'mon, Huber. Man up. Can't be that bad."

"This is the first stage," Alejandro said. "The *torero*, or matador as you call him, will test the bull."

The matador waved the gold cape in front of the bull, attempting to goad him into charging. The bull didn't seem interested. One of the assistants snuck behind the beast and jabbed it in the backside with what looked like a metal prod and then took off toward the matador. The animal bellowed at the man, who hid himself behind the matador. The bull ran straight into the gold cape as the matador sidestepped his gallop. Cheers erupted as the matador artfully dodged the angered bull several more times.

Huber raised his binoculars to his eyes and noticed the VIP box was now occupied. A middle-aged man with a thin mustache and dressed in a finely tailored suit sat clapping politely. Next to him, an attractive-looking woman appeared vaguely interested in the spectacle. Huber raised the binoculars a few degrees and spied Carlos and Mr. M. watching the man from directly above the box.

"He's there!" Huber shouted.

Scott and Alejandro fought over who got to look next. Alejandro pried the binoculars from Scott's hands and peered through the lenses.

"Do you know him?" Huber asked.

Alejandro shook his head. "No. I do not recognize the man."

"Lemme see." Scott grabbed the binoculars. "Whoa! Who cares about him? Look at that babe sittin' next to 'im."

One of the men on horseback suddenly came toward the bull with his lance. "What's happening now?" Huber asked Alejandro.

"He is the *picador*," Alejandro yelled above the crowd's cheers. "He will poke the bull between the shoulders, further angering him."

Huber felt nauseated as he watched the man on horseback jab the bull between the shoulder blades. The crowd stomped their feet and cheered. The bull charged at the

horseman, but he was too quick and got away. The matador got the bull's attention again by waving the gold colored cape. Its head drooped and it seemed more sluggish,
wounded, but still angry as a hornet.

Huber looked at Scott's face and without words, they
communicated what they thought. Scott's face had turned
white as a sheet. The men with the barbed skewers cautiously approached the bull. "What are they gonna do
now?" he breathed quietly.

"This is where the *banderilleros* will plant the skewers
in the bull's shoulders, slowing him down, preparing the
animal for the kill!"

The three men carrying the colorful, barbed skewers crept toward the angry, exhausted animal. The bull
focused on one of them and charged. As he did, the *ban-
derillero* sidestepped the bull and planted the skewer above
its left shoulder. The animal bawled in anger and pain,
slightly stumbling. While it was partially down, the other
man approached and planted the other barbed skewer in
its other shoulder blade. Another angry bellow emanated
from the animal, resulting in loud cheering that rattled
Huber's eardrums. The bull was temporarily stunned, but
it seemed to find a new sense of strength and somehow
pushed itself onto its legs. The crowd now cheered madly
for the bull.

"This is the final stage," Alejandro said flatly. "The
death stage."

Huber didn't want to watch but couldn't look away

from the spectacle. Not a sound escaped from Scott. Huber had never seen him look so pale. The matador threw the gold cape on the ground and retrieved a red one. As he unfurled it, the crowd went berserk. The matador waved the cape at the bull, and it charged angrily, the skewers bobbing in rhythm to its hoof beats. At the last second, the matador dodged the bull's attack by mere inches. The man did this several times. With each pass, the bull seemed to come closer to impaling the matador. Miraculously, he dodged the bull's horns each time without fail.

"*Estocada, estocada, estocada,*" the crowd chanted.

"What are they chanting?" Huber asked Alejandro.

It was difficult to hear him above the din of the crowd, but Alejandro yelled, "*Estocada* is the death blow. The matador will thrust his blade between the bull's shoulder blades and through his heart!"

Huber watched helplessly as the bull huffed by the matador one final time. The man raised his glimmering blade. Huber closed his eyes, looked away, and guessed by the roaring of the crowd that the deed had been done. When he opened his eyes, the bull was a motionless heap on the ground.

The crowd was now on its feet, stomping and cheering madly for the matador.

Scott took one look at Huber, stirred as if he were dizzy, then barfed his breakfast all over Huber's shoes.

The people surrounding them diffused in a circular fashion in a chorus of *ewwws* and *ughhs*.

"Sorry 'bout them shoes, Huber . . . couldn't help it."

"It's all right," Huber said. "It'll wash off. I guess you just need to *man up*."

Alejandro was suddenly upset. "No! Abuelo!"

Huber looked up, trying his best to rid himself of the dead bull's gruesome image he'd just witnessed. Inside the ring, Carlos was dancing, bare-chested, his small oxygen tank holstered at his side. He waved his shirt around his head in circles.

"What's he doing?"

"He's having one of his episodes! Abuelo must think that he is the matador!"

The whole stadium was in an uproar, laughing hysterically and pointing at the crazy old man. The real matador seemed upset at having the attention focused elsewhere. He pointed angrily at Carlos and yelled for security to remove the buffoon from the ring. A squad of personnel dressed in black with the words *seguridad* on their backs rushed out to remove him. Carlos waved his shirt in front of them as if they were bulls and dodged one of the men who charged. The man sprawled face-first into the dirt. The crowd bounced in delight. The announcer even got into it, narrating the old man's moves animatedly as Carlos successfully dodged another security officer. Four security guards surrounded him. Carlos eyed them all one by one and dropped the shirt. He then unloosed his oxygen tank from his side and wielded it like a weapon. Cautiously, the men approached and Carlos swung wildly, narrowly missing one of the men. They backed away as the crowd stomped and yelled in delight.

Alejandro held his face in his hands. "Oh . . . Abuelo," he lamented.

Huber caught something from the corner of his eye. He brought the binoculars upward. The man in the VIP box was rocking with laughter, and while he was distracted, Mr. Mendoza was slipping downward into the box behind him. Huber nudged Scott, who was still recovering from his sickness. "Look!"

Scott took the binoculars. Mr. Mendoza was hanging from a metal rod, his feet dangling five feet above the man in the VIP box. "Wait a second! Carlos is puttin' on a show . . . it's a diversion!"

"Hand those to me!" Alejandro demanded. He watched, holding his breath as Mr. Mendoza dropped from the air on top of the man in the suit. Arms and legs were flying everywhere as they struggled. The lady sitting next to him seemed to be yelling, but she couldn't be heard over the laughter of the crowd. She beat Mr. Mendoza's backside with her purse as the two men grappled. The boys continued to argue over who got to watch through the binoculars.

Finally, Huber yanked the binoculars from Scott's vomit-stained hands and brought them to his eyes. "Oh no!"

"What's happening?" Alejandro yelled. The VIP box was now full of men in suits, pulling Mr. Mendoza off the man. One held him in place as another slugged him in the stomach and then the face. Mr. Mendoza's head hung, unconscious, and they dragged his limp body through the curtains behind the box. The remaining men raked their eyes over the crowd to make sure no one was watching. Clutching the binoculars tightly, Huber's stomach dropped to his knees. One of the men pointed straight at him and yelled to the others. Several of the men in suits looked toward Huber, Scott, and Alejandro's direction and quickly exited the box.

"They're coming for us!" Huber yelled. "We have to get out of here, now!"

A sad moan swept over the crowd of spectators as Carlos was finally subdued. The security personnel began carrying him off the grounds. Roses and coins showered the old man as he waved triumphantly. The matador shook his head in disgust.

Huber, Scott, and Alejandro quickly ran for the nearest exit. As they turned the corner, they spotted the men in suits charging toward them. Turning around to run the other way, they slammed straight into another squad of men. The man sitting in the VIP box was among them and spoke to Huber before he could yell for help. "Do not yell for help, young one. Come with us," he said calmly. "Scream for help, and you will all suffer, including your friend you were watching through the binoculars."

The three boys eyed one another warily, but without a

word followed the man in the suit while his goons tailed behind.

● ● ●

The three boys were led to an abandoned lot adjacent to the stadium. The lot was cornered in on all sides so that there was only one entrance in and out. Muffled cheers reverberated off the thick-bricked walls from the stadium. A black Mercedes van was idling in front of them along with several fine automobiles. A symbol of some kind decorated the back door of the van. It was a yellow and blue shield topped with a knight's helmet. The man from the VIP box opened the van's back door to reveal Mr. Mendoza bound on the floor. His mouth was taped shut.

"Hey! Let him go!" Huber yelled.

"You're in no position to make demands," the man from the VIP box replied. "I thought the warning we sent you earlier was clear. Evidently, not clear enough. Search them," he demanded, pointing at the boys.

A swarm of suits started patting them all down and digging through their pockets. One man found Scott's pocketknife, and another took Alejandro's wallet. Each was also forced to give up his cell phone. Within seconds, they were smashed on the ground. The man patting Huber felt something metallic in his front pocket. *"¿Que es esto?"* He pulled out Grandpa Nick's gold coin, and the man stared at it, surprise registering on his face. He then tossed it to the man from the VIP box. "*Mira a eso.*"

The man eyed the coin pensively. "Looks remarkably familiar. Tell me, how did you come across this coin?"

"It was my grandpa's. He left it to me when he died. I don't know where he got it."

"*Mentiras! Lies!* Now I'll ask again—where did you obtain this coin?"

Huber met the man's gaze but said nothing.

"Don't tell them anything, Huber!" Mr. Mendoza said, after managing to free his mouth of the tape.

"Shut him up!" the man yelled to one of his cronies, who slammed the door to the van shut.

"Last chance, young one. Tell me or suffer the consequences!"

The man's demand was once again met with a long silence.

"Very well," he replied, going to the side of the van. He rapped three times on the door, and it slid open.

A behemoth of a man ducked his head beneath the door and stepped out. Inadvertently, Huber gasped and backed away. The man towered around seven feet and wore a finely tailored black suit with a red tie. Beneath the black fabric, the man's ropy arms and legs appeared to be frozen turkeys. His dark hair was shoulder length and parted down the middle. If the man hadn't been so massive, Huber would've thought his hairstyle looked a bit feminine. Covering the monstrous man's face, however, was a metal mask—the expression of which clearly conveyed wrath, anger, and hatred. The lips curved downward and the eyebrows formed a V shape. The only visible part of the man's face was his eyeballs, which appeared equally contemptuous. The man lumbered toward Huber in a slow, even motion. It was then Huber noticed the man's hands. He wore some sort of metallic gloves. They matched the sheen of his mask and made a whiny machine-like noise when he opened and shut his fingers. His beefy hands appeared like they could rip a person in two.

As he stepped forward, another person exited the van. In contrast to the colossal figure he'd just seen, this diminutive man was shorter than Huber and dressed like his partner in near identical attire: a fine black suit with a red tie. The man was bald on top but had some gray hair on the sides of his head. He also wore a metal mask. The only difference from the bulkier man's mask was that this mask resembled a sad and lonely countenance. The eyebrows were raised and lips closed inward as if the eyes were to the point of tears. The small man moved erratically and in jerky motions, almost hiding behind his larger compatriot like a frightened puppy. His cloudy eyes darted back and forth nervously.

Finally, a third man stepped from the van. He was of medium build, near five feet ten inches tall, and wore the same fine clothing and marks as the other two. His dark hair was short and slicked back. The countenance etched into his metal face was amiable and even, as if he had just heard a good joke and was on the verge of laughter. His eyes were dark and seemingly friendly. As he came forward, the other two parted in deference and allowed him to approach Huber first.

The man's voice was low and muffled behind the mask. "*Bienvenidos a España!*" he proclaimed. "*Yo me llamo El Rey Fausto,*" he said cheerily with a slight bow. "This," he pointed toward the muscled figure at his right, "is El Rey Matón and the smaller fellow to my left is El Rey Susurro. *Somos los tres Reyes de la Cofradía de Coronado*— the Three Kings of the Brotherhood of Coronado."

"Sounds like a ladies' club or somethin'," Scott said sarcastically. "How do I join? Dress up in a suit and wear a Halloween mask?"

The one called Matón stepped forward with a guttural growl.

"Matón!" Fausto raised his hand. Like an obedient dog, the giant hesitated and then obeyed. Fausto turned to Scott, walked toward him, and brought his metal face within inches of his. "You have a sense of humor, young one. That is good." He patted Scott's cheek with his white gloved hand. "You will need it where you are headed."

Scott didn't respond.

Fausto then inched toward Alejandro. "You . . . the grandson of Don Carlos *el Matador!*" The men around laughed heartily. "I have to give your abuelo credit. He is one of the most skilled men in Spain to wield an oxygen tank!"

"Do not speak ill of Abuelo!"

Fausto slapped Alejandro's face. Though his face still seemed friendly, the man's voice took on a harsher tone. "Your abuelo is a pesky fly, a fly that has pestered us long enough . . . you and your cousin are his putrid larva that we will squash before it hatches."

Alejandro glared, but with one look at Matón, he held his tongue. Fausto approached Huber. "And you . . . I saw you had a coin?" He grabbed it from the man, who had taken it from Huber. "This looks familiar. In fact, the striking is almost identical to some coins we recently brought here from America. Pray tell, friend, where did you find this golden token?"

Intimidated and frightened at his current predicament, Huber whispered, "It was my grandpa's . . . he found it in the mountains in Colorado."

Fausto leaned in closer. "Mountains, you say? Mountains in Colorado?"

Filled with numbing dread, Huber nodded.

"This coin came from *Tesoro de los Muertos*, didn't it, boy?"

Huber stood evenly, saying nothing.

"What is your name?"

"Huber Hill," he barely got out.

Fausto turned to his companions and held up the coin for the others to view. "Huber Hill here is in possession of a piece from *Tesoro de los Muertos*—the Dead Man's Treasure."

Whispering traveled through the group like electricity.

"I do not know how your grandfather ended up with this, but answer me, Huber Hill—who mined this gold piece from the heart of the earth?"

A long pause filled the alleyway. All eyes were plastered on Huber. He had to think fast and give the right answer. "The Spanish," Huber hesitated, not meeting the man's gaze.

"*Excelente!* The Spanish! Tell me, Huber Hill—who smelted the gold and molded it into coins like this one?"

"The Spanish," Huber repeated.

"Two for two! You are a bright one, Huber Hill. Final question—to whom does this gold belong?"

Fausto and the crowd anxiously awaited his answer. Huber closed his eyes, took a breath, and then said in a loud voice as brave as he could. "It belongs to the mountain."

A gasp swept over the crowd of thugs. Fausto slapped Huber across the face as he had Alejandro. "*Wrong!*" He held the coin up in the air. "Susurro! To whom does this gold coin belong?"

"*A España!*" the tiny king responded in a high-pitched voice.

"Matón!" Fausto pointed at the giant of a man. "To whom does this coin belong?"

"*A Coronado!*" the man bellowed in a deep voice.

The group in the alleyway cheered, clapped, and whistled.

Fausto came back and pointed to Huber. "From henceforth, you shall be known as Huber Hill the Thief! What do we do with a thief, my brothers? And those who keep company with them?"

"*Mátalos! Mátalos! Mátalos!*" they chanted.

Huber, Scott, and Alejandro's faces turned white. Fausto raised his hand and they instantly quieted. "Do not worry young ones. You will receive your due process *via la inquisición!*"

The group of cronies cheered and whistled again. Fausto motioned for Matón to bind the boys. As he did, Huber noticed a hooded figure appear on one of the rooftops overhead. The man raised his arm and tossed several small, spherical objects at the giant's feet. Confused, Matón gazed up. Suddenly, the pellets exploded and released thick, acrid smoke, saturating the air and making it impossible to see and difficult to breathe. Everyone coughed and wheezed as they wandered through the haze, colliding into each other.

Huber took the opportunity to bite the hand holding him and heard the pain-riddled result. "C'mon, let's go!" he yelled to the others.

In the confusion, Scott elbowed his captor in the stomach and Alejandro did the same. They coughed and weaved their way through the bumbling men and found each other a few klicks from the scene where the haze started to dissipate. Barely visible to his left, Huber noticed an open storm drain. "Over here," he whispered to the others. One by one, they climbed into the drain. From their hiding spot, they watched the Brotherhood's men run around frantically through the smoke.

"They've gone!" one of the men suddenly realized and yelled back to Fausto, who was still coughing from the smoke. A police siren sounded from somewhere near.

"*Vamos!*" Fausto roared. "We'll deal with them later."

Through the grate, the boys watched the men run back from the direction they'd come and pile into vehicles. The Three Kings entered the idling van once again.

"Mr. Mendoza!" Huber panicked. "They still have him."

"Nothin' we can do for him now," Scott said sadly.

The sound of screeching tires echoed through the drain and a sinking sensation overcame Huber as he thought of what tortures surely lay ahead for his Spanish teacher.

● ● ●

Paranoid, alone, and frightened, the boys wandered aimlessly around La Glorieta Stadium, constantly looking over their shoulders. Every few moments, a loud cheer would erupt as Huber envisioned another matador striking a blow. They decided it'd be safer to venture back inside the stadium's plaza where there were many people milling about. So far, they'd seen no sign of Hannah or Jessie.

"Do you think the Brotherhood got them too?" Huber finally asked.

"I do not know," Alejandro answered. "I hope not."

"If they did, I bet they threw 'em out of that van after five minutes," Scott joked. "That's about all I could stand from them two."

"Who do you think that guy was on the roof? The one who helped us get away," Huber asked.

"Wish I knew," Alejandro answered.

"Glad that dude showed up though. Otherwise, we'd be toast," Scott added.

Huber thought of his teacher. "We have to help Mr. Mendoza. There's no telling what's happening to him right now."

"How do ya s'pose we do that, Huber? We have no idea who took him, no idea where they went, and no idea what happened to Carlos or the girls."

"What happened to Abuelo?" Jessie said from behind, startling the boys. Hannah and Jessie were carrying a couple of small plastic bags. They'd been shopping around the plaza for hours.

Scott pointed at the girls' bags. "The old man gets arrested, Mr. Mendoza gets abducted, and we almost die while y'all go shoppin' for souvenirs? Nice."

Jessie dropped her bags. "What? Tell us what happened!"

The three boys took turns describing the events that'd just taken place, including Carlos pretending to be a matador and the mysterious stranger who'd saved them. Hannah and Jessie seemed beside themselves. "We have to find Abuelo," Jessie said. "I wonder where security has taken him."

"My guess is the *Cárcel* Salamanca," Alejandro answered. "The jail is not far from here."

Looking over his shoulder every few steps, Alejandro led them about a mile down the main thoroughfare until they reached the Cárcel. A guard stationed at the reception desk stopped them.

"*Perdóneme.* Can I be of assistance?"

Jessie spoke up. "Was there an old man brought here from the bullfight today?"

The guard smirked. "The same old man who trespassed onto the grounds," the guard said, pointing to a mounted television. Images of Carlos were playing repeatedly with the subtitle "Don Quixote de los Toros."

Jessie closed her eyes and sighed. "*Sí.* That's him."

"He is here. Are you relatives?"

"Yes," Alejandro answered. "We are his grandchildren."

"This way." The man beckoned them behind the desk. "You'll only have five minutes."

"How long will he be here?" Jessie said.

"I do not know. A few days, perhaps."

"A few days?" Alejandro became upset. "We are under his care! What are we supposed to do until he gets out?"

"Not my concern," the guard replied. He opened a metal door that led down a narrow corridor. Cells lined both of the walls. Grisly looking men stared them down. Their eyes were like sharks looking for a meal.

"Just keep walking. Don't look at them," Huber whispered to Hannah.

Finally, they reached the end of the corridor and found Carlos sitting on the edge of his bed within a lonely cell.

"Yesenia! Alejandro!" he cried

"Abuleo!" they ran and held his hands through the bars.

"Where is Señor Mendoza?"

"The Brotherhood has taken him," Huber replied gravely. "They almost got us too."

Carlos looked around nervously as if someone were eavesdropping. When they told Carlos about the hooded figure who'd aided in their escape, his eyes widened. "A letter was just delivered here to me just before you came."

"From who?" Jessie asked.

"The guard did not say. I opened it and it made no sense to me. Perhaps it is from this same stranger who is trying to assist us." Carlos went to his cot and retrieved the letter from beneath the mattress. "Here, read it." He slipped the envelope through the bars.

Alejandro took out the letter and unfolded it. Elaborate script decorated the face of the page:

You are not safe. Do not return home. The Brotherhood must be stopped at all costs. I will lead you into their stronghold and offer my help from the shadows. Gaining entrance to the Three Kings' place of hiding will require three separate keys. I have hidden them around the city in the event I am caught by the Brotherhood. By collecting all of the keys, you will prove your worthiness and ability to contend with the Three Kings. The first key is located "donde el astronauta asciende hacia al cielo." Make haste. Do not linger in any one place for too long.

~El Halcón

"The Falcon," Alejandro whispered.

Scott screwed up his face. "What the heck's that supposed ta mean?"

"The first key is located where the astronaut climbs toward heaven," Jessie answered.

"It's a riddle of some kind," Alejandro said pensively.

"No kiddin', Sherlock Holmes. I'm glad you're here to let us know," Scott shook his head.

"You must all work together to find these keys if you're going to save Master Mendoza and defeat the Brotherhood. You must do so without my help for now. Not to worry—no jail can long hold a true knight of Salamanca!" Carlos yelled out, his eyes going a bit wild. "Truth, honor, and valor will always prevail against evil!"

Several of the other prisoners in adjacent cells moaned and called for him to pipe down. The old man responded to their calls. "Can any of you stop the sun from shining? Stop the wind from blowing? Stop the waves from churning? Even so, my friends, you cannot stop the course of a righteous cause! Stand firm! Soon we will be released from this dungeon and breathe the free air. When that day arrives, I pray you will all ride with me and aid me in my quest!"

The other prisoners were now calling for the guard to shut the old man up. The guard opened up the cell block door. "What's going on in here? You!" He pointed at their group. "Time is up."

"You must depart here quickly," Carlos said. "The Brotherhood may be watching you. Try to decipher the Falcon's riddle. Between the five of you, I know you can complete this errand. I will make my escape soon and join you in this noble quest."

Alejandro stuffed the letter inside his pocket. Jessie grabbed her grandfather's hands and gripped them tightly. A lucid look returned to his face.

"Abuelo, we cannot leave you here," she said.

"Do not worry about me, Yesenia. I will be okay. When I am released, I will find you. Go! Seek out Pincho. He can help you in your mission. He is a noble squire whom I trust with my life."

● ● ●

After taking a cab to the opposite side of the city, they finally arrived at the tavern. Inside, Pincho was sitting around a table playing *Mus*, a popular Spanish card game. He glanced up, annoyed at being interrupted.

"What is it?" he growled.

"We need your help," Jessie said.

"Can't you see I'm busy? Where's your abuelo or should I say, *the mighty Matador*?" He laughed heartily.

"Abuelo is in jail," Alejandro answered.

Pincho chuckled and the others at the table joined in. "Yes," he said, "I assumed as much. I saw his antics all over the television. How long is he in the *cárcel*?"

"A few days at least."

Pincho smirked, staring intently at his cards. "What about your teacher? Mendoza, is it? Where is he?"

"The Brotherhood took him," Huber answered.

Pincho laid down his cards and glanced up. "What is this? A joke?"

"It's not a joke, Pincho," Jessie said sternly. "Señor Mendoza has been abducted. We followed your advice and went to the bullfight. Now look where it's got us. We went to see Abuelo in jail and . . ."

"Let me guess. He told you to come see me."

"That's right."

"I am not a babysitter."

"We don't need no babysittin'," Scott replied harshly.

"Then why have you come here?"

"We received information," Hannah said. "And it's not safe for us to return to Abuelo's house."

"Do you know anyone who goes by the name of *Halcón*?" Huber said.

The name caught Pincho's attention. He looked around nervously. "Halcón, did you say?"

They all nodded. Pincho searched the faces of the men surrounding the card table.

"Gentlemen, I fear I must throw in for the night. A very good game of *Mus*. You! Over there," he yelled and pointed to another man tilting precariously on a barstool. "Take my place." Pincho's belly receded off the card table as he stood from his chair. He pointed to a vacant corner. "Come with me."

As they sat around the deserted table in the corner, Pincho pressed them. "So . . . the Falcon has chosen to reveal himself to you? Tell me, what occurred?"

The boys took turns relating what had happened in the alleyway. Alejandro retrieved the letter from his pocket and handed it over. Pincho pored over the words, his eyebrows rising in surprise.

"You know who he is?" Huber pressed him.

"Where do you think I get all of my information regarding the Brotherhood? He is an ex-high ranking member of the order. He has knowledge of their comings and goings."

"How do you meet with him?"

"He finds me. I never request the meetings."

"And why would he go to you of all people?" Alejandro asked skeptically.

Pincho looked annoyed. "I do not know. One day I'm walking out of the bar and a man in a cloak and mask stops me . . . tells me he has information to share about the Brotherhood of Coronado. I tell him to shove off, that

I could care less about such things. He demands that I
share his information with Carlos Salazar or else."

"Why wouldn't the Falcon just go to Carlos directly?"
Hannah said.

"Do I look like I know? What is this? An interroga-
tion by children? He gives me information, and I pass it
along to Carlos."

"All for a price, right? Filthy *ladrón*." Jessie snorted.

"What?" He grinned. "Everyone needs to make a
living, *mi amor*! I have cats to feed."

"And bottles to drink." Scott pointed to Pincho's
empty bottle.

Pincho's smile faded.

"What do you make of the riddle in the letter?" Huber
asked.

"Hmmm . . . maybe I could tell you . . . for a price."

"Tell us!" Alejandro said angrily.

"Ten euros and I help you." He smiled a mostly tooth-
less grin.

The five huddled together to discuss the matter. They
turned out their pockets, and then Jessie emerged, slamming the money onto the table. "Satisfied?"

Pincho snatched the money faster than they could
blink and shoved it in his shirt pocket. "Well . . . I don't
actually know the answer to the riddle, but I can tell you
where to find it."

Scott and Alejandro looked at one another as if they
were both going to explode. Scott grabbed Pincho's bottle

and threatened to smash it on the ground. Patrons of the bar eyed the spectacle in the corner, amused. "Okay! Okay! Head to the library," Pincho squealed. "Just don't drop the booze! At the University . . . ask for Beatriz. She is the head librarian. She'll help you find your answers. Tell her I sent you."

"How do you know her?" Huber asked as the man wrestled the bottle free of Scott's grasp.

"She is my mother," he spat. "I'm certain she will find somewhere for you to stay the night." Pincho flopped back into his seat, red faced and cursing under his breath.

"Do you have a cell phone?" Huber asked the man. "Carlos told us we could trust you. You need to be able to contact us in case the Falcon visits you again."

Huber dug through his pocket and fished out a couple of more euros. He tossed them onto the table. Pincho grinned and unlatched a leather holder on his belt, pulling out a white brick with an antenna.

"What the heck is that?" Scott laughed.

"What? It's my phone!"

"That thing looks like it's from 1990."

"It is from 1990. So what? It works!"

"Jessie, give him your number," Huber directed. "The Brotherhood smashed my phone. If the Falcon contacts you, Pincho, call and let us know. We need to find Mr. Mendoza."

Pincho grinned and did a slight bow with his head. "I live to serve."

● ● ●

An hour later, the troupe had wound their way through the streets of Salamanca via taxi and foot until they reached the University of Salamanca. It was near dark, and the sprawling campus was a labyrinth of ancient-looking buildings amidst newer ones. Following the lit signs, they tromped past night students toward the mammoth library. Upon reaching the glass doors, they viewed a gray-haired woman just about to lock up on the other side.

"*Espere!*" Jessie yelled and pounded on the glass.

Startled, the woman gasped and mouthed "*cerrado*"—closed.

"*Por favor!*" Jessie pounded. "Pincho . . . I mean, Paco sent us!"

Upon hearing the words, the old woman stopped and reluctantly opened the door. "Paco sent you? My son? Who are you? What are you all doing here on campus so late? I wasn't aware the university was admitting so many teenagers."

"Please . . ." Huber pleaded. "We have nowhere to go and need help."

The old woman seemed ready to close the door but then opened it wide. "*Entren.*"

The inside of the library was like a monstrous cavern filled with books as far as the eye could see. A musty, papery smell permeated the air. Statuary and elaborately carved woodwork lined the walls and contributed to the warm, pensive atmosphere. The woman locked the door behind them and motioned for them to sit around a long table in the center of the room.

She sighed as she sat with them. "So . . . Paco sent you."

"Yes," Hannah replied. "So you're his mother."

"Unfortunately, yes," she hissed. "My name is Beatriz. How do you have the misfortune of knowing my son?"

A pang of pity shot through Huber at her words. The old woman evidently held no warm feelings toward the man.

"We met him at the tavern," Jessie said.

"Surprise, surprise. What were you doing in a tavern? At your age?"

"My abuelo told me to go there and find Pincho, I mean Paco," Alejandro explained. "He told us he could help us find the Brotherhood of Coronado." They took turns describing the events of the day, sparing no details about the bullfight, Mr. Mendoza, the Falcon, or brotherhood. They showed her the letter that had been given them. The old woman brought her glasses down upon her nose and eyed them like a hawk. She sat impassive, not revealing any clue as to what she thought of her visitors. "Well . . . that's quite a story you told just now."

"It's true," Alejandro said. "Every word."

She paused. "I believe you," she said, smiling a little.

"You do?" Huber said, unbelieving.

The woman nodded. "When you get to be my age, you can tell when someone is lying. You are no doubt sincere in your telling of the day's events. Not to mention the fact that I know of the Brotherhood of Coronado's evil deeds. They've been trying to infiltrate this university for years. Believe it or not, this structure has been standing since the twelfth century. There are many secrets contained within its walls. Secrets the Brotherhood seek. Any enemy of theirs is a friend of mine. Of course, one cannot vocalize such sentiments if she hopes to stay alive and kicking—or alive and *reading*, in my case."

"So, is it cool that we crash here tonight?" Scott asked.

"There are a few cots in the storage area behind the depository. You can stay there for a few nights. However, if you are caught, I will claim I never met you. You will be treated and prosecuted as trespassers."

They all nodded their understanding.

"What do you make of the riddle?" Huber asked.

The woman's eyes brightened considerably. "The answer you can no doubt find in this place." She pointed toward the walls lined with books. "Feel free to seek the answer. Now, I must retire to my home. I wish you luck in your mission." Her face suddenly hardened. "If you see that no good son of mine again, tell him his mother is still not speaking to him." Her facial muscles relaxed. "I will return in the morning. Stay safe. There is a refrigerator in the break room, next to where you sleep. Help yourselves. Take this key," she said, handing it to Huber. "Be gone before I arrive in the morning at 8:00. Lock the door on your way out." She then abruptly stood and exited the library, dimming the lights upon leaving. Huber locked the door behind her.

"This is incredible!" Hannah squealed. "Staying the night in a library that's hundreds of years old!"

"What are ya talkin' about? This is a nightmare," Scott replied. "Surrounded by books." He glanced at Alejandro. "Spanish ones, no less."

Jessie looked at Huber. "Well, shall we attempt to solve this riddle?"

● ● ●

Two hours later, the table was lined with books about astronauts and heaven. There was so much information, it was difficult to know where to start. Huber, Hannah, and Scott researched the ones in English. Jessie and Alejandro pored over the ones in Spanish.

Scott exhaled and slammed a book down about NASA. "This ain't goin' nowhere."

"I think we're making this too hard," Huber said. "Think about the words . . . where the astronaut climbs toward heaven. What comes to mind?"

"The sky," Hannah said.

"Yes, I agree," Jessie said.

Huber wrote the word *sky* on a yellow notepad.

"Right, so the key is somewhere up in the sky," Scott

said, shaking his head. He was munching on someone's leftover ham sandwich from the fridge. "That narrows it down. Guess all we gotta do is look up and we'll see it."

Alejandro pointed to a sign. "Cowboy, there is no food allowed in the library."

He took another bite from the sandwich. "I dunno Spanish. Can't read it."

"It's pretty vague," Huber said, conceding to Scott's point. "What else comes to mind?"

"Churches," Jessie said. "When he talks about heaven, anyway."

"Good." Huber scribbled the word *church* on a notepad.

"Maybe it's where a shuttle launches. Does Salamanca have a space program?"

Alejandro shook his head. "No, there is nothing like that here."

Huber blew out his breath. "Maybe we should just sleep on it."

"Wait!" Jessie stood up. She ran to a reference computer next to the librarian's desk. The screen flickered to life and she typed madly.

"*¿Que pasó?*" Alejandro yelled.

"I remember something. Papá took me years ago. Yes! I found it." She ran to a file cabinet full of old newspapers, archived by date. She found one dated from 1992 from the *New York Times*. She raced back to the table and flung it front of their eyes. "There! Look!"

It took a moment for Huber to realize what he was

viewing. The headline was in English and read, *Astronauts in Heaven?* Huber began to read the article aloud. "During the recent renovation of the facade of the Old Cathedral in Salamanca, Spain, the church, erected in the early twelfth century, received a modern token of the times. A mason took license to chisel the form of an astronaut ascending toward space."

"That has to be it!" Hannah said.

"Is not far from here. Less than five minutes." Alejandro became excited. "We can go there in the morning."

"All right!" Huber said excitedly. "Let's get some shut-eye and head out first thing."

● ● ●

Huber, Scott, and Alejandro filed into the dusty storage room that also served as break area for the library workers. A soda machine hummed and cast a soft yellow glow over the room. On the floor rested two cots. In an adjacent storage room, the girls had set up their cots.

"Hold up a sec," Scott said. "There's only two cots in here."

"Exactly," Alejandro replied. "One for me and one for Huber. Cowboys sleep on the ground."

"I don't think so, Rico. You wanna fight me for it? I'm game."

"How about we draw straws?" Huber suggested and fished through a drawer in the counter. He found some toothpicks and broke them in three different sizes. Holding them in his palm, he approached Scott and Alejandro. Scott pulled first, then Alejandro. Scott's was shorter than that of Alejandro. Huber opened his palm and compared his with Scott's. Scott was the loser.

"Fine!" he said. He then wadded up some dishtowels from the beneath the counter and tossed them on the floor. Using a tablecloth as a makeshift blanket, he lay down. Huber couldn't help but smile as he lay in the cot. Sleep found him quickly as he dived into the realm of dreams with the soda machine humming him there.

Sometime later Huber was startled awake by the sound of a book slamming shut within the library. He looked at Scott and Alejandro sleeping peacefully. They were out like rocks, their faces aglow in yellow from the soda machine. Huber arose from the cot and peeked outside the door. The library was dark. Faint light filtered in through the high windows, but not enough to see clearly. He looked toward the glass doors. They were still shut and locked tight. Another sound of a book falling from a shelf caused him to jump.

"Who's there? Hannah? Jessie?" he whispered.

There was no response.

Huber stepped into the library and crept toward the source of the sound. A swift movement caught the corner of his eye. A shadow that appeared like a person darted behind a bookshelf. "Who is that? Come out! Show yourself!" The shadow swept beyond another bookshelf to his left. Huber tiptoed forward. His palms were sweaty and the hairs on his neck were standing on end. Footsteps sounded on the other side of the bookcase to his right. Through gaps between the books, he could make out the dark figure of a person on the other side. Huber reached up and removed several volumes to get a clearer look. As he cleared away the books, two eyes stared back at his, one of them flickering an ethereal, blue light like the bottom of a gas flame. Salazar's decomposed face stared back, paralyzing him with fear.

"*Yooooo-berrrrr.*" Salazar's deep, distorted voice echoed through the library.

Huber thrashed awake in a cold sweat on his cot. The soda machine was still humming softly as the two others slept. He took a few breaths and convinced himself it was just a dream. Outside of the room, he noticed the low light of a lamp. He got up to investigate. Jessie was at a study table, texting on her phone. A fresh stack of books were in front of her. Huber wandered to her.

"Hey, why are you up so late?" he asked.

Jessie jumped and gasped. "Ay, Huber, you scared me to death." She flipped her phone shut and shoved it in her pocket.

"Sorry about that. I noticed the light. Who are you texting?"

"My parents. They called earlier and left a message. I texted them that we are having fun and everything is okay with Abuelo. I am also reading more on the cathedral for tomorrow. I couldn't sleep." She took a hard look at Huber, her eyes sweeping his countenance. "Are you okay?"

Huber sat across from her. "Yeah, just had a nightmare is all."

"About what?"

"Juan Salazar. Been having them for months now. Ever since what happened at Dead Man's Treasure. They're getting worse and worse. I've even started seeing him while I'm awake sometimes . . . in crowds and stuff."

Jessie reached her hand across the table and rested it on his. "It must've been terrible to go through that. But Huber, Juan Hernán is dead."

"I know. I just can't seem to shake him. It's like he's haunting me."

Jessie's eyebrows raised in compassion. "You know what has been haunting me?" She smiled.

"No. What?"

"That night in Abuelo's courtyard."

"What about that?" Huber stammered uncomfortably, knowing full well what she meant.

Jessie leaned across the table toward him. "When we were interrupted by Abuelo . . ."

"Oh . . ." Huber leaned forward ever so slightly.

As their lips came within an inch, Scott wandered into the library, his tablecloth wrapped around him like a cape. "Hey! What are ya guys doin' up?"

Huber fell back and sighed. "Nothing."

Scott smiled. "I see . . . doin' some late night . . .

research." He quoted with his fingers as he pulled up a chair next to them.

Jessie and Huber both blushed. "Why are you awake?" Huber asked, perturbed.

"Ya think it's possible to really sleep on the cold, hard tile in there? There's nothin' else to do. Figured I'd come out here and grab a book or somethin'."

Jessie smiled. "I thought you hated books."

"That shows ya how desperate I am for somethin' to do."

"Well, I am going back to sleep," Jessie said. She flashed a smile at Huber. "I'll see you in the morning."

She walked back to the room adjacent to the boys. Scott scooted next to Huber. His hair was all over the place. Huber slugged him hard on the shoulder.

"Ouccchhhh, what was that for?"

"Thanks for ruining the moment! Couldn't you have waited for five seconds longer to come in here?"

Scott rubbed his sore shoulder. "Told ya, I couldn't sleep. Ya like her, don't cha?" Scott shot his eyebrows up and down.

"She's okay . . . I guess."

"Want me to talk to her for ya?"

"Yeah, because you're so successful with the ladies. You got my sister to like you for what? Two days? And that's not hard. She likes practically every boy she meets."

"Shut up, Huber . . ." he said, sulking. "Ya think she likes Rico more than me?"

"Why don't you ask her?"

"Will you?"

"No way. I'm not getting involved in any of that. You just need to move on."

Scott's face fell. "I'll never meet anyone else like her."

"You're gonna make me puke. Honestly, can you hear yourself and what you sound like? Get over her."

"Easy for you to say."

"You want my sister to like you again? Act like you're not interested. My dad told me that's how he got my mom to marry him. He was lollygagging over her all the time and it drove her crazy. When he gave up and quit trying, she came back to him."

Scott's eyes lit up. "Ya may be onto somethin' there, Huber. I'm gonna try that. I'm just gonna treat her normal and not say or do nothin'."

"Good."

The two boys sat for a moment longer. "Well, I'm heading back to bed," Huber said.

"Yeah, all right," Scott answered as Huber walked back to the break room. "Hey, Huber!"

He turned around. "What?"

"Ya really think she likes Rico more than me?"

Huber shook his head in disgust and kept on walking. "You're hopeless," he muttered under his breath.

CHAPTER 7

THEY WERE ROUSED AWAKE by Alejandro at 7:30 sharp. After washing their faces, the five exited the library, careful to lock the door behind them, and made their way toward the Old Cathedral a few blocks away. Jessie, having researched the night before, related the edifice's history as they made the short, three-block journey. On their way, they stopped by a street vendor to purchase breakfast. The orange juice, eggs, and sausage seemed to liven their spirits.

Finally, they arrived and stood before the massive structure. It was one of the most beautiful buildings Huber had ever laid eyes on. The washed out, cream-colored stone façade was immense. On one end of the structure, a massive bell tower shot upward toward the sky. On the other, a cupola lower in elevation comple-mented it perfectly. Stone spires and masonry work were adorned throughout. Orangish-gray roof tiles added to the ambient effect. Eight visible buttresses helped support the arched roof.

Jessie continued on like a tour guide. "Amazing, isn't it? It was commissioned by King Ferdinand. They built the New Cathedral right next to the old one and integrated the two of them. That is why one side appears different from the other. The people needed a larger cathedral in the early 1700s but didn't want to get rid of the old one."

"So they added on," Huber said.

"Exactly."

It was difficult not to stand and gawk at all the intricate carvings of cherubs, devils, flowers, and myriad other masonry designs. Eventually, they found their way around to the north-facing façade of the cathedral along with its massive wooden door that kings of old would pass through. After raking their eyes over the carvings, Alejandro spotted the peculiarity they sought. "There! Look!"

About ten feet from the ground, the image of an astronaut was wrapped up seamlessly within the vines and leaves. The man clutched what appeared to be a tether in his hand. A tiny, rolled up scroll was tucked beneath his arm and the wall. "There's something up there," Hannah said.

"How are we supposed to get it down?" Huber asked.

"Dunno," Scott said. "Unless Spiderman is around, I think we're outta luck."

"I have an idea!" Jessie shouted. "Scott can be the base. Alejandro will climb upon his shoulders, and Huber can crawl up to Alejandro and reach the scroll."

"Don't you think that will attract some attention?" Huber said, looking around at the many pedestrians walking down the street.

"Perhaps. But the streets will only get busier as the morning goes on. Now is the best time."

Scott reluctantly agreed to be the base and squatted against the wall. He grunted and glared as Alejandro stepped within his palms and then onto his shoulders. Already some pedestrians were taking notice and darting glances in their direction. "Better make this quick, Huber."

Once Alejandro was standing on Scott's shoulders, Huber stepped into Scott's cupped hands and pulled his way up to Alejandro. Scott began to wobble under all the weight.

"Cowboy! Do not falter!" Alejandro yelled.

"Shut it, Spaniard! Maybe you should take it easy on those *tapas* . . . go on a diet or somethin'." Scott gritted his teeth. After shifting his weight, he once again planted his feet. Huber stepped into the hands of Alejandro, who boosted Huber even higher. Huber made the mistake of looking down. His head must've been fifteen feet from the concrete. The sensation was dizzying. He took a breath and clung to the stone wall. Tilting his chin upward, he locked his eyes on the scroll and reached out his fingers. It was just a half inch out of reach. Many people were taking notice of them now, some even snapping pictures of the human ladder.

"Hurry!" Hannah yelled, observing the onlookers.

"I can't reach it!" Huber responded.

Hannah came to Scott, whose legs were buckling under the weight. "Scotty, you need to push them up just a little more. Go up on your tiptoes."

"You wanna take my place?" he said through gritted teeth.

She stole a quick glance around her, then slowly kissed his cheek and whispered in his ear. "I know you can do it."

Scott seemed to gain the strength of ten men and pushed upward with all his might. Slowly, his heels raised off the ground, lifting Alejandro and Huber. Huber's fingers brushed the scroll once, then twice, then finally he grasped the paper. "Got it!"

Scott let out a breath and lost his footing. Alejandro stumbled, his foot coming off Scott's shoulder. His rear end landed on Scott's head, and Huber came crashing down on top of both of them. All three boys crumpled like a house of cards and fell to the ground. The crowd of spectators let out a gasp. Hannah and Jessie ran forward. "Are you okay?" Jessie asked Huber as he nursed a sore elbow. Hannah helped the other two boys, who were writhing on the concrete. There were some minor scrapes and bruises, but nothing serious. Scott stood and waved to the crowd. A cheer erupted and everyone clapped.

"Come on!" Hannah said. "Let's get out of sight and read the scroll."

The five darted around the cathedral's corner and untied the ribbon holding the small paper scroll. There was no key attached. Alejandro read the Spanish writing. "*La primera llave está en el campanario*—The first key is in the bell tower."

They all sighed collectively and looked up toward the looming bell tower. "How the heck we supposed ta get up there?"

Jessie spoke up. "May I suggest an alternative to climbing the outer wall?"

"Absolutely," Huber responded, still rubbing his grated elbow.

"Maybe this time, we take the stairs."

"We cannot just walk inside and climb up to the tower," Alejandro said. "The parish priest will see us."

"We will need to distract him . . . anyone feel like confessing?"

They all turned to Scott.

"Why's everyone lookin' at me?"

● ● ●

Upon entering the massive cathedral, Huber was overwhelmed by the artistry, architecture, tapestries, and ancient feel of the interior. Massive pillars supported an arched ceiling, which held breathtaking paintings of the divine. Tombs of former men of prominence were one side of the hall. Stained glass windows ran along the upper wall, casting a colorful radiance over everything. A wooden staircase led to a decorated pulpit and row upon row of empty pews stretched across the floor. It was something of a place of worship and a museum in one. How long must it have taken to erect such a building? The parish priest on duty noticed his visitors and approached them.

"What do we do now?" Huber asked nervously.

"Follow my lead," Jessie whispered.

"*Bienvenidos*," the priest said upon reaching them. The man was middle aged, no older than forty. "*¿Como les puedo ayudar?*"

"*¿Se habla ingles?*" Jessie asked the man.

"Yes, I speak English," the priest answered. "What brings you here today?"

"These are my friends from America," she said, indicating Huber, Scott, and Hannah. "I brought them here to visit the cathedral."

"Welcome." The man shook their hands. "What do you think of the Cathedral of Salamanca?"

"It's beautiful," Huber answered enthusiastically.

The man seemed pleased.

"Eh, it's all right," Scott added. Huber elbowed him as the man's expression morphed into something else.

"Is it okay if we sit for awhile?" Alejandro asked.

"Most certainly," the priest said, regaining his happy composure.

"If it is okay, our friend here would like to speak to you . . . privately." He gestured at Scott.

"Ohhhh?" the priest said.

"Yeah," Scott stammered. "I got some confessin' to do in that phone booth lookin' thing."

"I see. Come with me." He pointed to an intricately carved confession booth.

Scott approached the booth, opened the door, and looked back worriedly. The other four nodded approvingly and his head disappeared inside. Hannah had to suppress a laugh. Soon, the priest disappeared within the other side of the adjacent compartment.

"Now's our chance!" Huber said. "Let's get up there."

At the back of the interior, a spiral set of stone steps led upward. They were roped off with a sign that read, *prohibido el paso*. Huber and Jessie walked briskly toward the stairs. Alejandro and Hannah stayed behind as lookout.

"I think I know what that says," Huber whispered to Jessie. "I think we're about to break a big rule."

"Perhaps, when we are finished, you too can make a confession." She smiled.

● ● ●

The spiral staircase led upward and upward. It was dizzying and Huber had to force himself not to look down as the stairs shook beneath his feet. Finally, they emerged onto a wooden platform. A massive bronze bell, taller than both of them, hung lazily. They quickly assessed the area, but saw no sign of a key.

"Where do you think the Falcon hid it?"

"I do not know," Jessie replied.

Through slats in the stone, Huber could make out a sea of people milling about outside. "Hey, what time do you think—" Before he could finish his sentence, the bell began to move automatically. A massive *bong* almost shattered his eardrums. Dropping to the floor, Jessie and Huber covered their ears as the *bong* sounded eight more times. After the room stopped vibrating, Huber removed his hands from his ringing ears.

"Nine," she said.

"Yeah, thanks."

They continued surveying the tower. "We have to hurry," Huber said. "They're going to find us soon."

Jessie blew out her breath. "Hold on!" she lay on her back and slid beneath the bell. She stood up so only her feet were visible beneath the rim. Her voice echoed from inside as she said, "Found it!" She stooped down and crawled out, holding a large brass key in her hand. "It was tied with a small rope to the top of the clapper, along with this." She handed another rolled up scroll to Huber and quickly filed away the key into her pocket. "Let's get out of here."

Jessie and Huber flew down the spiral staircase, doing their best to mute their footsteps as they went. They emerged into the chapel and plopped down into a pew adjacent to Hannah and Alejandro just as the door to the confession booth opened. The parish priest clapped Scott on the shoulder, told them all good-bye, and walked to the alter, his shoulders inadvertently convulsing in laughter.

"Just in the nick of time," Huber said.

Scott's face was red, and he refused to make eye contact.

"Have you been crying?" Hannah said.

"No! My eyes are just red. Must be this Spanish air . . . full'a allergies and stuff. Did you guys get the key or what?"

"Yeah, and there was another note attached." Huber held up the scroll. "Let's head back to the library."

8

INSIDE THE LIBRARY, THE five crowded around a table as university students browsed through the bookshelves. Huber unrolled the tiny scroll and smoothed its edges over the wooden surface. The neat, stylistic writing was undoubtedly that of the Falcon.

"What's it say?" Huber asked Jessie.

"*Perlas de sabiduría se pueden encontrar en la casa de Santiago. X=-3, Y=5. La llave segunda se encuentra al sur.*"

Scott groaned. "Dang, is that math or somethin'? Here I thought we were gettin' away from school. Algebra ain't my strong suit."

"This one seems really difficult," Jessie added. "Let's take it one step at a time."

"What's it say?"

Alejandro translated. "Pearls of wisdom can be found in the house of Saint James, then the algebraic formula.

After that it says the second key can be found to the south."

"All right . . ." Hannah mumbled. "Let's start with the pearls of wisdom and Saint James. Sounds like another church."

Alejandro nodded. "*Sí*, Saint James is famous in España. It is said he traveled here to preach and was beloved by the people. Many say he was buried in our country after he was martyred."

"Buried here in Salamanca?"

"No." Alejandro shook his head, disappointed. "In Compostela, a few hours north and west of here."

"Rules that out, genius," Scott said, sneering.

Hannah kicked him under the table. "I don't see you making any contributions."

"I wonder if there are any churches or cathedrals here in Salamanca named after Saint James?" Huber asked.

They scoured the library shelves for a listing of churches in Salamanca. Before long, the table was piled high with tourist books and histories of religion in Salamanca. Each person took a book and quickly scanned the contents, searching for any churches related to Saint James. After an hour, discouragement colored their countenances.

"I'm not seeing anything," Hannah said. "There doesn't seem to be any churches or cathedrals related to Saint James in the city."

"Perhaps it is not a church we should be searching

for," Alejandro ventured. "Pearls of wisdom. What do you think of when I say the word *pearl*?"

"Ocean," Hannah said.

"*Sí*," Alejandro said excitedly, jotting the word down.

"Ain't no ocean round here, genius," Scott blew out.

"I'm getting tired of you just sitting back and criticizing everybody, Scott," Hannah scolded. "If you're not going to help, why don't you just leave?"

"Fine, maybe I will!" Scott shot up.

Patrons of the library stopped where they were and looked at him. Beatriz worked her way over to them quickly. "If you want to stay here," she said curtly, "I suggest you do not draw attention to yourselves. A library is a place of reverence and wisdom. Please keep your voices down or you'll be out on your laurels."

"Hold on!" Hannah said. "What did you say?"

"I said you'll have to go elsewhere if you cannot be reverent."

"No before that . . . a place of wisdom." Her eyes lit up. "We're sorry. We'll be quiet, won't we, Scott?"

Scott took a breath and sat back down, folding his arms and looking away.

"Pearls of wisdom can be found within the house of Saint James . . . are there any libraries in Salamanca named after Saint James?" she asked the librarian. Everyone's faces perked up at the question.

"Not to my knowledge, no."

Their faces fell.

"However," she continued. "There is another library close to here." She chuckled. "It is very peculiar. It's an old palace covered in seashells. The city converted it into a library years ago. We have a much larger selection of books here," she said defensively. "But I suppose the place has its charms."

"Seashells?" Huber said aloud.

"Pearls . . ." Jessie smiled.

"I see," Alejandro said excitedly. "Pearls are found within shells."

"What is the name of the library?" Hannah asked the woman.

"*Casa de Conchas* . . . House of Shells."

"That could be it," Jessie said.

"But what's Saint James have to do with seashells?" Huber said aloud.

Alejandro arose and fled down an adjacent row of books. A moment later, he returned with a periodical detailing the House of Shells Library when it was dedicated. He began to read aloud, "*Casa de Conchas* or House of Shells was originally a palace, designed by Rodrigo Arias Maldonado. Maldonado was a member of the order of— *listen to this*! Santiago! A brotherhood of knights centered around the teachings of the Apostle James. Maldonado decorated his palace with seashells, the symbol of Saint James in España."

"That's it!" Hannah said. "Why do seashells symbolize Saint James, though?"

Alejandro kept reading. "It is legend that after Saint James was beheaded by King Agrippa in Jerusalem, a group of Christian knights from Spain carried his body back to their homeland of Compostela to be buried. During their journey at sea, a massive storm wrecked the ship. The headless body of Saint James was lost, but days later washed ashore, undamaged and blanketed in seashells. Thereafter, Christians in Spain recognized the seashell as the symbol of Santiago or Saint James. I think we know where the second key is," he said, sitting back down and nudging Hannah.

"Now we just have to figure out what the rest of the riddle means," she said, nudging him back.

Scott watched this exchange and simmered in his seat. "So the Spaniard got lucky for once," he said roughly. "It's bound to happen. Well, we ain't gettin' no younger. Let's go and get this done with. Two libraries in one day . . ."

Jessie jotted down the address to House of Shells, and they briskly walked out the door.

● ● ●

After hailing a taxi, they shortly arrived at *La Casa de Conchas*. The building, a dullish brown, was decorated with chiseled seashells all over its exterior. Huber tilted his head and made out all the different patterns that the shells could make—triangles, squares, and rectangles. The effect was mesmerizing. They found their way to the south side of the building.

"X=-3, Y=5," Hannah repeated to herself.

"An algebraic expression," Alejandro said. "Coordinates on a grid."

"Yes." Hannah smiled with her eyes. "The shells form a kind of grid on the face of the wall."

"We just need to find zero!"

Scott pointed to Alejandro. "Think we found our zero right here." He chuckled.

Nobody laughed. Huber took Scott aside and whispered, "You're not going to win her back with comments like that. They just make you look like a jerk."

"I know," Scott said. "I just can't help it. I can't stand that guy."

"Because he showed you up?"

"No!"

"Just cool it, all right?"

Scott nodded and Huber turned to go back to the group. "Hey, Huber?"

Huber turned back. "What?"

Scott paused, his eyes darting to the ground. "Nothin' . . . never mind."

When they returned to the group, Hannah and Alejandro were pointing excitedly toward the wall.

"Find zero yet?" Huber asked.

"Yes!" Alejandro answered. He counted twelve columns of shells from the left, then twelve from the right. "The thirteenth column of shells represents the Y-axis. It's right in the middle of the wall!"

Hannah then counted seven rows of shells from the bottom and seven from the top. "The eighth row is in the middle horizontally. That's the X-axis. Where the two axes meet is zero."

"Ya kiddin' me?" Scott said. "I coulda figured that one out in two seconds."

"I thought math wasn't your strong suit." Hannah shook her head and muttered something under her breath.

"Okay, I see." Jessie transfixed her gaze on the wall and pointed to the shell representing the zero coordinate. "X=-3. That means we go three to the left of zero."

"Exactly," Hannah said.

"Y=5," Huber added. "So we go up— "

"Five from there," Scott finished the sentence for him. "Yeah, five up from -3. That's the one."

"Thanks," Huber said sarcastically. Hannah paid him no mind.

They all counted with their fingers until they landed on the same coordinate, twenty feet or so above the sidewalk. The sun peeked over an adjacent building and illuminated the south-facing wall. The shell at -3 and 5 glimmered in the sunlight. It was somehow different from the others. It was painted a different color. This particular shell was purple and stuck out like a sore thumb now that they looked at it closely.

"That's it!" Jessie said. "We need to get to that shell."

Scott glowered. "If you're thinkin' about doin' that human ladder thing again, forget it!"

"We won't need to. Look! There's a ledge beneath that window up there. If we go inside, one of us can go through it and step onto the ledge. Any volunteers?" Hannah asked.

Nobody spoke up.

"Fine. I'll do it. Let's head inside."

● ● ●

Inside *La Casa de Las Conchas*, there was a spacious courtyard full of people quietly conversing and reading on benches. A stone well rested smack dab in the middle of the yard. Huber wondered how many people must have drunk from that well over the centuries, including Rodrigo Maldonado who founded the order of Saint James. A bronze plaque of some kind decorated the face of the well. It was inscribed with the words *bebe del pozo de sabiduría viva.*

"What's that say?" Hannah edged closer to Alejandro while Scott bit his tongue.

"In *Inglés*, it says, 'Drink from the well of living wisdom.'"

"I see . . . very appropriate for a library. What a beautiful phrase."

Scott couldn't help but interrupt their conversation. "I'd rather drink Slurpees from the endless well of 7-Eleven."

Hannah didn't seem to hear him as her eyes stayed locked on Alejandro.

"C'mon, let's head up to the higher levels," Huber suggested.

They quickly ascended to the second floor and entered the building. The hallways were narrow and many doors lined the floor leading to different areas of the library.

As they walked further down the corridor, people thinned out until they were virtually alone. Upon reaching the south end of the building, they encountered large, double doors, intricately carved with cherubs and seashells. Just then, a male library worker rounded the corner and nearly plowed into them. He was tall, skinny, and seemed just a few years older than them, maybe in high school or barely in college. "*Bienvenidos, como les puedo asistir?*" the worker said sternly.

"*Buscamos un libro,*" Jessie replied quickly. "*Sobre Santiago de Compostela.*"

The library worker smirked suspiciously. "*¿Sí?*"

"*Así es,*" Alejandro affirmed.

He then looked at Scott, Huber, and Hannah. "*¿Americanos, no?*"

"*Sí, nosotros somos de Colorado,*" Huber answered in Spanish.

The young man seemed surprised that Huber responded in his native tongue. "Most Americans I meet here cannot speak a word of Spanish," he said. "Impressive." He then turned back to Jessie. "You seek a book about Saint James of Compostela, you say?"

"That's right."

"It would likely be on the north side of the building. Come, I'll escort you."

"That's okay. We can find our way."

"I insist," he said with a tone of finality.

"What kind of books are here on the south side?" Alejandro asked, pointing to the door.

"Special collections. You must have permission to enter there. Permission that *you* do not have. In fact, you could not enter if you wanted to." He grinned and pulled up an electronic key that was attached to his belt with an elastic cord. The key looked like a miniature credit card. "Now, come with me. I'll show you to the north side."

What choice did they have? The worker did an about-face and began walking down the opposite end of the corridor. Small bookshelves and chairs were interspersed throughout the hallway, almost forcing them to walk single file. Begrudgingly, they followed the worker who was now conversing over his shoulder with Jessie and Alejandro in rapid Spanish.

"We have to get that key," Hannah whispered to her brother.

"Yeah, good luck with that."

"I have an idea. I'm going to faint."

"What?"

"When I do, he'll come see if I'm all right. Grab the card off his belt when he does."

"No way can I do that without him noticing."

"Any better ideas?"

Huber didn't have time to respond before Hannah moaned and hit the deck with a hard thud. Everyone turned around. Hannah was sprawled out on the floor, seemingly unconscious.

"*¿Que pasó?*" the worker asked and hurried his way to Hannah.

"We've been walking around the city all day," Huber said. "I think she fainted."

"Let me see her." The young man pushed them all aside and bent down next to Hannah. The key was within reach, but it was attached with a metal clip to the man's belt. As the worker surveyed Hannah and jostled her, Huber took a breath and gently placed his fingers on the clip. The young man didn't notice. Steeling himself, he gripped the thing and tugged upward as softly as he could. It wasn't soft enough. The worker turned toward Huber and glanced downward at his hand, which rested on his waistline. His face turned red with anger.

"What are you—?"

A loud *smack* sounded from behind, and the young man crumpled to the floor next to Hannah, who now rose up. Scott, holding a large encyclopedia volume, looked satisfied. "Guess books *are* good for somethin'. Better hurry before he wakes up. Grab his key."

"Cowboy! Are you crazy?" Alejandro stammered. "We will end up in jail with my grandfather for this!"

"Better hurry before he wakes up then."

Huber snatched the key from the knocked-out library

worker. They bolted to the special collections door and waved the key in front of a black pad. The red light at the top turned green and the door *clicked*. Huber swung the door open, ushered everyone inside, and closed the door behind him. Inside, glass enclosed volumes and parchments decorated the room. The place was more of a museum than a library. Beneath one enclosure was the skull of a human being. Too bad they didn't have time to look around and find out who it had belonged to.

"There's the window to the south facing wall!" Alejandro pointed.

Hannah ran to the window, unlatched it, and pushed upward. As she did, a painfully loud blare almost burst their eardrums. The window had triggered an alarm. *Blllaaang, bllaaang, blllaaang.*

Huber covered his ears. "We are so dead!"

Hannah pushed the window up the rest of the way and stepped onto the sill. "There's only one way we're getting out of here! Looks like I'm not the only one going out the window now!"

Huber watched as his sister ducked her head out into the open air. She looked to her left. "It's right there!" She pointed to the purple seashell. Before Huber could stop her, Hannah stepped out onto the ledge and plastered her body as close to the window as she could, clutching the wall like a lizard.

"Hannah! What are you doing!" Huber yelled.

"We can climb down on the shells. Just like climbing

a rock wall," she yelled back. "The key is just over here. I can get it." She disappeared from view.

Huber stuck his head out of the window and watched as Hannah inched closer to the purple shell. Clinging tightly with her left hand to the wall, Huber held his breath watching Hannah lean to the right toward the purple shell.

"Hey, sis, don't look down."

"Thanks, that's very helpful advice."

Huber watched the purple shell tickle her fingertips. She reached a bit further and stumbled, her right foot temporarily losing hold of the shell upon which it rested. She lost control and fell backward. In those brief seconds, Huber pictured his sister lying flat on the sidewalk below. From this height, she'd likely survive, but be paralyzed from a broken back or neck. As she clawed at her hand-hold, Huber, without thinking, was outside. Instinctively, he caught the small of Hannah's back and pushed her toward the wall, steadying her body. Huber, clinging to the inside of the window with one arm, had caught her with his other.

"Thanks." She flashed a genuine smile. "I owe you a Coke."

"Can you reach the shell?"

"It's close!" Hannah leaned to her right once more. She caught the purple shell with her fingertips. "It's weird. The shell is hollowed out on the inside. I think I can open it."

Huber watched as she flipped it open as a person

would flip open a mollusk shell to retrieve a pearl. A silver key with a purple ribbon fell from the shell into her hand. "I got it!" she yelled above the blaring alarm. The shell snapped itself shut as she released it.

"Good! Can you climb down?"

"Yes, I think so. Follow me down!" Hannah said as she stepped onto a shell below her. She zigged and zagged between foot- and handholds like a mountain goat.

Huber followed, forcing himself to step beyond the ledge and onto the shells. An involuntary slip would result in near fatal injury. He refused to look down as he descended. Jessie followed close in tow, just above him. Alejandro and then Scott climbed out the window after the others. Luckily, the street below the south wall was currently deserted with only a few cars whizzing by. So far, it appeared as if no one had noticed the five of them scaling the House of Shells. Huber was three quarters of the way down now, only ten feet from the ground. Hannah had reached the sidewalk below. Scott was still near the top. Suddenly, the library worker who had been knocked unconscious shot his head out the window, holding the back of his neck. "*Allí están!*" he bellowed at someone on the inside. The man grasped for Scott, but he was just out of reach. "We will head them off below!" The man's head disappeared from view.

"Hurry!" Huber yelled as he dropped to the ground.

Hannah was ahead of him clutching the silver key, the ribbon still tied to its head.

Alejandro and Jessie both hit the ground running. Scott still had a little ways to go when several men burst out from some nearby the doors. The inside was still filled with the ear-piercing shriek of the siren. It didn't take long to spot them all. "*Allá!*" The librarian pointed.

"Scott! Let go!" Huber called. "We'll catch you!"

Scott, still ten feet above the ground, shook his head. "Just go!"

"Trust me!"

Alejandro was now at Huber's side. "Now! They're coming, cowboy!"

The men were racing hard toward them. Huber watched Scott take a breath and then fall backward from the wall. With Alejandro's help, Scott's body never hit the ground. It felt like catching a hundred pound sack of flour.

"Thanks," Scott muttered at Huber and Alejandro.

"Grab them!" one of the men shouted, now just feet away.

"Run!" Huber yelled.

The men from the library were fast, but not fast enough to keep up with their younger, more agile counterparts. Ducking and weaving through alleyways and side streets, they were soon out of sight of their pursuers. Reaching a deserted alleyway, they all collapsed against the wall, sucking wind, sweat wringing their faces. Hannah cracked a smile. "That was intense," she panted. "Reminds me of the time we ran away from Dad," she said, wheezing, "when he found out we backed his car into the garage door."

Huber smiled. "Yeah, I remember. He shouldn't have left his keys in the car. We were eight."

They all smiled and would've laughed if their lungs didn't burn so bad. Huber suddenly thought of his parents at home and sadness filled him. Since arriving to Spain, they'd called only twice and as far as Robert and Ellen knew, their kids were having the time of their lives studying Spanish all day long. Of course, it wouldn't do any good to call them and tell the truth now.

"Do you still have the key?" Alejandro asked Hannah after he'd regained his breath.

Hannah took out the silver key, still attached to the purple ribbon, from her pocket and tossed it to Alejandro.

"Looks very similar to the other key. Only this one is silver. There's something written here on the ribbon as well."

"What's it say?" Huber asked.

"It is the writing of El Halcón. It says, '*Ya que tengas las primeras dos llaves, la clave final se esconde donde el demonio enseñaba a sus alumnos. La oscuridad se ilumina el camino.*'"

"What's that mean?"

Jessie answered, "Now that you have the first two keys, the final key is hidden where—"

"The demon taught his students," Alejandro finished in an ominous tone.

"Where the demon taught his students?" Hannah repeated.

"Hey, I ain't goin' to no devil worshippin' site," Scott said flatly. "Count me out. Y'all can go there by yourselves. I'll stay in the library with the ol' lady."

"Is that it?" Hannah asked.

"No, there's more. The last part says that darkness will light the way."

Huber moaned. "That makes zero sense."

"More riddles," Jessie said. "It must be a physical location somewhere here in Salamanca."

"I'm noticing a pattern here," Huber said.

"What is it?" Hannah asked.

"The first key had to do with a church . . . heaven . . . up above. The second, a Saint. Now this one, a demon."

"I'd rather stick with churches and Saints myself," Hannah said uneasily.

"Yeah, me too, but we have to find the final key. Any ideas where to start looking?"

"Let's head back to the library. Maybe we can find some answers there."

CHAPTER
· 9 ·

THEY ALL FELT A bit safer back inside the library at the University. In fact, the place was starting to feel a bit like a second home. They'd been researching for hours about demons and Salamanca but hadn't found anything that particularly stuck out.

As they haphazardly turned pages, Pincho's mother snuck up from behind and slammed a thousand-page volume on the table, causing them all to jump in their seats. "I'd start by looking there," the old lady said.

"¿*Que es esto?*" Alejandro asked.

"It is a book. What do you think it is? I will leave you now."

"Wait!" Huber said. "You know the answer? Why don't you just tell us?"

"I wouldn't deny you the privilege of finding the answer for yourselves." She smiled and *swish-swashed* away.

Jessie traced her finger along the book's faded cover. "Dark Legends of Spain."

"What's in this book that can help us?" Hannah said.

"One way to find out," Alejandro said as he and Hannah reached for the book simultaneously. Their fingers touched and they both smiled awkwardly. Scott took a deep breath and restrained himself.

They flipped through the table of contents but saw nothing that correlated with the current riddle. Beatriz harrumphed from behind the counter. They all peered back at her. "Perhaps you'd have better luck using the index?"

Jessie turned flipped to the book's back and reached the index. "Let's think of some key words that pertain to our riddle."

"Stupid," Scott said.

Everyone rolled their eyes.

"Demon," Alejandro said.

"Nice," Hannah said with admiration.

"Waste of time," Scott added.

They turned and found ninety-six references to the word demon.

"There's too many," Jessie said. "Think of another word."

"Students," Huber said.

Jessie found the word in the index. "Forty-five references. Still too many."

"Salamanca," Scott said, still sulking.

"What'd you say?" Jessie asked loudly.

"I said Salamanca. If this place is here in the city, there'd prob'ly be somethin' about it, wouldn't there?"

Jessie thumbed a few pages back and found the word *Salamanca*. "Only five references! Very nice work, Cowboy!"

Scott bowed graciously. "Ain't as dumb as I look, now am I?"

Jessie flipped to page 567 and found the correct reference on the right hand column. Her voice trembled with excitement as she read, "There exists a legend in Salamanca, Spain, that seven students studied beneath the tutelage of a demon teacher." She eyed the others, elation beaming from her face. "For more regarding this legend, see *Marquis de Villena.*"

"Quick!" Huber said excitedly. "Find a book on Marquis de Villena."

Alejandro shot out of his chair. "I will find it."

Scott was on his feet too. "Not if I beat you to it, Spaniard."

Hannah laughed, "Right, Scotty, like you'll be able to find anything in here."

Alejandro was headed toward the nearest catalogue. Scott ran to one on the opposite side of the room, not really sure where to look. The Dewey decimal system was perplexing. He had no idea how to use it. Suddenly, the old woman's face appeared from behind a corner of a bookshelf. "Psst, here," she said and handed him a book labeled *Spanish Marquises of the 16th Century.*

Scott strutted back toward the table like a peacock and haphazardly dropped the book on the table. "Looky here. I think that's two for two."

"How did you . . . ?" Hannah said unbelievingly.

Alejandro was still fingering through index cards when Jessie shouted that Scott had already found the book. Crestfallen, Alejandro sulked back to the group. Scott grinned and flitted his eyebrows at him. Hannah opened the book to the index and quickly found a reference to Marquis de Villena on page 123. She read aloud, "Marquis de Villena is the most legendary of the seven students who were taught by a demon inside the Cave of Salamanca. In exchange for the Demon Maestro sharing his magic secrets, each student agreed to draw lots—"

"Hold up, what's a Maestro?" Scott said.

"You never paid attention in Spanish, did you?" Huber shook his head. "It means teacher."

"Oh yeah, I knew that."

Hannah sighed and continued, "The one who drew the shortest lot would be consigned to spend eternity in the service of the Demon Maestro. At the end of seven years of lessons, the seven students drew lots and the shortest fell to the Marquis de Villena. He was put in chains and forced to remain in the cave for all eternity."

The image of Juan Hernán Salazar rotting inside the mine at Dead Man's Treasure sizzled through Huber's mind, causing him to shudder.

"That's it?" Alejandro asked.

"No, there's more. One night, the Marquis hid himself in a large, empty vat the demon had once filled with water. When the demon came to bring the Marquis his evening meal, he opened the door to find his slave missing. In a panic, the demon assumed the Marquis had fled and rushed out to find him. In his haste, the demon left the door to the cell open behind him. The clever Marquis de Villena exited the vat and escaped. It is said that the demon still searches the streets of Salamanca for his missing prisoner by night and roams the tunnels beneath the city by day."

Alejandro's eyes widened. "*Aye caray!*"

"I wonder what the demon was teaching them," Huber said.

Hannah scanned the page further and answered, "It is rumored the demon taught his students the magic of alchemy or . . ."

"What?"

Hannah finished her sentence, ". . . the ability to turn common metals and objects into *gold*."

"Gold?" Alejandro repeated in awe.

"Does it say where the cave is located?" Huber asked.

"No," she said dejectedly.

"Great!" Scott jumped in. "Right back to square one."

Hannah noticed an American couple across the library, gawking up at the statuary within the library. In the woman's hand was a yellow tourist guide. "Be right back," she told the group, who was arguing about which book to find next. They didn't seem to hear her. She pushed her chair back, stood up, and approached the couple.

"Excuse me," she asked the woman. "May I see your guide for a moment?"

The woman smiled and handed Hannah the tourist guide. Hannah turned to the middle of the small book and handed it back to the tourist. "Thank you."

Hannah returned to the bickering group, "*La Cueva de Salamanca* or Cave of Salamanca! It's only a mile and a half from here to the north!"

The group stopped their hushed arguing. "How do you know?" Huber asked.

"Call it woman's intuition. Let's go before it gets dark. I don't especially like the idea of going to a demon's cave at night."

● ● ●

The sun was just beginning to set as they arrived to *La Cueva de Salamanca*—a partially recessed, arched tunnel that descended below the street about thirty feet. The ruins of an old church stood atop. One side led to an alleyway, and the other side to a doorway with stone steps that ascended up to the churchyard. There were several tourists milling about, snapping photos and reading guides about the site.

"I read in the guide that the church bricked off this cave and built over it, trying to erase it from the people's memory. Archaeologists rediscovered it fairly recently," Hannah said. "That's why it wasn't in the books we were searching."

"So, this is where the demon taught his students," Huber said aloud. "I wonder if there's any truth to that story."

Scott shrugged. "Probably. Demons teach us every day at school," he said. "This place is tiny though. I thought our classrooms were cramped. No way I coulda gone to school in here for seven years. But I guess we have to go for twelve years as it is."

"Sixteen if you get a bachelors degree," Hannah corrected him.

"Twenty for a doctorate," Jessie added.

"Good thing I ain't gonna be no doctor," Scott said. "Unless I can somehow earn a doctorate in awesomeness."

Hannah and Jessie both shook their heads.

"Look around," Huber directed them. "El Halcón must have left the final key here somewhere."

As the last of the tourists stepped outside of the small tunnel, the five scoured the inside, feeling their way around every nook and cranny of the bricked archway.

"It's not here," Huber said. "There's nowhere to hide anything."

"There's something we are not seeing," Alejandro ventured.

"Let us think for a moment," Jessie said. "The book said that the Marquis de Villena hid in a vat."

"But there's no vat in here," Hannah responded.

Jessie continued on. "The demon opened the door to find the cell empty. I wonder where the door was located originally."

"Wherever it was, it's long gone now," Hannah said, looking at both ends of the open tunnel.

"Maybe," Huber answered. "But maybe not."

"What do you mean, Huber?" Jessie asked.

"Think about it? Where do demons come from?"

"*El infierno*," Alejandro answered somberly. "From down below."

"Exactly!"

"I see!" Jessie said. "Look down. Perhaps the doorway is beneath us."

Everyone dropped to their hands and knees and diligently searched the cobble stone ground. The sun's light was fading, the tunnel darkening by the minute. A passerby walked by the tunnel and noticed the group crawling around on all fours. He chuckled and snapped a quick picture. Then a familiar voice caused Huber's head to snap upward.

"Dude! It's me!"

As they all looked up, Huber instantly recognized Willow—the man from the plane with tattered clothes and ratty hair.

"Oh . . . hey, Willow. Fancy seeing you here."

"Just broadening my horizons, bro. What are you guys doing crawling around on all fours like that? Did you lose a contact? I can help," he said, letting his backpack fall to the ground. He then dropped beside them and began searching.

"No, we're just looking for something."

"What?"

"It's hard to explain."

Willow smiled and nodded. "Yeah, I see. You're searching to find *yourselves*, aren't you?"

Huber eyed the others and silently pleaded for them to go along. "Exactly. We're searching for our inner selves, trying to figure out who we really are."

Willow pointed to Huber. "Dude, I respect that."

"And since you've already found yourself, there's probably not much point in you being here with us."

"Huber, Huber, Huber . . . haven't you learned anything I've taught you. The journey of self-discovery is never complete. I'll search with you, brother."

Scott piped up. "Hey, hippie, what's your deal, anyway? Did your mom drop you on your head when you were a kid or somethin'?"

Willow's smile faded. "I see your friend has some way negative vibes, Huber. It's kind of messing with my groove to be honest."

"Yeah, I know. You just have to bear with him."

"Dude, just tell him the truth," Scott said. "We're looking for a key."

"Ahhh," Willow said. "The key to what? Your soul? Your mind? Very deep stuff."

"Naw, dude. An actual key."

"Hmmm," Willow said. "I don't follow."

"Like the key to a door," Hannah said.

Willow nodded. "Like the door to imagination."

Huber shook his head. "Sorry, Willow, I wasn't completely honest with you. We are looking for an actual physical key. It should be here somewhere."

Willow looked hurt. "Huber, dude, I can't believe you were dishonest with me."

"Sorry," Huber muttered. "It's kind of secret stuff."

"Brothers shouldn't hold secrets from each other, Huber."

"Well, now that you know what we're looking for, I guess you can help us."

Willow nodded enthusiastically.

Sprawled out on all fours, they all continued to search the ground but couldn't find anything out of the ordinary. As the last rays of sunlight faded beyond the horizon, the cave dimmed until it was almost dark.

"Hey, hippie guy," Scott said. "You got a flashlight in that pack?"

"Of course I do."

"Break it out. It's gettin' dark in here."

Willow unzipped and dug into his bag. He fumbled a flashlight through his hands and clicked it on, shining directly into Scott's face.

"Hey! Watch it!" Scott rubbed his eyes.

Willow shone the flashlight all around the tunnel. As the light grazed the staircase and then drifted away from it, Huber noticed something odd just below the bottom step. It was a small design of some kind. It seemed to be glowing in the absence of the flashlight. Huber went to the step and dropped to his knees to take a closer look. The design had disappeared.

"Willow! Shine that light over here again," he yelled.

Willow complied, shining the light on the bottom step. There was nothing there. As Willow removed the light, the design reappeared and glowed brighter. Upon closer examination, Huber realized that the design was a carving of the same symbol that had decorated his grandpa's coin—the Crusader's Cross. Reflexively, he thrust his hand in his pocket, then remembered. A pang of anger and hurt welled up as he thought of his coin in King Fausto's possession.

"Over here!" he yelled to the others. "I found something! Willow, turn off the light!"

Willow clicked off the light and the others gathered around him. He pointed out the small symbol, glowing in the darkness. "Remember the riddle?" Jessie asked excitedly. "The darkness will light your way! Look around, the key must be here."

"Alejandro, do you still have the message?"

He removed it from his pocket and handed it over to Jessie. She recited it again with Willow's flashlight, *"Ya que tengas las primeras dos llaves, la clave final se esconde . . ."*

She suddenly stopped and slapped her forehead as if she'd come to a sudden realization. "Notice how he underlined the word *clave*?"

"What about it?" Huber said.

"*Llave* and *clave* both mean 'key' in Spanish, but they're different."

"How?"

Alejandro jumped in. "*Así es!* Brilliant! *Llave* is a key like this," he said, holding up the brass key they'd found at the church. "Clave is more like a key to solving a puzzle."

"Not physical," Hannah said.

"Exactly."

"Now we're getting somewhere," Willow said. "I knew you were looking for some kind of metaphorical key. Right on!"

Huber interrupted. "Look, the symbol is disappearing!"

Jessie took the light from Willow and shined it where the symbol had previously been. When she removed the light, it shone brightly once again.

"The light from the flashlight must charge it somehow. It's like those solar lights mom put in the yard," Hannah exclaimed. "The sun charges them up and then they glow at night. Shine the light around."

Jessie hastily shone the light in different spots, then removed the beam, hoping to see more hidden characters or symbols. Jessie shone her light in the middle of the floor and quickly removed it. Cursive letters briefly appeared, and then just as quickly evaporated.

"Here! I found something!"

The other four joined Jessie, directly on a spot in the middle of the cave. They counted to ten, then she removed the light. Glowing in bright green were the letters, "L-O-N-A-N."

"What does it mean?" Jessie whispered.

Suddenly, Michael Jackson's "Beat It" began playing. Yesenia retrieved her cell phone.

Scott shook his head. "What's that?"

"Michael Jackson. I enjoy his music," she said defensively as she answered the call. "*Bueno?*"

A few seconds passed before Jessie spoke, "*Sí, sí, ya tenemos la clave . . . ¿Cuando? . . . ¿Ahora? ¿Como sabe él? Okay, nos vemos pronto.*" She hung up the phone and then reported to the group. "That was Pincho. Somehow, the Falcon knows we've found the final key." She looked around and outside the tunnel. "He must be watching us somehow."

"What'd he say?" Hannah asked.

"He would like to meet with us. He awaits us at the tavern."

"Sorry, Willow, we have to go now," Huber said.

Jessie handed the man his flashlight. "*Gracias, señor.* You are very kind."

Willow smiled and shined the light on Scott. "Observe. *She* has some good vibes. You should try to follow her example." He then shone the light on the others. "Well, young ones, I'm so happy I could help you all with your journeys of self-discovery tonight. May the force be with you," he said, bowing somberly.

● ● ●

A half hour later, they arrived back at the tavern. Inside, Pincho was munching on some appetizers and downing a tall glass of something disgusting. He caught sight of them, let out a loud burp, and waved them over to his table. Several patrons eyed them warily as they made their way to the table. They crowded around the man, who seemed only about half drunk.

He smiled. "Hey there," he slurred. "How's life with my mother?"

"She's very kind, actually," Hannah answered.

"Yeah, how'd a guy like you come from a nice, smart lady like her?" Scott wondered.

"A fair question, my lad. I wasn't always as I appear. Believe it or not, at one time, I was a successful professor at the University."

"I don't believe it. What'd ya teach? Alco-hology 101?"

Pincho laughed raucously, then sobered. "History 101, actually . . . like my father."

"Father?"

Pincho looked up at Scott with vacant eyes, then turned a touch angry. "That's right! Everyone has a father! I grew up with my mother in the library and watching my father teach courses as a professor. It was natural I follow in his footsteps. We taught side by side for many years."

"Where's your father now?" Huber asked.

"Dead." He sighed. "At least we have no reason to think otherwise."

"Oh, I'm sorry."

"Don't you wonder why I've been helping you? Why my mother is helping you? My father discovered the truth behind the Brotherhood of Coronado years ago. He knew of their influence and was about to blow the lid off their whole operation when he disappeared. That was nearly twenty years ago."

"Why didn't the Brotherhood come after you and your mom?"

"My mother received a warning from the Brotherhood that if she continued prying into their business, her son would disappear as well. I received a similar warning about my mother. Since then, I've been working behind the scenes, but my mother is disappointed in what I've become. Says I've lost my soul."

Suddenly, thinking of Pincho as the comical village drunk wasn't so funny.

Pincho's phone abruptly beeped. He retrieved the giant white phone, pressed an oversized button, and brought the apparatus to his ear. "¿Sí?"

Undecipherable words filtered through the other side of the line.

"Okay, okay, I understand," Pincho said and hung up.

"El Halcón is ready to see you now. He is waiting in the alleyway behind the tavern." He pointed to the back door. "*Vamos*."

The five rose from their table and ventured out the back door one by one. The narrow alleyway was sandwiched between two tall, narrow brick walls. Trash cans and debris littered the thoroughfare. Huber caught a glimpse of a rat's tail beneath a wooden crate and shuddered. As Pincho exited the doorway, they heard the steel door lock itself shut upon closing behind them. They looked around but didn't see anyone.

"I don't see no Falcons," Scott said.

"I don't like this," Jessie said.

"Just wait . . . he'll be here," Pincho breathed nervously.

Huber hated the silence. The hair on his arms stood on end. They were startled when a cat jumped from a trash can, chasing the rat Huber had just seen. After regaining their composure, a hooded figure met their view, standing ten feet away, his face obscured by shadow and some kind of mask. Pincho wandered over to him and the Falcon whispered in his ear. His whispering was rapid and completely in Spanish.

"Well done," Pincho related on behalf of the man. "You've retrieved all three keys?"

Huber nodded. "You're the Falcon?"

The man gave an almost imperceptible nod.

"What? You can't talk to us yourself?" Scott scoffed.

The man whispered again to Pincho, who then relayed

the Falcon's words. "I must maintain as much secrecy as possible," Pincho translated. "You cannot hear my voice nor see my face."

"Yes, we have the keys," Hannah spoke up.

Pincho continued as the Falcon whispered in his ear. "Good. You will need all three to enter the Brotherhood's stronghold."

"What can you tell us about the Brotherhood?" Huber asked.

More whispers. "Their influence is ubiquitous. They seek to reclaim all of España's lost fortunes. The Brotherhood is patient. They've been plotting and plundering for many years, amassing great wealth for their final mission, which is to subvert the government, then use their resources to rebuild Spain's military and economic power." The Falcon paused and then whispered something else to Pincho. "Think about it, which currency is most recognized around the world?"

"*Oro,*" Alejandro answered. "Gold."

The Falcon nodded and continued whispering to Pincho. "With enough gold and treasure, the Brotherhood will usurp the government, then buy up power along with all of Europe's debts, ultimately subjecting them to a new kind of bondage, in effect setting up a new Spanish empire."

"We just came to take back Dead Man's Treasure," Huber said flatly.

Scott backed Huber up. "Yeah, we don't care about what happens over here."

The Falcon sighed, and his whispers took on a hardened tone. Pincho nodded and translated. "*Tesoro de Los Muertos* was just one treasure among many the Brotherhood has acquired and you should care about what happens here. Once the Brotherhood has seized power over Europe, where do you think they will focus their efforts next?"

Scott and Huber both shrugged their shoulders.

More whispering. "The New World. They will finish what they started with their conquest of America," Pincho related.

They all looked at each other, unable to believe what they were hearing.

Pincho continued translating the Falcon's words. "Before the Brotherhood of Coronado can put their final plans into motion, they seek one more thing—something beyond anyone's comprehension." The Falcon's tone became hurried, almost worried, as he whispered into Pincho's ear. "The Brotherhood of Coronado ultimately seeks to find the City of Cíbola. Their entire agenda depends upon it. The city made of solid gold that evaded Francisco Coronado so many years ago."

"My grandpa said that the Zuni just made those stories up," Huber interrupted, "to keep Coronado on the move."

The Falcon shook his head emphatically and kept whispering to Pincho. "That is what most believe. However, the Brotherhood is close to locating the city. The Zuni did lead Coronado away from Cíbola, because they knew as well as anyone what he would do if he found it."

"A city made of gold . . ." Alejandro whispered.

The Falcon continued through Pincho. "In 1539, Friar Marcos de Niza, told officers in Mexico City that the Natives had showed him something remarkable, a city constructed entirely of gold."

"I bet he was smokin' too much peyote," Scott said.

The Falcon ignored his comment and kept whispering to Pincho. "When Francisco Coronado heard the news, he set out with an expedition to find the city, drunken with greed. When the Natives heard that Coronado was coming, they led him away from the city, feeding him false directions and other lies. The Zuni led him further east, hundreds of miles away from Cíbola."

"Why didn't the Friar just tell him where it was?" Hannah asked.

"Without his Native guides, he could not relocate the city. Only those who are entrusted with the secrets are able to find it. Months later, Coronado and the Friar gave up the search and returned to Mexico City, failures. The Brotherhood seeks to rediscover Cíbola in order to redeem Coronado's name and fulfill their final mission."

"So the city actually exists?"

The Falcon nodded and whispered something else to Pincho. "It is said that over the years, the Zuni continue to guard the location, not to protect the city itself, but what lies at its center. This is what the Brotherhood truly seek."

"What is at the center of the city?" Hannah asked, intrigued.

The Falcon whispered and Pincho translated. "A staff."

"What's so special about a staff?" Huber asked.

"This staff has the power to change the world."

The five eyed each other skeptically.

The Falcon continued via Pincho, "It is said that Cíbola was once an ordinary village until Uhepono, the Zuni God of the underworld, disguised himself as a traveler and bestowed a gift upon one of its lowly residents named Lonan."

"Wait!" Huber interrupted him. "Lonan? That's the word we learned in the cave of Salamanca. The final key."

The Falcon nodded and continued his story through Pincho, "The traveler Uhepono gave Lonan a golden staff. On its end was a red, transparent stone, large as a human fist. Uhepono advised him that anything he touched with the stone would be transformed into solid gold. Lonan took the staff and sure enough, anything he touched turned to gold before his eyes. It did not take long for Lonan to become an incredibly wealthy and powerful man. He even turned his humble village into a shimmering city of solid gold. The people soon began to fear Lonan and his new power. Many tried to kill him and take the golden staff for themselves. Paranoid, Lonan went through his golden city in the night and touched every villager with his stone, turning them to gold where they slept. Soon thereafter, Uhepono returned in his true form as a demon of the underworld. Lonan was so lonely, miserable, and sorry for what he'd done, he begged Uhepono to take the staff away and end his existence. The God of the Underworld refused and relished in the man's misery. Resigned to his fate, Lonan arose, grabbed the tip of the staff with both hands, and was turned into gold where he stood. This staff, *El Baston de Oro* or Golden Staff still resides deep inside the heart of the city, its stone clutched eternally within the hands of the golden man, Lonan, or as he is known by us, *El Dorado*—the Golden One."

"That's impossible," Huber muttered.

The Falcon shrugged and whispered to Pincho. "Perhaps . . . perhaps not."

"Sounds a lot like the story of King Midas," Hannah said skeptically.

"And the story about the demon teaching students the magic of alchemy here in the Cave of Salamanca," Jessie added.

The Falcon nodded and whispered to Pincho. "Alchemy, the Philosopher's Stone, King Midas—many similar legends span the globe. While perhaps these stories occur within different places and times, along with gods and characters of diverse names, who is to say that the same being or source is not behind their origin?"

The thought caused everyone to take pause.

The Falcon continued through Pincho, "Once the Brotherhood finds Cíbola and the *Bastón de Oro*, there will be no stopping them. They will have infinite wealth and, as a result, infinite power. The city is among the most guarded secrets in the world. If the Brotherhood attempts to take the city, the Zuni will defend it. They will never willingly allow this evil to spread over the earth. The Brotherhood has been patient, planning their conquest for many years, building their private army and resources with fortunes like the Dead Man's Treasure. With your help, we will stop the Brotherhood's plans and I give you my word that the Dead Man's Treasure will be returned to its rightful place."

"What do you want us to do?" Huber asked.

The Falcon whispered in a resolute tone, making sweeping motions with his hands. Pincho translated. "The Brotherhood will soon make their move. During their conquests, they came across a golden tablet, which they say contains directions to Cíbola and Dorado. The only problem is they cannot read it. In the dungeons beneath their castle in Segovia, the Brotherhood is holding a prisoner—a Zuni girl by the name of Malia. She is one of only a few capable of translating the language. To my knowledge, she has not given in to their demands, but a person can only endure so much. She will eventually break and translate the tablet for the Brotherhood. We must reach her before she does. When you reach the Brotherhood's castle, I will not be far behind. We will need to work together. You will engage the Three Kings while I free the girl."

"You mean you need a diversion," Hannah said.

The whispering paused, then slowly resumed. Pincho related, "I would not put it that way, but yes, we will need to draw the Brotherhood's attention away from Malia. She is the key to finding Cíbola. All of the Brotherhood's ambitions depend upon her."

"What about us? How are we going to get away?" Hannah asked.

"And what about the Dead Man's Treasure?" Huber added.

"Trust me," Pincho translated. "I have put plans into motion that will allow you to escape with the Dead Man's Treasure intact. I just need you to provide the diversion."

"So, you expect us to just waltz on into the Brotherhood's castle and say 'Hey there, what's goin' on? We've come for your treasure?'" Scott asked.

"No," Pincho translated, "that would be suicide. There is a secret entrance to their hideout. An entrance very few know of. You will need to use the keys I left you. You've all proven yourselves worthy and capable of success. Do you have the keys?"

Alejandro held up the brass key. Hannah retrieved the silver one from her pocket.

The Falcon seemed pleased and whispered again to Pincho. "Good. You will need the silver and brass keys along with the keyword you've discovered. Go to the Plaza Mayor. There is a secret tunnel you must access. You can gain access by . . ."

Bright lights suddenly filled the alleyway from both

sides, blinding everyone. The sound of guns being loaded reverberated off the bricks from overhead. As Huber regained his sight, he saw red dots on his chest along with everyone else. From the light on the far side of the alley, a silhouette walked toward them. As he came closer, Huber recognized the man wearing a three-piece suit—*Fausto*. From the other end of the alleyway, Matón and Susurro approached the Falcon from behind. All along the roof- tops, men dressed in black clothing had their guns trained on the group.

"Very nice to see you again . . . *Halcón*," Fausto's muf- fled voice said from behind his metal mask.

"We've missed you," Matón said in his deep, gruff tone, cracking his mechanical knuckles.

"Time to come back home," Susurro squeaked, his voice almost sounding like he'd been sucking on a helium balloon.

El Halcón darted back and forth like a caged animal. Huber and the others huddled together, unsure of what would happen next.

"There's nowhere to go," Fausto stated amiably and motioned toward both alley exits. "You were once a Brother, Halcón. Come with us without a struggle and perhaps I will reward you with mercy. And you . . . *Pincho*. Quite a shame to see what you've become. At least your father possessed some dignity. If only he hadn't possessed stupidity in greater quantities."

Pincho glared but said nothing.

Susurro pointed at the group and tilted his head to one side. "What about them?" he asked, his high, troll-like voice echoing against the walls.

Matón slammed one of his meaty fists into the other. "I'll take care of them."

"No," Fausto said evenly. "They will be our guests. They've come all the way from America to see our country. Soon enough, we will come to visit theirs."

Huber glanced down at the red dot on his chest.

"Do not worry, young one. Only tranquilizer darts. We don't want to kill you . . . not yet. Yesenia," he said, pointing toward Jessie. "Thank you for your assistance. Now, come to me."

Jessie looked at Huber with teary eyes. "I'm sorry, Huber," she whispered and kissed him softly on the cheek. "I had no choice."

She broke away from the group and stepped toward Fausto.

"Wait . . . Jessie, what are you . . . what's going on?" he sputtered.

"Yesenia!" Alejandro shouted. "Do not go near that filthy beast!"

She turned toward her cousin. "I'm sorry, Alejandro."

"You've been helping the Brotherhood all along?" Hannah asked, unable to believe what was unfolding before her eyes.

Alejandro's face turned scarlet. "*Traidor mala!*" he yelled.

"I'm sorry," she whispered again and walked to
the side of Fausto, refusing to make eye contact with
anyone.

"A true patriot of España." He put his arm around
her shoulder. Suddenly, the steel door leading to the
tavern swung open and a swaying, intoxicated man
ambled into the open. Pincho stuck his foot out and
caught the door just before it closed. Dazed and confused, the drunkard searched the faces of the Three
Kings and everyone else around him. He then chuckled. "*Demasiado beber . . .*"

While distracted by the drunken man, the Falcon
retrieved several small pellets and smashed them to the
ground. Acrid, gray smoke billowed up from the pavement and burned everyone's eyes. Coughing wildly,
Fausto yelled, "Seize them!"

The men above the alley couldn't see where to shoot
their darts. Matón grabbed the drunkard and tossed
him like a rag doll down the alleyway. He then caught
a glimpse of Huber through the vapor and swung his fist
toward his head. Huber dodged the blow and Maton's fist
as it crashed through a brick wall with unnatural strength.
As he tried to dislodge his fist from wall, Huber made
out Pincho shuffling everyone inside the back door of the
tavern.

"Come! Now!" Pincho yelled. The smoke was dissi-
pating rapidly.

Huber made his way toward the doorway, but as he

did, the skinny king in the sad-looking mask stepped in front of him. Susurro dug into one of his suit pockets and when his hand reappeared, he held a tiny pile of white sand. Before Huber could react, he blew through a tiny slit along the mask's lips and the sand flew into Huber's face. Just as quickly, his vision blurred and the muscles in his legs refused to obey his brain's commands. Like putty, he slunk to the ground. Huber lost consciousness just as he saw the Falcon slam the door behind his companions and disappear through the haze.

● ● ●

Is this really happening? Hannah thought to herself as she struggled to find her breath.

"We have to do something!" she yelled to the others who had made it inside the tavern. Alejandro, Scott, and Pincho coughed their way into composure. The bartender was yelling for patrons to exit the tavern.

"Wait! Where's Huber?" Scott panicked.

"He did not make it through," Pincho wheezed.

"We gotta go back and help 'im!" Scott ran back toward the door. Hannah rushed to join him.

Pincho caught them both. "No! We cannot help him. Not now. In time."

"What do you mean in time?" Hannah shouted. "He needs help now!"

Hannah smelled Pincho's breath as he brought his

face to hers. "If we go out there and get caught, there may be *no one* to help us."

"Did the Falcon get away?" Alejandro asked.

"I do not know. We must take care of ourselves for now."

Suddenly, something crashed into the steel door—and the indent of Matón's meaty fist appeared.

"Come!" Pincho yelled as people in the bar scurried away like cockroaches. "We must hide."

Hannah watched as Pincho looked at the bartender, who nodded and waved them over. Behind the bar, he rolled up the rug he was standing on and pressed a button beneath the counter. A trap door fell open where the carpet had just been. "*Vaya con Dios*," he said and ushered them—Hannah, Alejandro, Scott, and finally Pincho— down the ladder. They descended a few feet and landed in a dirt crawlspace. They ducked down and crawled beneath the tavern floor. Alejandro barely cleared the space with the backpack the bartender had given him. Overhead, a loud *schwwaaamp* filled the tavern and then the sound of the door falling. Through tiny chinks in the planked floor, Hannah peered up and could make out Fausto entering the tavern. Dust rained on their faces as he walked directly overhead to the counter. Behind him, Susurro skulked, then Matón, and a dozen or so men, dressed in black clothing and ski masks. To Hannah's horror, Huber was draped over Matón's shoulder, bound and unconscious.

"They have him," she whispered frantically. Her

insides turned over like a washing machine. It was ago-
nizing to be so close but unable to help her brother. She
had to do something!

"Shhhh! Quiet," Pincho grabbed her shoulder. "Unless
you want to join them."

Hannah took a breath to calm herself. Despite her
instincts to bolt back to the tavern, her logical side told
her to keep quiet.

Overhead, they heard Fausto speak to the bartender.

*"Hola señor, tal vez nos puede ayudar. Sin duda, usted
vio a algunos individuos que entraron por la puerta antes de
nosotros,"* Fausto said cheerily.

"What'd he say?" Hannah whispered.

As quietly as he could, Pincho translated. "Dear sir,
I wonder if you could be of assistance. Surely, you saw
several individuals come through your door shortly before
we did."

"*Sí*, I saw them," the bartender responded in English.
"You owe me a new door."

Hannah guessed he spoke English because he knew
they were listening in on the conversation.

"I can grant you much more than a new door, my
friend, if you can tell me where they've gone." Several
metallic objects clinked onto the bar. Gold, Hannah
guessed.

"He's gonna give us up," Scott whispered.

Pincho slapped his hand over his mouth. Hannah
pinched his arm and twisted hard.

"That is a lot of money," the bartender said overhead.

"Simply a gesture of my goodwill," Fausto went on. "Tell us where they have gone and I will double it."

The bartender paused. The silence was unbearable. Finally, he answered. "*Sí*, I'll tell you where they went . . ."

Hannah almost began to hyperventilate. They were about to be discovered. Who knew what terrible things awaited at the hands of such men. As she lost hope, her body tensed and the bartender finished his sentence.

"They ran straight through that front door and down the street." He pointed at the door leading away from the tavern.

A profound sense of relief washed over Hannah. She allowed herself to exhale but not too loudly.

"He's lying," Susurro said in his high-pitched voice.

"Who are you to call me a liar?" The bartender feigned anger.

"*Somos los Tres Reyes*," Fausto said. "And you are lying. We have men posted all around the perimeter. They did not exit through the front door."

The bartender began stammering and stuttering. "Must've slipped past your men's gaze . . . must've . . ."

"Matón." Fausto flicked his finger at the bartender as if he were a irksome cockroach.

Through the gaps in the floorboards, Hannah witnessed Matón drop her brother to the floor, then clutch the bartender by the shirt. With his mechanical fists, the brute yanked him over the bar. With startling strength, the masked Spaniard flung the bartender across the room as if he were made of paper. The barkeep slammed into a cluster of chairs, smashing them to splinters.

"They are here somewhere," Fausto said calmly. "Find them."

A flurry of activity sounded above their heads. It would be only a matter of minutes before they were discovered.

"Open the bag and hand me the flashlight," Pincho whispered. "There is a way out."

As quiet as he could, Alejandro unlatched the leather backpack and looked inside. There were several red flares, a flashlight, water, and a dozen energy bars. He handed Pincho the flashlight. Crawling on all fours, they shimmied their way through the crawlspace, dust trickling down as the men above destroyed the tavern. Thirty feet ahead, Pincho shined the light on a round hole in the wall.

"Through the hole," Pincho whispered. "It leads into the wine cellar of the adjacent building."

One by one, they squeezed through the tiny opening like rats. They exited the small tunnel and landed on the other side within a darkened room. The cellar was pitch-black. In the darkness, Pincho heaved to catch his breath and swung the light around the wall. "Found it," he said and flipped the switch. Light suddenly dispersed the darkness. Racks and racks of wine bottles filled their view. Scott pulled one of the bottles from its slot. "Whoa! 1813!"

"And worth a small fortune!" Pincho growled, swiping the bottle from his hand and gently placing it back within its place. "There is a restaurant upstairs."

"How'd you know about this place?" Scott said.

"Tunnels like this run all through the city. Back in the day when the dictator Franco was in charge, many would need to flee his secret police."

"What are we supposed to do now?" Hannah snapped angrily.

"I do not know," Pincho said, worry written all over his face.

"I cannot believe Yesenia would betray us," Alejandro said, still in shock.

Hannah sighed. "I can't either. I'm sure she didn't have a choice. She must've been protecting you and your grandfather."

"There is always a choice," Alejandro said bitterly.

"I wonder how long ago they got to her," Hannah said.

"Probably 'fore we even got here," Scott answered. "We're thinnin' out. They got Mr. M., Huber, and probably the Falcon. Plus Jessie's on their side. The old man's in jail. We ain't got a chance."

"Still, we must try to assist them," Alejandro said.

"Did I say I didn't want to?"

"Plus if all that stuff the Falcon says is true about

Cíbola and Malia . . ." Hannah added. "The Falcon was just about to tell us how to reach the Brotherhood's castle. What did he say to do again?"

"He didn't," Scott answered. "All I caught was that we needed to go to some plaza."

"*Sí, sí,* La Plaza Mayor," Alejandro said. "I know where it is located."

"Take this," Pincho said, handing Hannah a folded paper and the flashlight to Alejandro. "The note is from Halcón. He left it just in case such an emergency were to occur. I must leave you now. Do not follow me. In ten minutes, walk upstairs and exit the building. I must see to some business of my own. The Brotherhood now knows I am conspiring against them. You are all on your own for now. Do not return to the library."

"You're leaving us?" Hannah asked incredulously.

Pincho looked to be in deep thought for a moment, then answered, "*Sí.* For now. Follow the Falcon's last clue. Stay safe. Keep to the shadows," Pincho said as he bounded up the stairs and out of sight. "*Ciao.*"

No one returned the gesture.

"Just the three of us." Scott looked at Alejandro. "This oughta be fun."

Hannah unfolded the paper and handed the note to Alejandro. "Alejandro, can you translate?"

"*Vaya a la plaza Mayor. A las diez, la senda del rey será iluminada. Entonces, resuelve las acertijos del demonio a pasar*—Go the Plaza Mayor. At ten o'clock, the king's pathway will be illuminated. Then, solve the demon's puzzles to pass."

Through the hole in the wall, distant voices were heard shouting.

"They've found the passageway! Quick, we've got to get to the Plaza Mayor!"

CHAPTER 10

HUBER WAS AT SCHOOL, listening to Mr. Mendoza give a Spanish lesson. Looking around, he realized he was the only one in the classroom. The windows were caked in dirt and grime. Unnatural, yellow light struggled to filter through them. Mr. Mendoza carried on as if he were addressing a large audience.

"*Clase. Repitense. ¿Como está usted?*"

Huber repeated. "*¿Como está usted?*"

Mr. Mendoza looked at Huber and smiled. "*Muy bien, Huber! Ahora responda a la pregunta. ¿Come está usted?*"

"*Estoy mal.*"

"*¿Porque?*"

"*Porque éste es un sueño. No puedo hablar español con tanta fluidez en la vida actual.*"

"*Excelente. Así es. Estás soñando. Póngase de pie.*"

Huber attempted to stand, but as he did, he realized

his foot was tethered to a chain in the floor. *"No puedo."*
Mr. Mendoza's face turned angry. *"Póngase de pie!"*
"No puedo levantarme!" Huber yelled back, frustrated.

Mr. Mendoza stormed over to where Huber sat chained
to his desk. Huber saw the back of Mr. Mendoza's head
as he dropped to the floor to inspect the chain. "Ohh . . .
lo siento," he said. His voice sounded different somehow,
deeper and distorted. *"Tienes razón."* As he brought his
head back up to look at Huber, the face was no longer that
of Mr. Mendoza—it was the decomposed face of Juan
Hernán Salazar. "Stand up, *jóven!"*

Huber startled awake, gasping for air. Where was
he? It was dark, nearly pitch. His brain was a bowl of
water being sloshed around. Dizzily, he tried to stand
but was instantly yanked back down to his sitting position. As his eyes adjusted, Huber realized his ankles were
chained to two rings in a concrete floor. Memories began
bursting like fireworks. The meeting with the Falcon; the
Brotherhood showing up; the smoke; and then . . . the
man in the sad-looking mask blowing powder into his
face. A dawning realization came upon him. He was in
some kind of dungeon. His voice was dry and hoarse as
he croaked, "Hello? Anyone there?"

"Hey there, *muchacho,"* a familiar voice answered.
"Got yourself into quite a bind again, I see. I'm afraid
you're starting to make a habit of it."

Huber's eyes shifted in and out of focus. He must've
still been dreaming because sitting against the wall in

front of him was Grandpa Nick, appearing just as he had within the cave at Dead Man's Treasure. The firelight from his lantern played shadows on his face. The musty, leathery smell of his cowboy hat brought a measure of comfort.

"Grandpa Nick," Huber muttered excitedly, but he was too groggy to raise himself from the floor. "You're here?"

"Temporarily," Grandpa Nick answered.

"I'm sorry. It's all my fault."

"What's your fault?"

"Hawk, Salazar, Mr. Mendoza—all of this. We should've never gone up in the mountains."

"Hogwash." Grandpa Nick flicked his wrist. "Everyone makes their own decisions, Huber. What happened to Hawk was not your fault. Before this journey is done, you'll bring honor to his sacrifice."

Huber's head was still swimming. "It's over," he despaired. "I'm going to be stuck down here forever."

Grandpa Nick removed his hat and brushed it off. "Listen closely. Very soon now, those men are going to come and put you through quite a tough time. Whatever you do, don't lose hope. No matter how discouraging things appear. No one is ever truly defeated until they've lost hope. Just remember that I'll be by your side. Don't give into them, Huber."

"Okay, Grandpa," Huber whispered as his grandfather went in and out of focus. He drifted off once again.

● ● ●

"Young one." A quiet, high-pitched voice floated over the air in what seemed like seconds later.

Huber's eyelids lifted. The effects of whatever drug Susurro had blown into his lungs seemed to have mostly diminished.

Shimmering faintly in front of him, the metallic, melancholy face of Susurro stood out in the darkness. Suddenly it shot forward to within inches of Huber's face. The man was no longer wearing a suit. He was decked out in a long flowing red robe. Beneath his robe were layers of finely tailored clothing, adorned with patterns and color—all vestiges of kingly glory. Atop his head, a metal, conquistador style helmet glinted from the torchlight outside the cell.

"Welcome, Huber Hill the Thief," Susurro said. "I hope you'll find your accommodations . . . satisfactory. It seemed like you were dreaming of something just now. Tell me all about it. Who is Grandpa Nick?"

Startled and revolted, Huber sank back as far as possible. "My friends? My sister? Do you have them?"

Susurro giggled like a schoolgirl. "They'll be joining you soon enough."

"Where's Mr. Mendoza?"

"Ah, ah, ah, we will ask the questions. Rest assured your teacher is unharmed . . . relatively. You are to be brought before the Three Kings shortly. I am here to give you counsel before your inquisition."

"Inquisition?" The word terrified Huber.

"That's right—you will be brought before the three of us. When standing at the dais of the Three Kings, do not resist or speak out of turn. Answer our questions honestly. If you don't, I cannot guarantee what King Fausto will do. You can imagine what kinds of tortures he's ordered Matón to perform upon those who do not cooperate with us. It will be easier for everyone if you are just forthright."

"Are you ready?"

"I'm thirsty." Huber tried to stall.

Susurro brought a bowl of clear liquid to Huber's hands. Huber dipped the bowl toward his lips and let the cool liquid flow into his mouth.

"Here . . . eat." Susurro handed Huber a piece of hard, partially molded bread. He was so hungry, he wolfed it down without thought.

"Your hands?" Susurro motioned Huber to hold them out. Huber complied and Susurro slapped a pair of heavy manacles over his wrists. He tightened them until they nearly cut off blood flow to his hands. The man then used another key to unloose the bonds around his ankles.

Susurro led him through his cell doorway and along a corridor of similar cells. One of them was occupied by a girl with long dark hair. As Huber passed, she didn't even look up. In the darkness at the end of the hall, he peered into another cell. Huber caught a glimpse of dirty feet that retracted into the shadows once he passed. Susurro continued toward the end of the cell corridor until they reached a winding set of stone steps. They spiraled upward and upward. Finally, they reached the top of the staircase and exited through a massive door into a chamber flooded with light. Huber's pupils constricted as he brought his manacled hands to his eyes. He slowly lowered them to observe a massive, ostentatious room set aglow by torch-light. The light was so bright because all around the perimeter of the chamber was treasure unfathomable—piles and piles of gold coins, hefty chests, crosses, jewels, and crowns. Elaborate tapestries and gilded wood carvings trimmed the chamber. The outer edges of the chamber were outlined with arches and columns striped in black and white. Intricate carvings and etchings adorned the room, decorated in red drapery. Centered toward the back of the room, a long table loaded with fruits, suckling meats, and vegetables caused Huber's stomach to rumble.

At the other side of the room rested three, dark wooden thrones upon a raised platform. The chairs were of exquisite workmanship—carved in Gothic style. The throne in the middle was raised slightly higher than the other two. Hanging above the center throne was a tapestry of some kind that pictured an eagle with wings outstretched. Across the eagle's chest was a shield bearing a crest. Upon the crest were the same lions and castles that had been displayed on the back of Huber's gold coin. A valance, located above the thrones read TANTO MONTA. A golden shield rested between the two words.

Susurro brought Huber to a small, blue glowing circle, ten feet away from the dais.

"Stand here," Susurro commanded.

Huber didn't dare do otherwise. He continued to take in the scene, amazed by the enormous fortune and obscene luxury laid bare before his eyes.

"I noticed you admiring my throne." Fausto's voice suddenly echoed throughout the chamber as he entered the room through one of the arches, followed closely by Matón. Long red robes flowed behind them. Like Susurro, upon their heads were steel, shiny helmets for crowns. They were dressed like kings from the fifteenth century, with high-collared gowns, gilded seams, and leather boots. Beneath their robes, fine-linen shirts protruded out of their finely embroidered doublets. Huber couldn't help but feel intimidated by their presence. Seconds after Matón, Jessie entered the room. She made brief eye contact with Huber, then averted her gaze. She came to stand next to Matón as if she were a servant. "It is the motto of King Ferdinand the Second of Aragon," Fausto said, pointing at the emblazoned writing above the throne. *"As much as the one is worth, so much is the other.* Tell me, young one, do you know what the word *Coronado* stands for?"

Huber shook his head.

"*Corona* translates to crown. *Coronado* means 'crowned one.' Now, tell me, Huber Hill, who are the ones that get crowned?"

"Kings," Huber answered softly.

"*Excelente,* boy. Susurro, Matón, and myself are all direct descendants of Coronado—the crowned one. Only Coronado didn't sit idly in a throne wearing a crown of gold and jewels. He was a warrior, an explorer." Fausto pointed to his gleaming helmet. "He donned the true crown of glory: that of a *conquistador.* Over the years we have risen through the ranks to become the Three Kings of Coronado's Brotherhood and just as Ferdinand, Felipe, and others, we will rule Spain and then the world with an *iron fist.*"

At his words, Matón slammed one of his mechanical fists into the other, sending a hollow *thud* through the room and a shudder down Huber's spine.

"The Brotherhood has been in operation for nearly 150 years, believe it or not. When one king dies, another worthy descendent takes his place. As you can see," he said, gesturing to the surrounding treasure, "we've been quite busy reclaiming what rightfully belongs to España." Fausto stepped upon the raised dais and seated himself in the center throne beneath the gilded eagle and stitched motto. Matón sat on his right, Susurro to his left. Fausto dug into his pocket and retrieved a gold coin, the same one that once belonged to Huber's grandpa. Fausto rotated it through his slender fingers. "*Tesoro de Los Muertos* was a great find. The treachery of Coronado's defectors and the Ute who tried to hide it from us is finally avenged. With your coin, the treasure is now complete."

"How did you find Dead Man's Treasure?" Huber asked.

Matón pressed some kind of button beneath the armrest on his throne. A jolt of electricity shot up through Huber's feet and throughout his body. Overwhelming pain filled his senses, taking his breath away as he dropped to his knees.

"Let me be clear, Huber Hill the Thief. *You* do not ask questions *here*." Fausto slammed his armrest. "Now stand."

Huber struggled to his feet. It was as if for a few seconds, the whole inside of his body had been on fire. The pain slowly ebbed away as he stood. The blue circle beneath him glowed with energy.

"However, since you asked, I'll tell you. We'd suspected for some time that *Tesoro de Los Muertos* was located near your home of Carbondale, Colorado. We'd been researching the area for several years, looking for the site, but we were missing one important key . . . *Pedro Salazar's map.*"

"Traitor to Coronado," Susurro hissed.

"Yes, a greedy thief." Fausto nodded. "We got the break we needed when we received word of that *idiota*, Juan Hernán Salazar, showing up in the area . . . supposedly he was aware of the map's location. He was watching you. The Ute were watching him. *The Brotherhood* was watching all of you."

"You killed Hawk," Huber said in contempt.

"The old Indian man? No, Huber, he caused his own death when he opposed us. As shall you, should you resist."

Huber couldn't stand the perpetual smirk etched across Fausto's metal face. "How'd you get it here?" he asked contemptuously and pointed to the chests he'd found within the mine.

Another electrifying shock racked Huber's body. He yelled out loud and dropped to the floor.

"Huber!" Jessie gasped and ran toward him.

"Stand," Matón bellowed.

Jessie ran to Huber and tried to help him up, but he slapped her hand away. "Get away from me," he whispered and stood. It was much more difficult this time. Jessie backed away, tears in her eyes.

Fausto's shoulders shook as he silently chuckled and turned toward Matón. "Some never learn." He then turned back toward Huber. "To answer your question, Huber—quite simple, really. We knew we wouldn't be able to smuggle the entire spoil of the Dead Man's Treasure out of the United States by air, so we transported the treasure to Florida. From there we loaded the chests onto one of our ships and sailed across the sea just as the conquistadors of old." He held up Huber's doubloon. "This single coin is worth about three thousand US dollars." Fausto then pointed to the wall opposite Huber's right where the chests from the Dead Man's Treasure sat. "Imagine how many coins are within those chests. The money we gain from this treasure will no doubt help us with our next conquest.

As you can see," he said, indicating the many other treasures littering the throne room, "*Tesoro de los Muertos* was just one find among many over the years. Now, we would like to ask you some questions, if you don't mind . . . how long have you been working with El Halcón?"

Huber looked down at the glowing blue circle and decided to answer. "Since we got here."

"I see. Was the Falcon in league with that crazy old man Carlos and his squatty sidekick, Pincho?"

Huber hesitated. Fausto reached beneath his armrest. Another shock enveloped his body. This one seemed twice as strong as the previous punishment. He screamed in pain. It felt like the tips of his fingers would explode.

"Stop!" Jessie cried out.

Fausto released the button. "Shall I ask again?" he said evenly.

Huber somehow pushed himself up. "Yes! Yes! He's been helping them all along."

"*Muerto*," Susurro jeered. "Death to El Halcón."

"*Mátalo*," Matón said.

"Halcón will pay for his trespasses," Fausto assured them. Then his shoulders once again lurched up and down. "But what say you to having a bit of sport with this one, first? Huber Hill the Thief, I am a merciful king. I will possibly spare your life. You will compete with one of our other prisoners in a series of challenges. The winner at the conclusion of the games will be allowed to survive. The other . . . not so lucky."

Huber thought of his Grandpa Nick and stared at Fausto rotating the coin within his hand. Taking a breath, he met the king's gaze. "And if I refuse to play?"

A pain unlike any Huber had ever experienced shot upward from his feet as electricity flowed through his body. With his jaw clenched, his body shook so violently, he could only scream in his mind. He was on the verge of passing out when Fausto released the button. Huber collapsed and knew he would not be able to stand again. Half conscious, he stared sideways at the three kings sitting upon their thrones.

Hazily, he heard Fausto's words. "Here are the terms: you will compete with the Zuni prisoner. Shall you prevail, you and the girl"—he pointed to Yesenia—"will live. Should you lose, both of you shall meet your demise, but the Zuni girl and your teacher, Mendoza, will survive. If you refuse to participate, you will all perish."

Jessie grimaced and looked at Huber with tears in her eyes.

"Matón, take Huber Hill the Thief back to the dungeon . . . put him in the cell with Malia—let them talk it over awhile and decide their fates."

● ● ●

Hannah's face burned with embarrassment as she trudged through the restaurant, caked in dirt and sweat. It was impossible not to garner a few curious stares. Once on the streets, Hannah found herself looking over her shoulder constantly, sure that any minute, a member of the Brotherhood would suddenly appear or she'd look down to find a red dot on her chest.

After taking a taxi a few miles to the south, they arrived at the Plaza Mayor, a grand square filled with cafés and small shops. At this hour of the night, the place was virtually deserted. All but a few of the shops and cafés were closed. Famished from their flight, they stopped to quickly eat a few *tapas*. After eating, they ventured onto the semi-darkened square, the stones wet from a light drizzle. Hannah, still reeling from what had happened, found it difficult to focus. How could Jessie have done this? Alejandro seemed similarly distracted.

"It just doesn't feel right, does it?" Hannah said. "What Jessie did."

Scott pointed to Alejandro. "How do we know he ain't on their side too? Cowardliness seems to run in the family."

"Be quiet, Scott," Hannah warned. "Alejandro is on our side."

"Well, I don't trust 'im. I think he's a conniving back-stabber just like his no good cousin."

Alejandro's fist struck Scott's face just as he finished his sentence. Scott tumbled backward but didn't fall. A dab of blood smudged his lip. He wiped it with the back of his hand, looked at it, and grinned. "I've been waitin' for this, Spaniard."

"Stop it, you two!" Hannah demanded and stepped between them. "There's no need for this. The last thing we need to do is turn on each other."

"Get outta m'way, Hannah," Scott said tersely with a crazed look in his eye.

"Let's go, cowboy ... *Mano a mano*," Alejandro crowed and lifted his fists like a boxer.

Hannah did her best to constrain Scott. "Please ... don't," she pleaded.

"You sidin' with him?" Scott asked her.

"We're all on the same side, Scott! Just cool it! We need to keep our heads!"

Scott finally threw his hands up. "Fine."

Alejandro did the same. As Hannah let her guard down and stepped away, like two powerful magnets, Alejandro and Scott collided, arms swinging.

"I'm gonna knock your *cabeza* plumb off!" Scott yelled while the two tumbled in a wiry mass of flesh and bone.

Alejandro landed several shots to Scott's kidneys, dropping him to his knees. As he landed on the ground, he threw his fist into Alejandro's gut, knocking the wind out of him. Hannah didn't dare get in between them now. "Stop!" she yelled furiously.

Alejandro charged at Scott and the two landed on the damp, stone pavement with a groan. They grappled until Scott got Alejandro in a headlock and squeezed. Alejandro gasped for air.

"Scott! Stop it! Now!" Hannah shrieked.

Alejandro threw his elbow, tagging Scott above the eye. He moaned in pain, then released his grasp.

"Alejandro! Please don't!"

The two boys slowly rose to their feet and stared each other down, nursing their wounds. Simultaneously, they let out a shriek and crashed together again. This time, it was Alejandro's turn to grip Scott in a headlock. Hannah panicked as Scott's face turned scarlet. Flailing his arms wildly, he jabbed his hand backward and thumbed Alejandro in the eye, causing him to release his hold and fall on his back. The two writhed on the ground, unable to arise.

"Okay, enough!" Hannah yelled. "What's wrong with you two?"

"Truce?" Alejandro gasped, rubbing his sore eye.

"Truce," Scott repeated on all fours, trying to recapture his breath.

Hannah walked in the middle of them and shook her head, disgusted. "I was wrong to ever like either of you. You can both go take a hike. I'll help Huber on my own!"

The two, bloodied boys lay on the wet pavement, sucking wind as Hannah receded to the front of the plaza.

"Stupid boys," she muttered under her breath. As she ruminated on her disgust for what she'd witnessed, her eyes grazed the elaborate statuary and columns. Above her in the tower, a giant clock was nearing ten o' clock. She gazed up at the clock and walked backward, almost tripping on her shoelace when it dawned on her. The riddle! *At ten o'clock, the king's path will be illuminated.*

"Stupid boys!" she yelled. "Get over here!"

Scott and Alejandro stood up and gingerly cantered over to where she stood. "It's almost ten o'clock!" she said excitedly.

"So what? I know it's past your bedtime," Scott said in a nasally tone, plugging a bloody nostril.

Alejandro held his side. "*Sí, sí, sí.* The riddle!"

"Yes." Hannah seemed to forget her anger at the two. "In a few minutes, it will be ten o'clock. The king's pathway will be illuminated!"

"So what do we do?" Scott asked. "Sit here with our thumbs up our noses 'til ten o'clock?"

"Do you have a better idea, cowboy?"

"Can't say I do seein' my finger's already up m'nose."

The three stood shoulder to shoulder, watching the clock overhead anxiously as it ticked toward ten o'clock. Finally, the long hand reached the twelve. The bell above the clock swung and chimed. One . . . two . . . three . . . four . . . five . . . six . . . seven . . . eight . . . nine . . . then ten.

Hannah braced herself for the unexpected, but nothing happened. They all anxiously eyed their surroundings, but absolutely nothing had changed. The long hand ticked past the twelve. Hannah sighed.

"Well, that was awesome," Scott said.

"Maybe it means ten in the morning," Hannah ventured.

"So we should just camp out here in the dark until tomorrow morning? No thanks."

"Perhaps you are right, Hannah, but we cannot go back to the library," Alejandro said. "So where do we go?"

As Alejandro was finishing his sentence, Scott suddenly ran from them and shimmied up a nearby column toward a first-story balcony along the plaza's perimeter.

"Scott! What are you doing?" Hannah yelled.

"I ain't stayin' outdoors all night. I noticed there's a window open up here. Maybe we can get in."

"So we can get arrested for breaking and entering?"

"If we go to jail, we'll be safer there than wanderin' round the streets waitin' for red dots to show up on our chests."

"The cowboy has a point," Alejandro said.

Scott made his way up the column and toppled over the balcony. Seconds later, his head appeared over the edge. "C'mon up, I can't fit through the window. But maybe that skinny Spaniard can."

After double-checking to ensure the coast was clear, Alejandro clawed his way up to the balcony followed by Hannah. When they reached the portico, Hannah noticed the small opening leading into a dark room. The bottom of the window was about four feet off the patio. Perhaps Alejandro could slither his way through.

"Go on then." Scott motioned to Alejandro.

Alejandro looked at Hannah as if seeking approval.

"Go ahead," she urged. "I don't want to stay out here all night either. You can do it."

Alejandro pulled himself up to the bottom of the cracked window. There was a gap of just over twelve inches. He pushed his head through, then his shoulders. Wiggling his way forward, his stomach cleared the space, but then he stopped.

"What's wrong?" Hannah shouted.

"I'm stuck!" they heard him yell from the inside, his legs kicking like a jackrabbit. "Help!" he cried frantically.

"I got this," Scott said as he gripped Alejandro's feet and pushed.

Alejandro yipped in pain. "Stop pushing!"

Scott smiled at Hannah and pushed even harder. Seconds later, Alejandro's legs shot forward through the window and a loud crash sounded on the inside. A moment later, the door to the balcony opened. Hannah and Scott stepped inside, drew the curtains, then found the light switch. As the room lit up, they realized they were in some kind of posh office suite. A fine mahogany desk was in a corner. Expensive-looking paintings lined the walls. Hannah smiled with the other two upon seeing a most blessed sight—three separate leather love seats, arranged in a U Shape. It wasn't a bed but infinitely better than the cold, hard ground.

● ● ●

Morning came too soon as sunlight filtered through the office windows and landed on Hannah's face. She opened her eyes groggily, then shot upright. There were footsteps in the hallway just outside the office. She shook the others awake. "Time to go," she whispered frantically. "Now!"

Startled, the others were quickly on their feet. Hannah moved for the balcony door when the sound of a key clicking against metal caused her heart to skip a beat. She flung open the patio door and stepped out. Scott followed in close pursuit, then Alejandro. As she went to close the door, she saw the door leading into the office open. She dropped to her hands and knees, but wasn't able to close the balcony door completely. She stepped to the side of the windows and prayed whoever had come through the door hadn't seen her and wouldn't notice the open balcony door. "Quick! Over the edge!" she mouthed to the others standing against the wall on the other side of the door.

The three flung themselves up and over the stone balcony, climbing down to the lower portion and hanging on for dear life. Hannah's breath escaped her as she viewed a woman's hands curl over the top of the balcony. Her face came into view as she gazed upon the square. All she would have to do is look down to discover the trespassers. She spoke to someone behind her.

"Must've left the balcony door open last night. Lucky we didn't get robbed."

The woman then disappeared from view. Hannah let out a sigh of relief and scooted her way over to the nearest column and began her descent toward the ground. A few people milling about in the plaza noticed the three climbing down the column and pointed suspiciously. As Hannah dropped to the ground, an older gentleman approached her.

"*¿Que hacen?* What are you doing?"

Hannah tried to think quick. "Free running," she said, remembering a YouTube video she'd seen of young people climbing and dropping from buildings within an urban environment. "Just getting some exercise and messing around."

The man seemed to mull this over, then threw up his hands. "I do not understand young people!" he harrumphed and then walked away.

Hannah sighed in relief and looked at the clock above the square. A little bit after nine.

"Well, we may as well get some breakfast while we wait for ten o'clock."

● ● ●

After getting a quick bite, the trio made their way to the clock and watched anxiously once again as the long hand ticked across the twelve and the bell began to chime. The bell rang ten times and once again, nothing noticeable happened.

Hannah sighed as the sun peeked above the tower and cast a ray of light into the square.

"I do not understand!" Alejandro said. "Halcón's riddle said that at ten, the king's pathway would be illuminated."

Hannah's mouth dropped open. She broke off in a trot across the square.

"Hey! Where you goin'?" Scott yelled after her.

"Illumination!" she yelled. "Follow me!"

Scott and Alejandro tailed after her.

Hannah reached the other end of the square and stopped. A smile stretched across her face. She was right! The boys reached her, panting. She pointed down at the small tile, seemingly glowing in sun's morning ray. Upon the face of the tile was a glazed etching of a crown.

"See? Illumination!" she said, a bit too proud of herself.

"At ten, the king's pathway will be illuminated!" Alejandro beamed.

"So what do we do now?" Scott asked.

The three dropped down to investigate the tile more closely. Upon closer inspection, they noticed small notches below the crown.

"Keyholes!" Hannah exclaimed. "Alejandro! The key!"

Hannah watched in excitement as Alejandro took out the brass key and inserted it into one of the holes. It didn't fit. He tried the other hole and it matched up perfectly. Turning it clockwise forty-five degrees, they heard what sounded like chains and gears rumbling below them.

"Hannah, hand me your key now." He stretched out his hand.

She dug out the silver one and placed it in his palm. He inserted it into the vacant slot and also turned it to clockwise, and more rumbling ensued. The grinding sound stopped and a three-foot square door dropped to their right, just inside the recess of an archway. Alejandro removed the keys and they stealthily moved toward the opening. Hannah retrieved the flashlight from Alejandro's bag and shined it into the seemingly endless black void while Scott kept a lookout. Inside the small door were stone steps that led down into a shaft.

Alejandro was the first to step inside. Hannah took a breath and followed him, then called out to Scott to join them. This all seemed remarkably familiar to the feeling she'd had upon entering the mine at Dead Man's Treasure.

Once inside the passageway, the steps led down to a wider opening and stone steps that descended even further. A rope dangled from the ten-foot ceiling at the top of the stairs. Scott impulsively tugged on it. The sound of gears and clanking once again filled their ears and the door behind them sealed itself up followed by a few more *click* and *clacks*. Ahead lay darkness and dripping sounds.

"I don't think we're gettin' out the way we came," Scott said.

Hannah shook her head. "Just a word of advice for the future, just because you see a rope doesn't mean you should pull it, you dope."

"I can't help it," he answered.

Alejandro shined the light in front of them. The steps continued downward as far as the eye could see. "Now all we need to do is find *el demonio* . . . the demon."

A low, rumbling, sound wafted their way from somewhere down below.

Scott looked at Hannah. "Well, you said I need to act more like a gentleman. Ladies first."

CHAPTER
• 11 •

EXHAUSTED AND STILL RECOVERING from his inquisition, Huber couldn't walk as Matón dragged him back to the dungeon.

Matón used a key from a ring attached to his belt to unlock a cell, just a few down from Huber's original. With his mechanical fists, the brute slid the iron bars away effortlessly and tossed Huber inside. He then entered the cell and pointed to a vacant set of manacles cemented in the floor toward which Huber crawled. A girl, wreathed in shadow, was slumped across the floor, her long, dark hair hanging over her face. Matón secured Huber's feet to the manacles and twisted them tight, until they dug into his skin. "One hour," Matón threatened. "If you refuse to comply with King Fausto's request, you'll both be executed upon my return . . . and nothing would please me more." He then smashed his oversized fist into the wall above Huber's head causing a shower of orange sparks. Dust and rock shards sprayed across the cell. Matón left, slamming the iron door shut.

Once Matón was out of earshot, Huber looked toward Malia. So far, the girl had said nothing. Through the dim light, Huber could see her stomach moving evenly.

"Hey," Huber said, trying to start the conversation. He wondered if the she was asleep. "I'm guessing someone told you about Fausto's deal."

The girl stirred but still didn't respond.

"I don't know what to do . . . if we refuse to cooperate, we both die along with my friend and teacher. If we play along, then only one of us will die. If I win, then Jessie survives, but you'll die. If you win, then Mr. Mendoza lives, but I'll die. There's really no good outcome."

The girl still didn't respond. In his discomfort, Huber continued rambling.

"I'm not afraid to die. I've been close to death before. Last summer, in the mountains, this crazy guy . . . Juan Hernán Salazar hunted us in the wilderness. I thought for sure I was dead a bunch of times. If what you they say is true about you and Cíbola, then at least if one of us survives, maybe we can stop the Brotherhood from finding it."

The girl stirred again and sat up. Her hair still dangled in front of her face.

"I know you've been stuck in here for a long time. At least my friend and sister got away. Maybe they'll come for us. I'm pretty sure the Falcon got away too."

Suddenly the girl parted the hair from her face and scurried forward. "The Falcon? You've seen him?" she asked excitedly.

"Yeah," Huber said, taken aback. "He's been helping us."

Malia laughed so hard she was on the verge of tears. "Then he lives. There is hope he'll come for us."

"He told us about you—said that you were side by side for months down here."

"Yes! We kept each others' spirits up. As you can imagine, we got to know each other quite well. Then one day, Susurro left the Falcon's cell door open a second too long. I distracted him and the Falcon knocked him unconscious. Unfortunately, Susurro did not have the key to my cell. The Falcon promised to return and rescue me from this awful place. That was months ago. I assumed he was either dead or had forgotten about me."

"He's alive and well." Huber smiled. "He could be on his way to help us as we speak. If we play Fausto's games, perhaps it will give him and my friends the time they need to find us."

Malia nodded. "Yes, we will play along. But what if they do not arrive in time?"

"They will," Huber assured her and then tried to convince himself. "They have to."

Malia seemed to consider this and for a moment hope lighted her eyes.

"So, how did you . . . ?"

"End up here?" she finished his question from the shadows. "I was stargazing on top of a mesa near my home. Next thing I know, there's a dart sticking out of my arm. Then the next thing I remember is being on a boat. It's all hazy."

"The Falcon said the Brotherhood took you because you can translate something?"

"I am one of few who are able to read the ancient Zuni language of Cíbola. We are chosen from birth, taught the language, but are to never share it or allow anyone to know." The girl dug around her clothing and tossed an object toward Huber. He flinched and ducked, the metallic object clanking off the wall and landing next to him.

Huber picked up the object and realized it was a solid gold scorpion.

"The scorpion has been passed down through my family for as long as anyone can remember," she said. "They say it comes from Cíbola. That it was turned to gold by Lonan himself. My father gave it to me."

"So how did the Brotherhood find out you knew the language?" He tossed the gold scorpion back.

"I've been trying to figure that out. No one except my immediate family and a few others know that I'm able to read the language."

"Maybe someone betrayed you."

Malia's eyes smoldered. "My family nor my tribe would *ever* betray me!"

Huber reeled back. "Hey, sorry . . . I'm just saying they had to find out somehow."

An awkward silence was exchanged, then Huber resumed the conversation. "The Falcon says the Brotherhood wants you to translate a tablet?"

"Yes. They want me to decipher a golden tablet which they believe holds directions to Cíbola and El Dorado's Golden Staff."

"Does it?"

"I don't know. I've never looked at it. Whenever they try to force me, I close my eyes. They've made me go hungry and left me down here for days without light or contact. It will do them no good. I will die before helping them."

"Have you ever been there? To Cíbola?"

Malia shook her head. "No. Only the Zuni chief is allowed to visit the city. The location is kept secret from all others."

"How did the Brotherhood end up with the tablet?"

"I wish I knew."

Huber nodded in respect and couldn't help but admire the girl's resolve. She had been down here for many months and hadn't broken. He'd only been in this place for a few hours and was already feeling the pressure.

A few minutes passed before Matón and Susurro's steps echoed down the corridor. The two kings, adorned in their regalia, arrived at their cell.

"So . . ." Susurro squeaked. "Had time to chat? Have you come to a decision?"

"Yes," Huber said. "We will play Fausto's games on certain conditions."

"You are in no position to bargain!" Matón growled.

"Then I suppose you can just kill us both now and not have any fun."

Matón and Susurro looked at one another. Finally, Susurro turned back toward Huber. "What *conditions?*"

"If I agree to play, I want to see Mr. Mendoza and then Yesenia."

"What do you think, Matón?"

Matón shrugged his muscled shoulders.

"I will arrange for you to meet with your friends. Don't go anywhere," Susurro cackled.

Ten minutes passed before the two lesser kings returned, carting Mr. Mendoza along with them.

"Mr. Mendoza!" Huber yelled through the bars.

Mr. Mendoza appeared haggard, dirty, and exhausted, but otherwise unharmed. He grabbed Huber's hands through the cell. "Huber! How did you end up in here? Why didn't you have the sense to go home?" he said angrily.

"We weren't going to leave you here!"

"You should have," he said in a hard tone, looking back at Matón. "Where are the others?"

"Jessie betrayed us. I was caught. The others got away."

"What do you mean Jessie betrayed you?"

"She was working with the Brotherhood all along. She's probably the reason you're here too. She must've tipped them off at the bullfight."

"Why would she do such a thing?

"Says she was protecting Alejandro and Carlos. The Brotherhood threatened to execute them if she didn't. She now appears to be a prisoner too, just not in a cell."

Mr. Mendoza shook his head. "I can't believe this. I don't know how . . . but I'm going to get us out of here. Just do whatever they say for now. Got it, Hill?"

Huber nodded. "Fausto is setting up some kind of game between me and Malia." He pointed toward the girl.

"Who is she?"

"Long story. I don't have time to explain, but we're going to compete in some sort of game. If I win, Jessie and I will be free, but you and Malia will . . ."

"I see," Mr. Mendoza whispered. "Yes, I see."

"If she wins, then you'll both go free they say. But we'll . . ."

Mr. Mendoza nodded and squeezed Huber's hands. "Well then," he said, "let's hope an alternative solution presents itself."

"Where are they holding you?"

"I don't know. They blindfold me every time I'm moved. When I remove the blindfold, I'm in small room in complete darkness. Once in awhile, they bring me food and water . . . and a bucket. I go up a lot of steps, so it's got to be somewhere high in the castle."

"Time's up!" Matón yanked Mr. Mendoza away from Huber's cell. Mr. Mendoza looked back and nodded. "Don't lose your head, Hill."

Susurro and Matón prodded Mr. Mendoza up the stone steps. Some minutes later, Matón returned with Yesenia. At first, she refused to look at him but finally did.

"Huber," she whispered. "I . . ."

"How could you do this? How could you believe anything they said? You think your cousin and grandpa are safe?" He snorted. "They'll kill them anyway. You know that, don't you? We're just tonight's entertainment. After they get tired of it, they'll be rid of us."

"I know that now. I'm sorry. I shouldn't have helped them."

"So you're a prisoner too, I gather."

"They keep me in a room here in the castle. I am fed gourmet food and given everything I ask for. However, I am a prisoner just the same."

"Sounds like you have it pretty rough compared to us down here." Huber shook his head and looked at Malia.

"Fausto says you've agreed to the games."

"What choice do I have? If we refuse, then we all die, remember?"

A tear ran down Jessie's cheek. "I'm so sorry, Huber. After what I've done, I don't deserve to live."

"When did they get to you?"

"Shortly before you arrived in Spain. They must've been watching my email somehow."

"That's who you were texting in the library late at night, wasn't it?"

"Yes. I was just scared, Huber. I didn't know what to do."

Huber tried to stay resolute in his contempt but softened. "I know. Who's to say what any of us would've done? But my grandpa always said that you should never make a decision out of fear."

Jessie nodded in response and took his hands and leaned in close. Huber did the same, so they could be out of earshot. "Please forgive me." She kissed his cheek through the bars and slid her hand over Huber's.

"Get back!" Matón ordered. "Time to go!"

Before the brute tore Jessie away from Huber, she leaned in close and whispered in his ear, "Be careful."

CHAPTER
· 12 ·

HANNAH PEERED DEEPER INTO the darkness, not knowing where it would lead them. This must have been what it was like when Jonah was swallowed by the whale. Step by step, Hannah, Alejandro, and Scott dived deeper into the void, the beam of the flashlight barely penetrating the abyss ahead of them. Hannah was sure that any second, a monster or something worse was going to jump from a corner or grab them from behind. The air grew noticeably cooler.

"How far down do you think this thing goes?" Scott asked.

"*El infierno* . . ." Alejandro smirked.

A low rumbling sound followed his words. Hannah instinctively pulled herself next to Scott. Just as quickly, she detached herself.

"Sorry," she breathed. Her tone became more resolute.

"Don't get any ideas. It was just an involuntary reaction."

The rumble sounded again.

"What is that sound?"

"*El demonio*," Alejandro whispered, wide-eyed.

"I don't know, but the closer we get, the louder it's gettin'. You may wanna stay close to me a bit longer," Scott said.

"By which you mean, you want to stay close to me. No thanks. I'll take my chances with the demon."

The tunnel descended even further and narrowed. Finally, the bottom came into view. The stone steps ended at a dirt floor that leveled off, but the tunnel continued horizontally.

"I wonder how far below the city we are," Alejandro said. "I never knew such tunnels existed."

They trudged onward through the darkness, the rumbling sound amplifying as they progressed.

"You don't really think there's a demon down here, do you?" Scott asked.

"I thought you didn't believe in things like that," Hannah chided him.

"I don't . . . I mean, I didn't."

"*Demonios* are real," Alejandro insisted. "When my great-grandmother was very old, she met one while picking oranges in the grove. She used to tell us all about it when we were children. She said the demon came and demanded the orange harvest or he would curse her family and the land. She told him to take the oranges.

He devoured all of them from the trees and afterward the trees never produced fruit again. I had many nightmares about it."

"I didn't know demons liked fruit," Scott said. "Thought they'd be more into meat and potatoes."

Alejandro shook his head. "Do not mock me, cowboy."

Hannah took a breath. "For our sakes, I hope she was senile and dreaming."

Alejandro shrugged. "Perhaps, but one can never be sure."

Suddenly, the light from the flashlight faded and died, plunging the troupe into complete darkness. Not looking ahead, Scott suddenly bumped into something that clanked and rattled.

"Ouch!" He rubbed his head and stepped back. "What the heck was that? Grab a flare."

Alejandro ruffled through the pack and found one of the flares. He tore it open and a low, red light illuminated their surroundings.

Color drained from Scott's face, and he limped backward. Hannah let out a scream as did Alejandro. Hanging straight in front of them was the skeleton of a man cast in the red light. Tattered rags clung to his dusty bones. His corpse was suspended from the ceiling with chains and irons. His remains flapped against the stone wall at being disturbed. This is where the tunnel ended. A wooden board hung around the deceased's neck. There was some kind of inscription upon it. After regaining their composure, they approached the skeleton cautiously.

"I thought we were done with things like this," Scott said. "I'd be just fine if I never saw a skeleton again."

"Me too," Hannah agreed.

"What's that board say, Rico?"

Alejandro brought his light to the board. "It says, *Marquis de Villena.*" They all eyed each other somberly. "Beneath his name it reads, *tal es el destino de aquellos que juegan con demonios*—Such is the fate of all who trifle with demons."

"So the demon finally caught up with him," Scott said gravely.

"Or that's what someone wants us to think," Hannah added. "I think it's a scare tactic."

A loud rumbling sound came from behind the wall that held the skeleton bound, causing them to startle and jump backward.

"Well, it's workin'."

"*El demonio* is behind that wall," Alejandro stammered.

"I'd just as soon not find out," Scott said. "Besides, there ain't no way to get past it. Might as well turn back."

"Over here!" Hannah yelled out.

Alejandro moved the flare in Hannah's direction Standing ten feet from the hanging skeleton in the corner was a life-size statue of a horned demon, his forked tongue sticking out grotesquely. Toward the base of the statue was a kind of grid with rotating, ivory dials. Upon the dials were different letters.

"It's like a gargoyle," Hannah said as the boys approached.

"There's another inscription near the dial," Alejandro said. "It says, '*Yo soy el demonio que otorgó el poder de oro* . . . I am the demon who bestowed the golden power.'"

"Shoot, what was that guy's name?" Scott said. "The demon guy that gave the golden staff thingy to that one dude who turned the city to gold."

"Yes," Alejandro continued. "The one who Halcón told us about."

"It started with a 'U.' "

Hannah eyed the ivory dials and counted how many letters there were. "There's seven letters. I think I know how to spell it."

"U . . . H . . . E . . . P . . . O . . . N . . . O."

As the last letter locked into place, a loud *thwackkk* sounded within the statue and beyond the wall. Suddenly, the base of the statue began to move, grinding against the floor and rotating counter clockwise. Moments later, the statue ground to a halt, revealing a narrow entrance hidden behind the wall.

"A secret passageway!" Hannah said.

"Are we sure we want to go in there?" Alejandro whispered.

"We've come this far . . . Might as well."

"If I get eaten by some demon, Hannah, I ain't ever forgivin' ya." Scott then turned to Alejandro. "Too bad we didn't bring any oranges."

One by one, they squeezed through the narrow passageway behind the statue. On the other side, the cavern was illuminated by glowing torches. It was obvious people had been there recently. The floor upon which they were standing was cemented and flat. Up ahead of them ten feet away, the floor gave way to a horizontal trench. Inside the trench, rail ties and tracks stretched onward in a parallel fashion in both directions as far as the light could penetrate.

"This is a platform!" Hannah said. "Those are tracks down there!"

The platform started to vibrate as a sound rumbled toward them in the darkness.

"Shoot, I don't like the sound of that."

"*Es el demonio.*" Alejandro's eyes widened.

Hannah pointed to a small crevice in the wall. "Over there! Hide!"

It was tight, but all three managed to fit within the small space and looked onward as the vibrations rattled their teeth. Alejandro dropped the flare to the ground and extinguished it with his foot. There were now only two left in the pack. Sparks flew through the air as a railcar came into view and skidded to a halt. Two men, wearing black leather armor and metal helmets, stepped out of the car. Their faces were concealed with black mesh. One of them walked toward the opening they'd just entered through. So far, they hadn't been detected.

"*Oyyy!*" the man shouted to the other. "*La puerta está abierta.*"

The two men looked around nervously. Hannah, Scott, and Alejandro held their breath.

"One of the brothers must've left it open by mistake," the other responded. "Go up toward the plaza, I'll stay here."

"*¿Porqué no vayas tú?*"

"Because . . . " the man answered, hefting a burlap sack, "I'm in charge of this. I'm not leaving *you* here with it. Now, go!"

The man shook his head and slipped through the doorway, leaving his companion alone in the railcar. He seemed to be just out of earshot.

Careful to keep her voice down, Hannah whispered as quietly as she could. "Where do you think that railway goes?"

"I am guessing to the Brotherhood's castle," Alejandro answered.

"Or maybe to Hogwarts." Scott shrugged.

"Now's our chance. We've got to get on that railcar."

"Umm . . . in case you haven't noticed, it's occupied at the moment."

"Then we'll have to *un*-occupy it."

Alejandro's brow scrunched. "How will you do this?"

"Like this." Hannah grabbed Scott, turned him around, and boosted him in the rear with her foot, causing him to stumble out in the open and fall to the ground.

"Hey! You! Stop!" the man shouted from the railcar and jumped out in pursuit.

Scott scrambled to his feet and shot a menacing glare at Hannah before the faceless man tackled him.

"Now!" she yelled to Alejandro, who nodded.

The two of them jumped from their hiding spot, pouncing upon the back of their unsuspecting victim. Alejandro got the man in a headlock and Hannah noticed feathered darts attached to his belt. Quickly, she grabbed one and jammed one into the man's neck. Seconds later, he slumped to the ground, deep in slumber.

"What if he'd a killed me?" Scott shouted and dusted himself off. "Think ya kin just use me as fishin' bait?"

"I had to, Scotty. I knew you'd never go along with it if I told you my plan."

"Dang right, I wouldn't. What's your plan now? What's gonna happen when he wakes up and his friend comes back? Ya don't think they'll realize where we've gone? I ain't goin' one more . . . "

Before he could finish his sentence, Hannah shoved him toward the cart.

"There's no time to argue. We have to go before the other one comes back."

Hannah stepped inside the railcar followed by Alejandro. She pointed to a lever. "Looks simple enough. Push it forward."

Alejandro put his weight into the lever and slowly it released. The railcar started inching forward.

"Okay, now pull it back."

The cart grounded to a stop. "Scotty. Get out and

give us a push. When we get some momentum going, jump in."

"How come you think you can just boss me around?" he asked, irritated.

"Well, out of the three of us, you are the strongest. It just made the most—"

"Can't argue with that." Scott was out of the cart and pushing before Hannah could finish. As he pushed, the mine cart gradually gained momentum. They were just beginning to pick up speed when a frantic voice shouted from behind, "*Alto!*"

Scott peered over his shoulder. The man's companion had returned. He jumped onto the track and raced toward them. They were picking up speed but still going slow enough that the man was gaining.

"We've got to go faster!" Hannah shouted. "Scott, push harder. Run!"

"I'm goin' as fast as I can," he grunted, pumping his burning legs. "It ain't easy pushin' all this weight. You guys need to quit eatin' so many *tapas*."

Hannah picked up one of the several burlap sacks from the floor of the car. Each one was about the size of a bowling ball and just as heavy. "We need to make ourselves lighter!" she yelled and lugged the small sack over Scott's head and into the path of the oncoming man. As the sack hit the rail, it split open, spraying gold and silver coins upward. This temporarily slowed the man, who was now only fifteen feet away.

"Is that . . . !" Alejandro's mouth dropped.

"Yes!" Hannah shouted. "Now, help me!"

The man was only ten feet away from Scott. The car continued gaining speed. Hannah watched as Alejandro hesitated but then picked up a sack of coins and tossed them over, landing just in front of their pursuer. Their assailant stumbled over the bag but stayed up. The car was speeding up and Scott appeared to be having a hard time hanging on.

"Jump in, cowboy!" Alejandro yelled and pulled on Scott's arm.

Scott heaved himself up and into the car.

Hannah threw another bag over the edge and the man dodged it. He was only five feet away—close enough that the three could hear him breathing. The man leaped and grabbed onto the back edge of the railcar, his feet knocking against the ties as it shot forward. The man pulled his torso up over the lip of the car. The railcar came upon a sharp decline and descended fast. Suddenly, the kiddie ride had morphed into a rollercoaster. The man was still halfway in, halfway out of the car, struggling against the speed of the railcar. The car hit a bump, sending them all a few inches from their seats. The man's grip loosened as he was thrust upward, but he grabbed onto Alejandro's shirt, jerking Alejandro out of the car with him. Alejandro grabbed the back of the car as the masked man hit against the ties and bounced like an apple core thrown from a car window. Hannah closed her eyes, not wanting to see. She feared Alejandro would soon share the same fate. Hannah watched Alejandro try to pull himself up, but he was now in the same predicament as their assailant. His legs were flying behind him like a kite in the wind, the momentum gradually peeling away his grip from the car.

"Stop!" he tried to yell, but his cheeks filled with air before any words escaped.

Hannah got the message and pulled on the brake lever. Sparks flew everywhere, but they were going too fast. The friction did little to slow them. Hannah gritted her teeth and pulled harder. The bottom of the lever was glowing bright red and it broke off in her hands. Helplessly, she held it, staring at the smoldering end.

Alejdandro groaned, his arms giving out more and more. One by one, his fingers peeled away from the railcar, his feet occasionally bouncing off the wooden ties below. Hannah threw the lever overboard and grabbed one of his arms. Scott grabbed the other. The acceleration was too much for them to pull him back inside on their own. Hannah's eyes locked with Alejandro's, and they both knew that at any second he would be roadkill.

"We gotta pull 'im up together. On three, pull with everything you've got!" Scott shouted above the din of the rails and wind. "One, two, three!" Together, they planted their feet and heaved backward. Alejandro toppled over them into the railcar, gasping and laughing at the same time, grateful to be alive. The car continued to accelerate.

"*Gracias, gracias,* cowboy!" he yelled and kissed Scott on both cheeks.

"Don't make me throw ya back out!" he yelled, wiping his face.

Alejandro took Hannah's hand and kissed it. "*Gracias,* Hannah."

The car kept speeding forward, nearly bouncing off the rails as it hit dips in the track. Each time, they held their breath, fearful they wouldn't land back on the iron.

"We're gonna flip over!" Scott yelled at Hannah. "If ya wouldn'ta made us get in this death trap, this wouldn'ta ever happened."

"Maybe if you weren't so obstinate, I wouldn't have had to make all the decisions."

"I ask again, why ya gotta use big words like that? You know how much I hate it!"

Alejandro peeked over the front edge of the car. A hundred feet away, the track ran straight through a blockade of wooden crates and barrels.

"*Amigos!* Stop arguing, please! We're about to die!" he yelled and pointed forward.

Scott and Hannah stopped bickering for a moment and looked in his direction.

"Son of a monkey!" Scott said as they slammed into the blockade like a bowling ball hurling into a set of pins. Splinters of wood flew overhead as they clung to each other and huddled as close to the floor as they could get. The barricade did little to slow the speeding cart as it jostled, tipped to one side, and slowly came back down to meet the rails once again.

Hannah laughed as she hugged both of them. "We made it!"

Scott even hugged Alejandro, a sight Hannah never thought she'd see. "I sure am glad that the last image of my life wasn't your ugly mug." He laughed.

Hannah was silent as she stared forward.

"What's up, buttercup?" Scott asked as he sat up next to her.

What was up was the fact why the blockade was put in place. Just up ahead, the iron rails careened off a rocky ledge in a tangled, wiry mess. Beyond the ledge, a gulf of blackness awaited them.

The smiles and laughter faded. "Well . . . shoot." Scott looked at Hannah with melancholy eyes. "It was nice knowin' ya."

CHAPTER •13•

TRYING NOT TO PANIC, Hannah guessed there were mere seconds before the railcar would go flying off the track. The flare revealed one final blockade set up to impede their progress toward the chasm.

"What do we do?" Alejandro yelled above the whistling wheels.

"We jump," Hannah responded.

Scott and Alejandro both shook their head emphatically.

"When the car hits the blockade, it will slow us down. It's our only chance!"

The car was only fifty feet away from the blockade. The never-ending gulf awaited just beyond, eager to swallow them up.

"Fine," Scott said. "No time to argue."

"Here it comes!" Alejandro yelled. "Duck!"

The car smashed into another set of obstructions. Wooden crates and water barrels exploded over their heads, dousing their clothes with cold water. The precipice was just another twenty feet in front of them. The car was still going fast, but it had slowed considerably.

"Now! Jump!" Hannah yelled as she threw her body out of the car.

She landed hard but used her momentum to somersault along the gravel to the side of the track. Watching helplessly, she saw Alejandro hand Scott the flare, nod, then jump, not landing near as smoothly as Hannah. He bounced and scraped along the cinders.

She then watched Scott toss the flare from the car and leap just as it hit the end of the line. The vehicle flew over the edge, its wheels whistling through the air as it disappeared into the darkness. Hannah brought her hands to her mouth as Scott collided with the ground and rolled with his momentum, skipping across the gravel like a stone over water. Seconds later, a loud crash came from somewhere below as the car dashed against the rocks.

When Scott finally skidded to a stop, his feet were dangling over the edge. He moaned and pulled himself forward. His clothes had been torn, revealing angry red flesh below. "Dang," he said, wincing as he moved. "Now I know how roadkill feels." He stumbled to his feet and worked his way over to Hannah and Alejandro, who were also nursing wounds. Hannah seemed to have fared best and Alejandro the worst. Scott and Hannah eyed one another, then raced to help Alejandro. Together they braced his arms and pulled, causing him to yell out in pain. They quickly dropped him back to sitting position. From his pack, Hannah retrieved the final flare and tore it open.

Alejandro gritted his teeth and tore away his tattered pant leg, revealing a cut that was bleeding pretty badly.

Scott dry heaved and looked away. "I think I'm gonna barf."

Hannah examined the wound. "It's not too deep. You might need stitches though."

"Steetches?" Alejandro repeated.

"For now, we'll have to wrap it up as best we can. Scott! Tear off some of your shirt. We can use it as a bandage. Alejandro, this is going to hurt, but we have to do it. Here, bite on this," she said, handing him a loose piece of wood.

Scott nodded and tore cloth away from one of his sleeves. Using the clean side, she wrapped Alejandro's calf. He winced in pain.

"Geez, how'd you know to do that so good?" Scott asked.

"Health and Physiology. You should take it sometime instead of Mr. Simonton's weight lifting class."

"You kidding me? Gotta keep these guns loaded." He kissed his right bicep. Alejandro spat the wood piece out of his mouth. "Hello?"

"Sorry," Hannah said and tugged the cloth tighter, finishing the job.

"*Gracias*, Hannah." He moaned as he got up. "Ay, it still hurts."

Hannah blushed but was secretly pleased with how cool she kept in the situation

"Quit bein' a baby," Scott said, interrupting her thoughts. "I'm the one who had to tear up my shirt."

Hannah glared upward, then bent down to cinch the makeshift bandage tighter. She tore a few more pieces of cloth away from Alejandro's shirt and wrapped it again. Hannah sighed. "It'll have to do for now. We'll need to get you real medical help when we can."

"I will be okay," Alejandro said with a determined stare. "We need to help your brother and the others."

"Can you walk?"

"*Sí*, I can walk," he managed to get up and limp forward.

"He's like a horse with a broken leg," Scott said. "It'd probably be better to put him down, get him outta his mis'ry."

Alejandro glared. "*Gracias* for your concern, cowboy. Only the source of my misery does not stem from the leg—it comes from listening to you."

"All right, all right," Hannah interrupted. "Let's head back to the platform we passed."

Limping along, they passed the first barricade they'd crashed through. To their right was the platform with another stone statue of the demon propped up against the wall. They pulled themselves up onto the platform and approached cautiously, fearful of being watched.

"It must be another passageway. I wonder where it leads," Hannah said.

"Nowhere good, I dare say," Scott answered. "What's it say, Rico?"

Alejandro limped toward the demon where more ivory dials awaited with an inscription etched above them. He read aloud, "*La ciudad de oro*," it reads. "The city of gold."

"Cíbola!" Alejandro and Hannah said in unison and laughed.

"I knew that too," Scott interrupted. "Y'all just said it before I had a chance."

"By all means, cowboy, go ahead and enter the name into the dials."

"All right," Scott nodded and approached the statue. "Let's see . . . starts with an S."

"*Ehhh*," Hannah said in a buzzer imitation.

"'C,' I meant to say." He turned the first letter to *C*. "The next one was . . . *E*."

"Wrong again, cowboy." Alejandro chuckled, then grimaced as he stepped too quickly.

"Fine, so I ain't the best speller. What is it then?"

"I," the other two answered.

Scott turned the second dial to *i*. "Okay, the rest is easy—b-o-l-a. I know that much"

"*Muy bien*, cowboy. You spelled half a word."

"Yeah, I can spell half another word too—*w-i*. The last two letters are *m-p*. Put 'em together and whatdaya got?"

"Wimp?" Alejandro answered.

"Exactly," he said, pleased. "A wimp says what?"

"What?"

"Just ignore him, Alejandro. Scott, put in the rest of the word."

Scott rotated the white dials in place until they read, "C-I-B-O-L-A."

The grinding sound started up again and the statue moved outward, revealing a hidden passageway.

"Sure you don't wanna stay here, wimpo?" Scott asked Alejandro.

Before Alejandro could come up with a comeback, the sound of another railcar filled the chamber.

"Must be more Brotherhood goons," Hannah said. "What do we do?"

"Should we run or fight?" Alejandro asked.

"Fight," Scott and Hannah answered in unison.

They absconded behind the statue and waited. The railcar's brakes ground the vehicle to a halt. Alejandro peeked around the corner of the statue and raced out as fast as he could with his hurt leg.

"What's he doin?" Scott's eyes became saucers.

Hannah and Scott ran after him out into the open platform. Hannah couldn't believe her eyes. Inside the railcar were the people she least expected to see. Pincho stepped out. Then reaching backward, he helped someone else out of the cart.

"Abuelo!" Alejandro yelled and ran to his grandfather.

"There you are!" He laughed, attaching his oxygen tank to some kind of pack slung around his shoulders. The old man was decked out in his leather armor and brandished a sword at his side. "I wouldn't miss this adventure for anything. Jails cannot contain knights from accomplishing their just duties."

"Especially when those knights can afford to pay hefty bail bonds," Pincho mumbled.

"How did you find us?"

"The senses of a knight never fail him!" he said. "Indeed, I used my keen faculties to lead us here!"

"*We* pieced together the instructions Halcón left for you," Pincho said. "And when I say *we*, it was mostly *me*."

"Yes, my squire. You were somewhat helpful, I admit. Now onward! Let us fulfill our destiny and defeat the Brotherhood of Coronado!" Carlos yelled and stepped back inside the cart. "*Vamos*," he said, pointing his sword toward the precipice they'd all just avoided.

"Abuelo . . . this way." Alejandro indicated the door behind the statue.

● ● ●

Huber hadn't been afraid as he'd marched through the dungeon and up the stairs, but now that he and Malia were standing before the Three Kings, his hand began to shake. It had to be late afternoon. After spending the previous night in the dark, cold cell, Huber was glad to be up and moving around, but he dreaded to think of what Fausto had cooked up. Within the throne room was a legion of faceless minions, also brandishing steel helmets, loitering about in anticipation of the games. Jessie sat in a chair next to Matón, unbound, yet a prisoner all the same. Huber could feel Jessie's eyes on him, but he ignored her and thought of Grandpa Nick. He stood a little straighter. Fausto raised a hand and the room fell deathly still. He turned his silver face toward his captives.

"*¡Bienvenidos mis hermanos a un jeugo especial!*" Fausto bellowed.

A loud cheer erupted throughout the room as men began placing bets on who would win, or rather who would live and who would die. Matón motioned for them to sit at a small round table toward the center of the room. The table was covered in red felt. Wooden cups, dice, and cards rested upon it. Two chairs sat opposite each other and above each chair, long sharp skewers dangled above like chandeliers. Each one must've weighed a hundred pounds. Huber eyed the steel spikes and looked at Malia, who was also focused on the tools of their demise.

"Very well," Fausto said, and the crowd of soldiers fell silent. "Here are the rules. There will be a total of three *juegos* or games. The one who wins two of the three will survive along with his corresponding companion. For each game lost, the blades of justice will fall closer toward the criminal!"

Cheers and applause raced through the crowd. Fausto raised his hand to quiet it. "Should Malia the Zuni win, she and the American teacher, Mendoza, shall live."

Boos and jeers followed the statement. Apparently, the men were not happy that the Zuni girl had refused to cooperate with the Brotherhood's demands of translating the tablet.

"Should Huber Hill the Thief prevail, he and his friend," he pointed to Yesenia, "shall be allowed to leave the castle unharmed."

A cheer erupted. Evidently, the men in general were rooting for Huber and Jessie.

"The first game . . ." He paused for drama and raised his hands high in the air, ". . . will be *Engaño!*"

Huber turned to Malia. "What's that?"

"I've seen some of the guards play it in the dungeon. In English, it's called Deception or Liar's Dice."

"Great . . . a game I've never played."

"It's a game of chance."

Fausto looked on the players. "Are you familiar with the rules?"

Huber shook his head.

Susurro approached them and started to explain the rules. "Each of you will receive five dice. Place the dice within your cup and turn it upside down on the table. You are only allowed to look at your own dice. You will then call out a number, one through six, and how many dice you believe carry that number on the table whether it be your own or your opponent's. Let us suppose you have one 5, two 4s, one 2, along with a 6. You may decide to tell the truth or lie to fool your opponent. You decide to tell the truth and call out 'two 4s.' Your opponent may believe you or she may not. In this case, let's say she calls you 'mentiroso' or *liar*. You both reveal your dice whereupon she will know you were telling the truth, since she has no fours, there really are only two 4s on the table. Your opponent loses one of her dice. If she were to have a single four beneath her cup, she could counter by saying 'three 4s.' It would then be up to you whether you believed she was lying or not." Susurro turned to Malia. "This time let us suppose you roll three 1s, one 3, and one 4. You tell your opponent that you possess 'two 3s.' He calls you a *mentirosa*. You both reveal your dice, showing you only had one 3 and he has none. You lose the round and one of your dice. Understand?"

Huber and Malia nodded. The rules seemed simple enough.

"There are additional rules to consider. You must always up the ante. If you believe your opponent when he tells you he has three 4s, then you must tell him that you have additional 4s to add. Or you must choose a higher number. You can say you have one or more fives or sixes, if you want the play to continue. Do you understand? Are you ready to begin?

They both nodded and glanced at the blades of justice dangling overhead. Huber forced himself to look down at the table, ignoring them. Matón strapped their legs and torsos to their chairs so there could be no escape.

Huber looked Malia in the eye. She met his gaze and both could see the worry written across the face of the other.

"*Jugamos!*" Fausto shouted to the applause of the many spectators.

A wooden cup with five dice was placed before Huber. The same was done for Malia. Huber picked up his wooden cup, shook the dice up, and slammed it down on the table. It was kind of like playing Yahtzee, but he'd never played Yahtzee with his death looming over his head. Of course, there were times Hannah lost where he thought she might kill him. Where was Hannah now? Malia threw down her cup as well. Huber was allowed to go first. He lifted his cup from the table and looked at the results: two 5s, one 6, one 1, and one 3.

"Two 5s," he said, looking at Malia, trying to tell her with his eyes that he was telling the truth.

"Three 5s," Malia answered after looking at her own dice.

Huber thought it over. Either Malia had another 5 and was telling the truth or she was lying. It was also possible she had more than one 5. Looking into the girl's eyes, he couldn't tell if she was telling the truth or not. Huber took a guess. "*Mentirosa.*"

Malia lifted her cup. She had two 1s, three 2s, and one 5. She had been telling the truth. Laughter and cat-calls ensued from the soldiers looking on. One of the men snatched away one of Huber's dice. He was down to four. They shook again. It was now Malia's turn to go first.

"Three 1s," she said, her face inscrutable.

Huber didn't know what to do. He looked at his own dice. He had no ones. He'd either have to call Malia a liar or up the ante. Huber had two 2s, one 4, and one 6.

"Two 2s," he replied.

Malia nodded. "Three 2s."

If Malia really had three 1s, this meant one of her two remaining dice was really a two or she was lying. Huber decided to up the ante again. "One 4."

Malia quickly responded, "One 6."

Huber had to think quickly. "*Mentirosa*," he said again.

Malia unveiled her dice. There was no six. Another loud cheer from the crowd echoed through the chamber. One dice was deducted from the girl. They were both down to four.

They shook again. Because Huber won the last round, it was his turn to start. He rolled three 1s, and one 5. "Three 1s."

"*Mentiroso*," she responded.

Huber lifted his cup to reveal three ones. Malia lost another dice. She was down to three. They shook again. This time Huber rolled two 2s, one 3, and one 6.

"One 6," he said.

"Three 6s," she responded.

"*Mentirosa*," Huber said, sure of himself.

Malia uncovered her dice, showing two 6s. With Huber's one 6, that totaled three on the table. Huber couldn't believe it. He lost a dice and the crowd moaned in disappointment. They were both down to three. They shook their cups again and slammed them on the table. This time Huber got two 4s and one 5. It was Malia's turn to start.

"Three 3s," she said.

Huber thought it unlikely that she rolled that many threes with just three dice. "*Mentirosa*."

Malia uncovered her dice. Indeed, she had rolled three 3s. The crowd moaned again as Huber lost another dice. *Down to two.* He shook the cup again, rolling one 1 and one 4. Malia went again. She looked at Huber as if trying to convey a message telepathically.

"One 5."

Huber didn't have any fives or sixes but decided to bluff. "Two 5s."

"Three 5s."

"*Mentirosa*."

Malia and Huber revealed their scores. There was only one five on the table. Malia lost another dice. They both now only had two dice. They rolled again and tipped their cups to see what they'd scored. It was now Huber's turn. He had one 6 and one 4.

"One 6."

"Hmmmm . . . *mentiroso*," she said coolly.

Huber lifted his cup, revealing his six. Malia lost another and now only had one die. They went again. This time Huber rolled a one and four. "One 2," he called out.

"One 3."

"Two 3s."

Malia appeared to be mulling it over, trying to guess if Huber really had a three under his cup. "*Mentiroso*," she said. Huber popped his cup off the table and lost another die. They both were down to one. The crowd was getting excited, starting to argue over who would win. They both shook and slammed their cups on the tabletop. It was Malia's turn. It all came down to this. She looked at Huber solemnly with tearful eyes. "One 6," she croaked.

Huber lifted his cup, also revealing a six. He sat for a moment. There was only a one in six chance the girl was telling the truth. However, he could turn it back on Malia by telling the truth. If she called him a liar, she'd lose. There was no way to up the ante from this point, so if Malia believed him, it'd be a draw and they'd roll again.

"Two 6s," Huber replied to the astonishment of the crowd as they adjusted their bets. Gold and silver coins were being exchanged like candy. Even the Three Kings were on the edge of their seats.

Finally, she replied, "*Mentiroso*."

They both lifted their cups. Both had one six. Malia had lost.

The crowd burst forth in applause, jeers, and cheers,

some lamenting their losses, others celebrating their gains.

Fausto raised his fist to quiet the crowd. Silence was immediate.

"*Buen hecho*, young one. Huber Hill the Thief has won the first game." Pressing a button beneath his arm rest, the long metal spikes above Malia rattled, shook, and zoomed downward a few feet, but were stopped before falling all the way onto the girl. The spikes clashed and clanged together. Malia grimaced and shut her eyes tight. Huber watched helplessly and prayed the chains would hold the weight. Slowly, they swung lazily back into place, knocking into each other like the wind chime in his backyard.

Fausto stood and chuckled. "Are you both ready for the next game?"

● ● ●

Hannah was impressed that despite being old and hooked up to an oxygen canister, Carlos moved like a young athlete through the narrow corridor.

"I wonder how far this tunnel goes," Pincho muttered.

"I don't know, but I get the feeling we're going to have company soon," Hannah said.

"I think our odds are pretty good," Scott said. "An old man, a drunk, and the three of us versus a small army."

"We won't need to fight," Carlos said.

"What do ya' mean, we won't need to fight?"

"Just trust me," Pincho answered. "All the arrangements have been made, but we need to get to the castle quickly."

"What do you mean all the arrangements have been made?"

"It is better we not say right now," Carlos answered cheerily. "Forward! Onward, young knights!"

Moments later they arrived at a massive cavern at the end of the tunnel. Another large statue of a demon rested in the center of the room. A large double wooden door, laced with iron loomed behind. A black, powder-coated chain ran through the handles.

"It's locked tight," Alejandro lamented, examining the padlock holding the enormous chain in place. "We need a key," Alejandro said.

"Look!" Hannah yelled, after examining the statue. There were more dials beneath an inscription, just like the others. "The inscription reads *A entrar, dime el nombre del Dorado.*"

Pincho translated. "To enter, give me the name of the Golden One."

"That one dude who turned himself to gold?" Scott said.

"I'm guessing that's the one," Hannah responded.

"What was his name? Conan?"

"Lonan," Alejandro said, his limp slightly improving. "The key word that Halcón said we would need to enter the castle."

"That's right, knew it was somethin' like that."

Hannah rolled the six dials—*L-O-N-A-N*. A gold key dropped from the demon's mouth onto the ground. Picking up the key, she wandered to the door and inserted it into the lock. With a click the lock unlatched. The chains binding the door fell to the side.

"Prepare yourselves for what lies beyond that door," Carlos said with excitement. "Perhaps sorcerers, giants, or even wizards." His eyes grew wide. "Maybe even the grand enchanter himself!"

"If that's true, let's hope we die quickly," Pincho muttered.

"Each must die sooner or later," Carlos responded. "We shall do so valiantly!"

"I'd just as soon die later," Pincho added. "And cowardly."

"Each of you," Carlos said, pointing to Scott, Hannah, and Alejandro. "Stay behind us. Pincho . . . open the door."

Pincho took a deep breath and swung it open.

● ● ●

Within the throne room, Huber and Malia awaited the next game.

Fausto silenced the crowd and thumbed Huber's coin within his fingers as if deep in contemplation. "The second *juego* will be *Monte*!"

The crowd chanted wildly, "*Monte, Monte, Monte!*"

Huber eyed Malia curiously. "What's *Monte?*"

"It's another game of chance—this time involving cards. Neither of us can influence the outcome."

"Susurro!" Fausto yelled over the din. "You will be the broker."

Susurro grabbed a wooden chair nearby and sat it between the two players. He snatched up the deck of cards from the table and shuffled them in a flash.

His high voice squealed, "Each of you will receive four coins."

Susurro signaled one of his cronies. The man leapt to a nearby treasure pile and gathered eight gold coins and stacked four in front of Huber and four in front of Malia.

"After I shuffle the cards, I will remove one card from the top, one from the bottom, and place them both face up." He demonstrated. "I will then place the remaining stack in the middle. I will turn the stack over, revealing the suit of the bottom card. Before doing so, you will both place bets on which card—top or bottom, you think will match the suit of the *monte* or card on the bottom of the stack. You must both place one coin each round on the card you believe will match. If the *monte* does not match either card, we will replay the round. The first to lose all of their coins will lose the game. Ready?"

Huber thought he understood, so he nodded. Malia did the same. Taking the card on top, Susurro placed it face up. A queen of hearts. Huber noticed these cards were ancient looking, almost hand drawn. Susurro retrieved the bottom card and placed it beneath the top one. It was a four of spades. Huber now had to choose the card he thought would match the *monte* or card resting at the bottom of the stack. Huber took a guess and placed a coin on the queen of hearts. Malia chose the four of spades. The crowd waited in anticipation. Susurro turned the stack over, revealing an eight of spades. The spectators jeered and jostled one another. Susurro took Huber's coin. He was down to three. Malia still had four.

"I'm sorry, Huber," Malia said. "I did not mean to win."

Susurro reshuffled the antique deck and repeated the process of displaying a top and bottom card. This time, the bottom card was an ace of diamonds, the top a six of clubs. It was now Malia's turn to go first. She placed her coin upon the ace of diamonds. Huber did the same. Susurro flipped over the deck to reveal the *monte*. It was a King of clubs. They'd both lost. Susurro laughed and snatched up both coins. Huber was down to two. Malia had three.

"I wouldn't follow her again," the Sandman King said through his mask before reshuffling the deck.

This time the top was a four of hearts, the bottom a jack of spades. Since neither won the last round, Malia went first again, placing her bet on the four of hearts. Huber took Susurro's advice and placed his bet opposite Malia. Susurro revealed the *monte*—a seven of spades.

Huber had won this round. The crowd was ecstatic as Susurro slid Malia's coin away with his long fingernails. They both now had two coins remaining.

Susurro repeated the process. This time, the top was a queen of diamonds, the bottom a three of hearts. "Place your bets," Susurro squawked.

Here goes, Huber steeled himself and placed a coin on the three of hearts. Malia placed her coin over the queen. Susurro lifted the deck to reveal a ten of diamonds. Most in the crowd moaned, others cheered. Susurro slid Huber's coin off the table and into his pocket. Huber now only had one coin compared to Malia's two. Huber prayed that he would lose this round. If he ended up winning, his life would be spared, but Mr. Mendoza's and Malia's would be snuffed out. He couldn't let that happen. They had to buy more time. But what could he do? There was no way to cheat in a game of chance.

"Huber Hill is down to one coin!" Susurro squealed at the spectators, holding up his index finger. Matón's shoulder jostled upward in a deep belly laugh. Fausto sat in his throne, impassive, watching the game with seeming indifference as he rolled Huber's doubloon along his knuckles. Whispering and murmuring traveled like electric current through the crowd as Susurro dealt another hand. The top card was a two of spades. The bottom card was a six of clubs. Malia placed her bet on the six of clubs, Huber the two of spades. Susurro flipped over the deck in the middle. The card on the bottom was a jack of spades.

Huber had won. He sighed in disappointment as Susurro grabbed Malia's coin instead of his. They both only had one coin left.

"What's the matter, Huber Hill?" Susurro whispered. "You almost seem disappointed you won."

Huber answered his question with a hard stare. Susurro brought his face close to Huber. "It's as if you *want* to lose . . ." Susurro abruptly stood. "Master Fausto! I believe our competitor here desires to lose the competition!"

Matón now spoke up and belted out. "Yes . . . he must be trying to *protect* someone." He pointed toward Malia.

Catcalls and whistles swept through the crowd. Fausto stopped fiddling with the doubloon and raised his hand. The crowd went immediately silent. Fausto looked at Huber, then Yesenia, then toward Malia with his ever-smirking countenance. Both girls' faces took on an apprehensive look as they glanced back and forth between Fausto and Huber.

"So . . . it is a true love story," he said evenly.

The crowd laughed in delight.

"Well . . . this certainly makes things interesting, doesn't it, boys? The young boy, willing to sacrifice himself for the Zuni? Luckily, there is no way to win or lose by your own accord, Huber Hill the Thief. As in life, *all* is left to chance. Deal the last hand, Susurro."

The crowd waited in anticipation. Susurro placed the two cards on the table. The top was an ace of spades, the other a seven of clubs. Huber wavered between the spades and clubs. Finally, he settled on the seven of clubs. Malia placed her coin on the ace of spades. Whichever suit the *monte* was would reveal the victor. Susurro turned over the deck. Jessie cupped her hands over her mouth. On the bottom was a jack of spades. Malia had won! Huber couldn't help but smile as Susurro took away his last coin. More boos and cheers echoed through the chamber. Huber and Malia had now both won one round. The metal spikes lingering over Huber's head dropped sharply, but stopped halfway down as the weighted restraints kicked in. Huber winced and tried to keep the image of himself as a shish kabob out of his mind. One more game to go. They were running out of time.

King Fausto looked over the crowd and quieted his minions. "There is one more round. The ultimate game of chance. Whoever shall win this game will be victorious. Should Huber Hill the Thief prove victorious, he and his treacherous friend shall survive." He pointed to Jessie. "Should the Zuni prevail, she and the teacher will live while the others perish."

Yesenia looked at Huber with a worried countenance.

Fausto continued, "Each competitor will have a 50/50 chance of survival in this game." The King of the Brotherhood held Huber's gold coin high in the air. "*This is the coin which Huber Hill the Thief stole from Tesoro de los Muertos!*"

The crowd booed and jeered as Fausto arose and

rotated it for everyone to see the light dance off its shiny surface.

"Only fitting that *this* is the coin which shall decide his fate."

Whispers of anticipation rippled through the crowd.

Fausto raised his hands high in the air as if calling down fire from the sky and cried, "*Victoria . . . justicia . . . esas son las calidades de la Cofradía.*" Fausto turned toward Huber. "Victory . . . justice . . . these are the qualities of the Brotherhood. Huber Hill the Thief will be allowed to call the coin. Which side will you choose? The crusader's cross or the coat of arms?"

Huber looked at Yesenia, unsure, then at Susurro who nodded for him to choose.

"The cross," Huber replied steadily.

"Very well. *Buena suerte!*"

Elation swept over the crowd as Fausto flipped Huber's coin high through the air. Huber detached himself as he watched the coin rotate in the air and land on the ground. It rattled and bounced off the stone floor and, in what seemed like slow motion, reverberated to a stop. Grandpa Nick's doubloon would decide his fate. It was too far away for Huber to see the end result.

Complete silence invaded the room. The Three Kings arose from their thrones and approached the coin with excitement.

"We have our victor!" Fausto shouted out. "Coat of arms! Malia is the victor. Mendoza and the Zuni shall live. Huber Hill the Thief and the girl, Yesenia will die!"

The crowd burst forth in cheers and jeers. Huber looked at Yesenia for what he was sure the last time and managed a half-hearted smile. Tears stained Jessie's cheeks.

Huber took a breath, closed his eyes, and waited for the steel spikes hanging above to fall.

● ● ●

Hannah had braced herself for the worst as they'd entered the door. To her relief, there had been no one waiting on the other side. Instead, they stood at the bottom of a flight of stone steps that went upward a hundred feet or so. At the top of the stone staircase, there shone a shaft of light. Carlos and Pincho were slow going up the steps and urged the others forward. Hannah, Scott, and Alejandro loped up until they reached the top and then abruptly stopped. The shaft of light was coming from a long corridor of some kind. On both sides of the corridor, rusty bars served as confinements to shallow cells. A guard, dressed in a Brotherhood uniform and helmet, paced up and down the hallway, a key ring dangling at his side. Hannah and the others ducked their heads from view and pressed their backs against the wall to keep from being seen. The guard walked past them, their presence undetected in the shadow of the stairwell. They signaled Carlos and Pincho to step lightly as they came up the stairs, and they finally reached the top.

"There's a guard," Hannah whispered. "This must be the Brotherhood's dungeon."

"Maybe Huber and Mr. Mendoza are down here somewhere," Scott said.

"Hmmmm . . . the lair of the enchanter. We shall set the captives free," Carlos whispered. "We'll need to take out that ogre." He pointed to the guard. "I'll take care of it."

Pincho shook his head. "Delusions of grandeur, old man. What are you going to do, *viejo*? Stay back in the shadows. You'll hurt yourself."

"*Sí*, Abuelo. It is better for you to stay behind us."

Carlos ignored their comments and danced up the stairs and burst into the cell corridor.

"What's he doin'?" Scott said.

From their vantage point, they saw Carlos dancing as though with a partner. The guard, now making his rounds back the way he came, noticed the peculiar old man.

"*Allá! Paré!* What are you doing, *viejo*? How did you get in here?" He sprinted toward Carlos.

Carlos stopped dancing and stroked his chin. "So sorry, ogre. Is this the way to Madrid? I must've taken a wrong turn. I'll just go back the way I came." He did an about-face and entered the stairwell.

Carlos passed the group and positioned himself against the wall once more. As the guard stepped through the darkened stairwell, Carlos stuck his foot out, sending the guard sprawling down the hundred-step staircase, crashing and thudding all along the way.

"Not it!" Scott said.

"What do you mean, cowboy?" Alejandro asked.

"I mean I ain't goin' down there to get them keys."

At the bottom of the steps, the guard landed, unconscious.

"So lazy." Hannah rolled her eyes and ran down the stairs.

"Fine, guess, I'll come with."

Moments later, they reached the guard and took his key ring. Scott then dragged his unconscious body through the wooden door and locked it behind him.

They regrouped with the keys and entered the prison corridor.

"Strange there's only one guard down here," Pincho pointed out.

Carlos agreed. "*Sí* . . . very strange."

Suddenly from somewhere up above, a loud ruckus vibrated and echoed downward. It sounded like a crowd cheering.

"Must be a party or somethin' goin' on up there."

"Good, they will be distracted. Let's find Huber and Mr. Mendoza, then get out of here."

They searched the cells around them but found them empty.

"There's no one here," Alejandro said, frustrated.

Up above, another thundering applause sounded. Scott and Hannah eyed each other gravely.

"We need to get up there!"

On their way out of the dungeon as they passed the final cell, something scurried from Hannah's view into the shadows. She stopped abruptly.

"Wait! There's somebody in this one."

Everyone halted and stood before the bars.

"Hello? Huber? Mr. Mendoza?"

A small voice answered, "No."

"What's your name?"

"Doesn't matter," the voice said quickly and quietly.

Pincho approached the cell. "Come out of the shadows. We're enemies to the Brotherhood and therefore friends to you."

"It's a trick," he answered coldly. "You are spies, aren't you? Sent by Fausto here to test me?"

"No trick. We have no part in the Brotherhood. Hannah, give me the key."

Hannah gave Pincho the key, and he unlocked the cell door. The man didn't stir.

"Come. We'll help you get free."

Like a wounded animal, an emaciated old man crept from the shadows. Dirt caked his skin and hair, his clothing blotched by sweat stains.

"Is this real?" His mouth gaped through a long beard.

"Yes, we are quite real, fair maiden," Carlos boomed. "Come into the light!"

"Maiden?"

"He gets confused sometimes," Alejandro said.

The man rattled his chains in the shadows. Alejandro took the guard's keys and entered his cell. The man scuttled away against the wall like a cockroach. Alejandro bent over and tried several keys before finding the right one to unlock the captive's shackles. With a *click*, the lock came undone and fell to the floor. With his skinny ankles free of their bonds, the man stood but wobbled. Alejandro caught him before falling and helped him step forward.

"What is your name, old one?" Alejandro asked as he exited his confines.

"My name? It's been so long since anyone has asked me that . . . my name is *David*. Yes, that's it! David. Who are you?"

"I am Alejandro. This is Hannah, Pincho, Carlos, and the cowboy . . . I mean, Scott."

"Pincho?" He looked at the squatty man with vague familiarity. "You look familiar . . . "

"My actual name is Paco," he said, staring at the old man. Suddenly his eyes widened. "David, you say?"

"It cannot be . . ." the frail man said. "My son?"

Pincho took a step forward. "*Padre mío*? You're alive!" he shouted and embraced the old man. "The Brotherhood said they'd killed you long ago." Tears flowed down his cheeks.

The old man's eyes danced. "Oh, some days I wished

they had my son, but not now." He embraced Pincho and stroked his son's head.

"You've been here for twenty years?" Hannah asked, unable to fathom that much time in such a foul place.

"Has it only been twenty years? Feels much longer than that . . . the Brotherhood said they would release me from mortality when I begged mercy of the Kings and kissed their feet. Each day they tempt me, but each day I refuse."

"A valorous maiden indeed." Carlos stroked his goatee thoughtfully.

"Your mother?" David asked Pincho.

Pincho released his father. "She is well. Still at the library."

The old man saddened. "How I wish I had a book to read."

"You soon will," Pincho said. "Hundreds of them. Come, we'll help you escape."

"I'm guessing since you thought I was dead, I'm not the reason you're here."

Hannah answered, "We've come to rescue my brother, Huber, and our Spanish teacher, Mr. Mendoza. Have you seen them?"

David nodded. "Yes, I've seen them."

"Wonder where that one dude is . . . what's his name? Calzone? We could really use his help right now," Scott said.

"Halcón," Alejandro corrected him.

"Yeah, that's it. Man, I could really go for a calzone right about now though."

"He was a prisoner here too, wasn't he?" Hannah asked.

"*Sí.*" David nodded. "He was a prisoner here for a short time. The two of us never actually spoke, but I've heard the guards tell stories of his escape."

"Do you know what's going on up there?" Pincho asked his father.

The feeble man nodded. "I overheard the guards say they had something special planned for the Zuni girl and the American boy."

"Have you seen another girl?" Alejandro asked. "Yesenia is her name. Is she here? I must get to her!"

"There was another girl," David answered. "She was here this morning . . . came to speak with the boy before he was paraded upstairs." He pointed with a shaky finger. "She wasn't a prisoner."

Another booming sound of laughter and jeers echoed down the stairway.

"It is time!" Carlos thundered as his eyes glazed over. "Arise knight and knight-esses." He squinted at Hannah. "The Brotherhood's end is near and we will vanquish the grand enchanter along with all his minions to the abyss in one fell stroke! Are you with me?"

The others looked at one another and then at the old man hesitantly.

Finally, Pincho nodded and shouted. "*Sí*, I am with you Don Carlos *de los Toros!*"

"Yes!" he yelled and nodded. "What say you?" He pointed his sword to Scott, narrowly missing his neck.

"Whoa! Watch it with that thing. Sure, I'm with ya I guess."

"*Maravilloso!*" he exclaimed then pointed to Hannah.

"Yes, I'm with you!"

"*Excelente!* And you fair maiden?" He directed the point of his blade at Pincho's father.

David looked at Pincho. "And I thought I'd lost it . . . Yes, I am with you Don Carlos!"

"*Muy bien!*" Carlos turned to Alejandro. "And you . . . *mi nieto* . . . are you with your abuelo to the end?" he asked softly.

Alejandro nodded. "*Sí*, Abuelo . . . I am with you. But we must have a plan! To walk up there unprepared is suicide."

Carlos eyed Alejandro's tall, slender frame as if he were sizing him up.

"*¿Que, Abuelo?*"

Carlos nodded, "Yes, I believe you'll fit just right."

"Fit just right? Into what?"

He turned toward David. "Fair maiden, we will need your help."

·14·

HUBER DID HIS BEST not to tremble as King Fausto stared down upon him with amusement, his finger hovering over the button that would rain down hundreds of pounds of sharp steel. Malia was still chained to her seat opposite Huber, her eyes downcast. Huber was a rabbit caught in a deathtrap. He assumed Fausto would savor this for all it was worth. "Before we release you from this mortal frame, young one, is there anything you'd like to say?"

Huber forced himself to look straight into the face of Fausto. "I want to say good-bye to Mr. Mendoza."

"I will pass along your message. What would you like me to tell him?"

"Tell him I'm sorry. I never meant for any of this to happen, I just . . ."

Suddenly, the door to the throne room burst open.

A Brotherhood solider was dragging a frail old man by the arm. His skin was caked in dirt and his hair was long and matted. Huber recognized his feet as belonging to the person he'd passed in the cell block earlier.

Matón stood up. "What's going on?" he thundered. "Why is the prisoner out of his cell?"

A soldier, cloaked in the garb of the Brotherhood, approached the throne. He sounded young. "*Yo tengo algo que decir.*"

"*¿Que es?* Can't you see we're busy?"

"*Está listo besar los pies de los reyes.*"

The room fell still as if the air had been sucked out in a vacuum.

Fausto arose, seemingly uninterested in Huber for the moment.

"Is that right, old friend? You're finally ready to kiss the feet of the Three Kings and be free of your shackles forever?"

The old man's head dropped in a nod. "*Sí,* I am ready, but only if you release the boy."

Fausto seemed to consider his proposition. Finally, he answered. "Come forward . . ."

Huber noticed that the soldier ushering the old man seemed to have a slight limp.

"David," Fausto beckoned the old man. "Come."

David came before the three thrones and dropped to his knees.

"I must say, *viejo,* I never thought this day would

come." He laughed. "Go on, then. Begin with Susurro."

David bent forward and brushed his lips over the King's boot. Susurro giggled in delight. The crowd loved it and shouted their approval. The old man then shuffled to Matón on all fours and kissed his foot likewise. He growled his approval, then booted the old man, sending him sprawling backward on the floor. The crowd erupted in applause. David regained himself and kneeled before Fausto. Slowly, he came forward and kissed his foot.

"Arise," Fausto said.

The old man complied.

"The Three Kings of the Brotherhood recognize your allegiance and shall release you from imprisonment via death. Tonight you shall be freed."

"And the boy?" he asked.

"He shall join you in your freedom," he said.

The spectators crowed and whistled their approval. Several faceless soldiers apprehended David and bound his hands behind his back.

"No!" Malia screamed. "Stop! Let them all go and I'll do what you ask!"

Fausto perked up, raised his hand, and silenced the crowd. The king suddenly seemed to forget the old man and Huber altogether. "Susurro! The tablet! Matón, the machine!"

The two lesser kings sprang into action, disappearing into adjacent rooms. All eyes homed in on Malia as she sat in her chair. Susurro reappeared with a thin, golden tablet etched with strange markings. Matón wheeled in a large polygraph machine—a lie detector.

"We will ensure you are giving us the correct translation. Should you lie, we will know."

"Do you accept my conditions?" she asked.

Fausto looked at Matón, then Susurro. A silent understanding passed between them.

"We are agreed. All the prisoners shall be released unharmed, if you deliver the correct translation to us."

A murmur swept through the Brothers assembled. Matón proceeded to hook her up to the machine by wrapping a Velcro strap around her arm and attaching diodes to her forehead. Susurro brought the tablet and set it before her on the card table. A scribe appeared next to Susurro, ready to jot down her words.

"I want the prisoners released first. A token of good will."

"No," Fausto answered flatly.

"Then the deal is off."

Matón growled and raised his mechanical fist.

Fausto raised his hand to stop him. "I will release one prisoner. Whom do you choose?"

Malia eyed Huber, Yesenia, and David. Her eyes landed on Yesenia. "The girl."

Jessie looked up at Fausto. "No! Not me! Release Huber!"

"Go!" Fausto motioned toward the door leading out of the throne room.

Yesenia was ushered to the door, passing Huber on her way out. She laid a hand on his shoulder but couldn't bring herself to look him in the eye. She then passed Matón and Susurro. A couple of guards threw open the door and tossed her out.

● ● ●

Hannah rounded the corner and grabbed Yesenia in the hallway once the soldiers had gone back inside the throne room. Hannah then dragged her to the adjacent armory where Scott awaited.

"It's you!" Jessie exclaimed. "You came! Is Abuelo here?"

"Yeah, traitor, we came, but not for you," Scott spat. "Where's Huber?"

Carlos stepped into view from behind a set of armor.

"Abuelo!"

"Good to see you again, my dear. You played your part masterfully. I know it must've been difficult to keep up the facade."

The old man seemed to be more lucid all of a sudden.

"What are ya talkin' about?" Scott said in bewilderment.

"Hannah, Scott, I am sorry for our deception. I knew Yesenia was working with the Brotherhood. In fact, I encouraged it."

"What? Why?" Hannah asked, unable to believe what she was hearing.

Carlos ignored her question and turned to Jessie. "Were you able to make the switch? Did you get the real one?"

Jessie nodded and tapped her stomach. It made a tinny sound.

"*Excelente, mi amor!* We will gather Malia and the others along with the Dead Man's Treasure."

Scott turned to Hannah. "What the heck they talkin' about?"

She shrugged.

Carlos went on, now seemingly completely in control of his thoughts and the situation. "Yesenia, take the others and get out. Don't go through the main gate. There's a door down the hallway to the right that will lead you to the gardens. It should not be difficult to escape with most of the soldiers occupied in the throne room. Stay to the shadows. Beyond castle walls, to the south about a kilometer, you'll find Beatriz in a large white van waiting. Just as we talked about earlier."

"*Sí, Abuelo. Entiendo.*"

"Good, now go. Take Scott and Hannah with you. We'll see you soon."

Jessie turned toward Scott and Hannah. "Come with me. We must go."

"No way. I ain't leavin' without Huber," Scott said defiantly. "I don't even know who you are? Why should I trust you?"

Carlos gripped Scott by the shoulder. "You must

trust us. If you want to help your friend, you will do as I say. Now, go! Yesenia will need your help in escaping from the castle. For now, the Brotherhood's eyes are drawn inside that room. There is no time to argue, do as I say!"

Hannah spoke. "Fine, we'll trust you."

"But if anything happens to Huber, I'll make sure you pay." Scott put his finger on Carlos's chest.

Carlos chuckled. "I admire your passion, brave knight! Your friend is lucky to have you. He will survive, I promise you."

Jessie trotted off down an adjacent hallway. Scott and Hannah reluctantly followed.

Carlos turned to Pincho. "Well, my old friend. Are you ready for a battle of epic proportions? To face danger and possibly our untimely deaths?"

Pincho grinned and nodded. "Untimely for me, you mean. *Sí*, Don Carlos, I am ready. I would follow you into battle anywhere."

● ● ●

Within the throne room, Huber, along with the rest of the onlookers, watched anxiously as Malia gazed upon the golden tablet.

Susurro bent low toward Malia. "Begin," Huber heard him whisper.

Malia studied the tablet and traced the carvings with

her finger. "It's a story. One I've heard many times from my father and grandfather."

"Do tell," Fausto hissed.

Malia inhaled deeply. Matón watched the polygraph closely. "It is the story of Lonan and Uhepono. It is written by Lonan's own hand. I will now translate—Be it known that any who seek what lies within the heart of Cíbola, will come to ruin. Listen to my tale and do not follow in my footsteps.

"For many years, I lived in peace within my village. However, I wished to rise above my fellow man and be exalted. One day Uhepono, the God of the underworld, disguised himself as a traveler and bestowed a gift upon me: a golden staff topped with an amber stone. Uhepono told me that anything I touched with this stone would be turned to gold. I took the staff and found Uhepono's words to be true. Anything I touched turned to solid gold before my eyes. The people worshipped me as a God and called me the Golden One."

"*El Dorado*," many of the soldiers in the room murmured, transfixed as Malia told the story.

Malia continued, "I transformed my humble village of Cíbola into a shimmering golden city. Some of the people desired my gift for themselves. Others feared me and my new power. Many tried to kill me. Others cursed my name and sought rebellion. To avenge these wrongs, I went through my city in the night and touched every sleeping being with my staff, turning them to gold where they lay. Soon thereafter, Uhepono returned in his true form. Miserable, defeated, and alone, I begged Uhepono to take the staff from me. The God of the Underworld refused and continues to relish in my misery, inhaling my despair as it were sustenance.

"I can no longer endure his presence nor my own. I, Lonan, the once lowly villager, write my own story and solidify my words in gold upon this parchment with my Golden Staff—these are my final words before I turn the stone on myself."

"*El Dorado*. It is true!" the crowd kept whispering.

Fausto raised his fist in the air. "Continue."

"I will guard the Golden Staff eternally within the clutches of my hands, deep inside the heart of my fallen city, Cíbola. To enter my domain, you must possess the keys of knowledge and answer correctly the riddles of my seven golden sentinels. Only then will you possess this cursed stone and staff. I bid you farewell and should you find my golden vestige, remove the staff from my hands at your own peril. To find the city of Cíbola, you must . . ."

"Yes, yes?" Susurro stammered impatiently.

"What does the rest say!" Matón slammed his fist upon the table, splintering it from end to end.

"That's it," Malia squeaked. "It ends there."

The tone of the crowd grew hostile. Fausto arose from his throne and stalked toward Malia. "We have spent years obtaining this tablet. I know it holds the location of Cíbola. Matón, is she telling the truth?"

Matón growled and looked upon the polygraph. "The machine says she is telling the truth. She must be fooling it somehow."

"It cannot be," Fausto said distantly. "I was assured this tablet contained the key to Cíbola's location."

The crowd grew more angry by the minute. Huber and Malia glanced at each other, then at the spikes overhead, unsure of what was about to happen.

Fausto pointed toward Malia, Huber, and then the old prisoner, David. "Dispose of them immediately. *Todos!*"

The door to the throne room suddenly burst open. A tall, lanky form decked out in leather armor ambled through the door, an oxygen tube running to his nostrils. To his side was a portly, bald fellow. The sight seemed to throw everyone off guard. Even Matón staggered back a bit, unsure.

"What is this?" Fausto said curiously.

The gallant knight gazed upward, full of confidence and grace.

"Carlos! Pincho!" Huber yelled upon seeing the welcome sight.

"By the order of his majesty, King Ferdinand, I demand you to depart his former castle and release these prisoners into my custody along with the spoils from the Dead Man's Treasure!"

The room laughed uproariously at the comment. Pincho looked side to side nervously.

"King Ferdinand has been dead for hundreds of years,

my friend. This castle is no longer his. We are the new Kings of España," Fausto proclaimed. "I do not know how a crazy old fool found his way into our stronghold." Fausto looked at Matón, who hung his head. "Come to think of it, you look familiar. Ah yes, I do recognize you. *You* are the loco who tried to fight the bulls in La Glorieta Stadium! The one all over the television. Don Carlos de los Toros!"

Fausto's comments drew laughter from among his many minions.

"I challenge you to a duel!" Carlos shouted above the noise.

The crowed quieted is response, then more laughter echoed throughout the chamber. Pincho looked as if he wanted to crawl into a hole.

"A duel? Are you joking, old man?"

"*Mano a mano!*" Carlos declared.

"I've got more important things to deal with, viejo."

"I know where the real tablet lies," Carlos replied. "The authentic one . . . with the location to Cíbola."

The crowd went silent. Fausto's head turned in surprise.

"What do you mean, *real* tablet?"

"That one there?" he said, pointing to the table. "A fake. Forgery. Counterfeit. Fool's gold! I know because I had Yesenia plant it here. Your prisoner translated it correctly. Only this tablet is missing the last section inscribed on the real tablet. That section is now in a safe location.

You want it back? Accept my duel. Shall I win, you will set the prisoners free and deliver the Dead Man's Treasure into my custody. I'll then give up the tablet. A few measly lives along with one single treasure is surely worth an entire city of gold. Shall I lose, the tablet, the treasure, and all our lives shall be in your hands. What say you, *honorable king*? Not afraid of an old man, are you?"

The soldier who had brought David to the throne room, tore off his helmet and mesh mask. "Abuelo! What are you doing? Do not trifle with these men!"

A slew of soldiers immediately detained the imposter. Huber's jaw dropped as he looked upon Alejandro.

"Do not worry, Alejandro. I will be all right. The honorable king of the Brotherhood will surely not refuse such a boon. Now," he said, turning to Fausto, "do you accept or not? You must swear an oath by Coronado's name to abide by my terms. Nothing less."

"What kind of duel do you have in mind, *viejo*?"

"Rapiers." He unsheathed his sword and swung it wildly almost losing his grip. "Fencing rules. No stabbing. The first to score five points wins the duel."

The crowd resumed their laughing as the old fool seemingly could barely hold the blade, let alone fence.

"And when I trounce you, how do I trust you will tell me the location of the real tablet?"

"I always keep my word. However, take Pincho here as collateral if you like. He'll be your servant. Consider him a gift."

Pincho looked up as if he'd been slapped in the face. "What? We never . . ."

Carlos winked. "Yes, and an excellent servant he'll be."

"Your wish and doom are granted, old man. Matón! To the armory! Fetch me a rapier. Let's end this quickly."

"Swear it!" Carlos demanded. "By Coronado's name!"

Fausto paused, then looked upon the faces of his soldiers. "I swear to your terms *por el nombre de Coronado*."

● ● ●

Minutes later, Huber, still bound to his chair, observed Matón return, bearing a rapier, sharp and thin. Fausto removed his cloak and faced his elderly opponent, still adorned in leather armor, already laboring to breathe, the oxygen tank attached to his back.

"A touch scores a point," the old man reminded the king. "The first to five points wins the bout. Are you sure you don't want to wear armor?"

Fausto looked around and chuckled, ignoring the man's question. "*En guarde*."

Huber was surprised as Carlos's legs spread apart and he brought the fencing sword to be parallel with his nose, suddenly seeming to gain a sense of balance and adroitness. The two circled one another like two cats ready to spring.

Fausto took the first shot, coming at Carlos with

lightning fast speed. Huber wanted to look away but couldn't. Relief washed over him as Carlos nimbly evaded the thrust and deflected the blade. Huber couldn't believe how agile the old man had become.

"Impressive, *viejo*," Fausto said, regaining his balance.

"I may have neglected to mention that in my younger days, I was champion fencer at the University of Salamanca." Carlos slashed his rapier through the air, clashing with Fausto's.

The swords clanged as each parried and countered. Carlos saw an opening and tagged Fausto in the chest, just above his right pectoral muscle. The blade cut through his clothing leaving a quarter-sized flesh wound. Fausto cried out in pain and stumbled backward.

"One point for Don Carlos!" Pincho cheered and gave a thumbs-up to Huber. The soldiers stepped toward him and he quieted, darting his eyes between them.

The onlookers were aghast, seemingly unable to believe their eyes. Surely, they hadn't expected to see their king bested by a harmless old man.

"I advised you to wear armor," Carlos said.

Fausto, enraged at the comment, slashed wildly at the old man. Carlos parried and deflected each of his blows and caught Fausto across the stomach leaving a thin red line the length of a pencil. Once again, Fausto took pause to nurse his freshest wound.

"The first rule of fencing," Carlos tutored him, "is to never let your emotions get the best of you."

"*Dos puntos* for Don Carlos de los Toros!" Pincho shouted and raised his fingers.

Huber felt himself hope just a little. Perhaps he would get out of this place alive.

"You will pay for that, old man." Fausto resumed his stance and gathered himself. This time he waited for Carlos to strike first. Carlos took a jab, missing wide left. Fausto came around and tagged his rib cage with the sword. The armor protected the old man from any harm. The crowd cheered wildly. "*Un punto,*" Fausto said and did a slight bow to the crowd.

"A lucky shot." Carlos grinned.

The two circled each other clockwise, each daring the other to strike first. Finally, Fausto's rapier whizzed through the air. Carlos caught it with his own blade a mere inch before it touched his shoulder. The old man slid his blade to the hilt of his opponent's, then pushed forward, causing Fausto to stagger. Carlos saw his opportunity and sliced into Fausto's thigh. The King of the Brotherhood dropped to one knee and the crowd collectively drew their breath.

"A king kneeling to me?" Carlos feigned shock, attempting to goad his opponent further. "What an honor!"

"*Tres puntos!*" Pincho bounced with excitement. "*Dos más y tienes la victoria!* Two more for victory, Don Carlos!"

Carlos, turned to Pincho and nodded in satisfaction. As he did, Fausto charged forward and sliced Carlos's right bicep where the armor failed to protect. The old man winced and quickly brought his blade up in defense, struggling to hold up the rapier with his wounded arm. The crowd cheered for their king.

Huber winced himself, imagining the pain.

"Cheap shot!" Pincho shouted.

"Three to two," Matón shouted back.

The two men resumed their positions and locked eyes. Fausto came forward and easily knocked Carlos's blade out of his wounded arm and tagged the armor on his other shoulder.

"Three to three," Susurro shrieked gleefully. "They are tied!"

Carlos was visibly shaken. Suddenly his eyes glazed over and his expression turned to one of confusion. His head darted back and forth around the room, taking in his surroundings.

"No, not now," Huber whispered to himself.

"¿Dónde estoy?" Carlos mouthed. "Who are you?" he asked the king.

"Is this some kind of trickery?" Susurro hissed. "Pick up your sword, *viejo*. Finish what you began."

Matón picked up Carlos's sword and forced the hilt back inside his hand. The massive king's physique startled the old man. "Ah! Giant!" He stepped back, causing a ripple of laughter to travel through the crowd. Carlos scanned the audience with his eyes. "Demons!"

"Old man!" Fausto yelled after him.

Carlos turned to face Fausto. "Oh, thank goodness. So good to see a fellow knight. Please help me slay these demons and this grotesque giant!"

"Don Carlos!" Pincho yelled. "He is no knight, he is your enemy! Come to your senses. I am *not* going to be a slave here because of you!"

"A talking donkey?" Carlos said upon viewing Pincho curiously. "I've never seen such a thing in all my days. Must be the work of the Grand Enchanter!"

More laughter ensued from the crowd.

"Enough," Fausto said and brought his sword to the startled old man.

Carlos, seemingly unsure of himself, no longer resembled the master fencer. He now appeared like a frightened child. He managed to parry two of Fausto's attacks out of sheer defensive instinct. The third attack struck Carlos in the head, lacerating the scalp near his temple. The old man cried out in pain and skirted away as if trying to flee. The men in the crowd closed in and blocked his escape, pushing him back in the fencing area. Huber couldn't watch any longer.

"Four to three for Fausto!" Matón thundered.

"Stop!" Huber yelled from his chained position beneath the looming spikes. "You find honor in defeating an old man suffering from dementia? Coward!"

As Huber called the king a coward, the spectators quieted and focused in on him. Matón walked briskly toward him, crackling his mechanical knuckles. He raised his fist high and was about to slam it down on Huber's face when Fausto stopped him.

"Matón! No! Such a blow would knock the boy unconscious. I want him to be awake and watch the remainder of our match."

Matón hesitated but finally unclasped his fist and brought it to his side with a growl.

Carlos was handed the sword again as if it were some foreign object he'd never held before.

"Carlos!" Huber yelled.

Carlos looked at the boy as if he strained to recall where he'd seen him before.

"He's the wizard in disguise! The Grand Enchanter!" He then pointed to Malia. "He's holding this fair maiden against her will. You must defeat him to set her free."

Carlos's eyes went from confusion to certainty as he gazed upon Fausto. "You will unloose the maiden, Enchanter!"

Fausto brought his sword up in a defensive position. Carlos tossed his sword into his left hand and charged toward the king with a shout. Huber witnessed a flurry of steel on steel as the rapiers clashed and whizzed through the air. Carlos ducked as Fausto swung at his head. Using his off hand, Carlos was slower than before, but still agile. He sliced into Fausto's other leg, dropping him again. Pincho, Huber, and Alejandro cheered. "Come on, Abuelo!" Alejandro yelled. "One more and you will defeat him!"

Fausto struggled to his feet. He stabbed forward several times, narrowly missing Carlos's form. They both went for the other's midsection simultaneously and their swords became entwined. Carlos pulled back, broke free, and swung his blade upward, catching the bottom edge of Fausto's bearded metallic mask. The mask flew off his face along with his helmet, leaving a deep gash in the man's cheek. Fausto fell to the floor, holding his face.

"*Cinco puntos* for Don Carlos de los Toros!" Pincho yelled and ran toward Carlos. "The old man has won! I will not be your slave!"

"Back! Talking donkey!" Carlos warned with his rapier.

"You won!" Huber yelled. "You defeated the Grand Enchanter!"

"I did?" Carlos shouted. "*Que maravilla!*"

Suddenly, a squad of Fausto's goons grabbed Carlos and Pincho.

Fausto, unmasked, was still in front of Huber on his knees. Huber could only see the back of his head and the side of his bloody hand pressed against his laceration.

"You made a deal!" Huber said to the king. "You were beaten fair and square. Release us. You swore upon Coronado's name!"

Fausto stood up and turned toward Huber, still holding his cheek. As Huber saw Fausto's face, the breath went out of him. His brain could not register what he was seeing.

"No, Mr. Hill. I don't think I'll be honoring that deal."

"Mr. Mendoza?"

"You got me. Feels a bit awkward, I admit."

"*How?*" Huber stammered.

"I've been king of the Brotherhood for ten years, Hill."

"But you're our teacher."

"And you were such a good student. We'd been searching for the Dead Man's Treasure for many years. We knew it was in western Colorado somewhere. I even went so far as to apply for a teaching job at the town's middle school so I could spend my time looking for it. Believe me, being reduced to teaching Spanish 1 to young brats like you every day wasn't easy, but it was the best disguise I could think of. When that buffoon Juan Hernán Salazar showed his face in town, I knew something was up. I must say, I never expected someone like you would have possessed the map. You see, Salazar followed you. The Ute followed him. I followed all of you. I bided my time a few weeks before taking the treasure. I notified my brethren here in Spain shortly after your discovery and within days, reinforcements arrived. We went up the mountain, opened up the skull's mouth, and took what rightfully belonged to us. On our way down the mountain, we met minor resistance from that old Ute man and some of his friends. They posed no challenge."

Huber's eyes moistened and he breathed hard as he thought of Hawk. "You filth!"

"I had my men trek the treasure to Florida where it was

loaded onto a barge along with some *other* precious cargo," he said, indicating Malia. "I returned after the summer to tie up any loose ends. I became suspicious when a study abroad program was advertised within the school . . . to take place in Salamanca of all places. My suspicions were confirmed when the three of *you* were selected. Why do you think I insisted on coming along? Of course, it was near my time to return to España anyway. And it's good to be home!"

The crowd erupted in cheers and applause.

"We trusted you!"

Mendoza grinned. "Yes, well, you probably shouldn't trust anyone these days, Mr. Hill."

"So, what are you going to do now?"

"The location of the real tablet is inside that old man's disturbed mind somewhere. We'll get it out of him one way or another. We have our *methods* for extracting information. Plus we still have the key." He pointed to Malia. "You cannot stop the Brotherhood of Coronado, Huber. A noble effort, but you were foolish to try. I do wish you hadn't have gotten involved. You and your sister were always such good students. I can't say I'll miss Mr. McCormick all that much. Matón, go ahead and finish the boy off."

Matón's shoulders gyrated up and down as he chuckled in delight. "*Con placer*," he said, approaching Huber, but he stopped short upon seeing a peculiar sight. Sitting upon Fausto's throne was a hooded figure, watching the scene, his face shrouded by a black mask, flickering in the firelight. Huber instantly recognized Halcón.

"Rey Fausto!" Matón bellowed and pointed, momentarily forgetting about Huber.

"It's him," Susurro gasped.

Mendoza, now holding a rag to his cheek, smiled up at the Falcon.

"Well, if it isn't the infamous Halcón . . . *the Falcon*," he spat. "I'm surprised you dare show your face here. You know what fate awaits traitors and mutineers."

The Falcon said nothing. Mendoza skulked toward his throne. "Have you come to pay penance? To seek forgiveness for your trespasses? Perhaps the Brotherhood can afford you mercy if you swear allegiance to me and aid us in our quest for Cíbola. I wonder what you'd say to that?"

The Falcon said nothing, keeping his gaze down at his feet.

"Quite a foolish move to come here all alone. Can't you see you're surrounded?"

El Halcón raised his right hand in the air. As he did so, half of the faceless soldiers in the room removed their helmets and masks. Their hair and skins were dark. Huber thought he recognized one or two of them from the mine at Dead Man's Treasure. A stunned silence pervaded the room. The Ute men suddenly and quickly stabbed feathered plumes into the necks of the soldiers, who only moments ago assumed these men were their comrades. Seconds later, they fell to the floor unconscious.

One of the Ute men stepped forward. He was bulky, broad shouldered, and cut an imposing view. He shouted, "We've come to reclaim the Dead Man's Treasure!"

"And who are you?" Fausto sneered.

"I am Eagle Claw. Son of Hawk—the good man you murdered in your heist."

"I see," Fausto said evenly. "It was nothing personal, friend. He was just in the way."

"In addition to the treasure, we will take the prisoners as well." Eagle Claw pointed to Huber, Malia, Pincho, and Carlos.

Matón growled. Susurro's beady eyes scanned the room for an escape. Mendoza smiled, the blood from his wound now drying. "Take the treasure . . . take the prisoners . . . they're yours. Everyone but her," he said, motioning at Malia.

"All the prisoners," Eagle Claw repeated.

"Come, let us be reasonable," Fausto addressed everyone in the room. "I am offering you a way to avoid bloodshed. Take everything and everyone but the girl and you will leave here unmolested. Refuse and you will all be slaughtered before you ever leave this castle. *I promise you.*"

Malia looked at Huber, her eyes round as saucers. "Please," she gasped, "I can't go back."

"You will unhand the maiden, evil Enchanter!" Carlos called out.

"We'll take our chances," Eagle Claw said. He pointed at the three large chests, brimming with gold. Handfuls of Ute men darted toward the treasure chests, hefting them upon metal carts that had since been wheeled into the room. He then pointed toward Huber and Malia. A separate group of men unbound them and ushered them toward Carlos and Pincho.

Fausto grimaced. "You've made a grave mistake, Halcón. You won't get far."

"Let's go," Eagle Claw said, walking to the door.

"You hear me!" Mendoza seethed. "You will all perish. Such is the fate of all those who cross the Brotherhood!" He then addressed Huber and the others. "Be cautious of who you trust. Has *the Falcon* told you much about himself? Has he told you—"

The Falcon raised his right hand high in the air. Instantly, a slew of feathered plumes shot through the air and pierced the Three Kings. Susurro fell first, then Matón, and finally Fausto.

"Why don't you just kill them now?" Alejandro said, perturbed. "You know they will pursue us."

"Others will simply take their place," Pincho said. "We must defeat the Brotherhood at its core. Draw them out. We best leave now. We won't have much time."

The Ute men once again disguised themselves with their armor and helmets. Alejandro did the same. With his back to the group, Huber watched as Halcón bent down, slipped off his mask, and took Fausto's, slipping it over his face. Huber craned his neck to try and catch a glimpse of the man's face but couldn't. He then donned the helmet and robe and began leading them all out of the throne room.

"Wait!" Huber said and cautiously approached Fausto. Never before had he been so scared to approach his teacher. Mendoza was snoring softly. Huber reached into the deceiver's pocket and withdrew his grandpa's doubloon. He quickly slid it into his own pocket where it belonged. "Okay, we can go now."

Close behind, the disguised Ute rolled the chests down the corridor. Huber, Malia, Pincho, David, and Carlos were prodded along, pretending to be prisoners. As Carlos ambled down the corridor, Huber noticed the old man become more lucid. Gazing upon Pincho with hazy eyes, he asked, "What happened, Pincho? It seems like seconds ago I was battling Rey Fausto . . . now I'm here." He scanned the front of their garrison, spotted Fausto's mask, and touched the wound on his head. He then looked down at his bonds. "It appears that I lost."

"No, my friend. You bested King Fausto. Everything went according to Halcón's plan. We're on our way out," Pincho said under his breath.

"*Excelente*," Carlos whispered enthusiastically. "So Fausto . . ." He gestured toward Halcón with his chin.

"Is locked in the throne room behind us."

The assembly marched beyond the Brotherhood soldiers standing guard. None of them dared question where the group was going with Fausto at their head. Finally they reached the massive drawbridge, which was

closed. Halcón motioned for the guards stationed there
to open it.

One of the guards tiptoed toward Halcón, eyeing the
treasure and prisoners.

"King Fausto, I beg your pardon for asking, but it
is against all rules to open the bridge after nightfall. In
addition, all prisoner and treasure transfers are to be con-
ducted through the tunnels."

Huber froze.

The Falcon stared hard at the guard, saying nothing.
It did the trick. The man gulped and returned to his post.
"Of course, you are the king."

Men on both sides of the drawbridge began crank-
ing levers in unison. The latticed portcullis began to lift
upward, albeit painfully slow. The massive door finally
crested to a point where Huber could see the stars outside.
On the other side of the bridge spanning the dry moat,
a large white van sat idling, its rear facing the bridge.
Finally, the portcullis locked in place overhead. The back
door to the van opened up. Huber wanted to jump for joy
as he saw Hannah, Jessie, and Scott. The guards standing at the door grabbed for their walkies, but before they
could reach them, feathers were sticking out of their
necks. They crumpled to the ground instantaneously.

"*Vámonos!*" Yesenia shouted from the van. "We need
to hurry!"

Hastily, the men wheeled the carts containing the
Dead Man's Treasure to the van. It took two of them on

both sides of one chest to lift it inside. The back of the van sagged beneath the weight. As they lifted the final chest into the van, a loud, screaming alarm began to sound. Huber looked behind him and from a distance could see a slew of soldiers led by Mendoza, Susurro, and Matón racing toward them.

"They're coming!" Huber shouted.

"Go!" Eagle Claw said to them. "We have accomplished our mission. Return the treasure to its resting place and the girl to her people. Keep her safe. We will buy you time."

Halcón and the Ute brandished their arms and stood their ground just outside the drawbridge.

"Go!" Eagle Claw urged Beatriz, who was driving the van. "Drive to the coast of Campostela. Pier twenty-three. If we survive, the Falcon and I will meet you there at dawn!"

The librarian nodded. Pincho and his father were the last to enter the van. The three rows were crammed with people. Beatriz made eye contact with her husband through the rearview mirror. *"David! Is that you?"*

The old man nodded. "Sorry I never made it home for dinner, my love."

"Step on it, *madre!*" Pincho shouted. "We'll have time for a reunion later!"

The old woman slammed the gas pedal. The tires of the van screeched forward.

"How did you get in here?" Huber asked his sister.

"Beatriz told the guards she was a caterer delivering food for a festivity."

"They bought that?"

"I don't think they do now." She pointed through the windshield.

The gate leading out was now closed and the guards were leveling rifles at the van.

"Don't stop!" Alejandro shouted.

"Duck!" the woman yelled as the van lurched toward the gate.

Bullets thudded into the van and several flew through the windshield. The van was rocketed by an impact, but the vehicle's momentum kept going. Everyone slowly brought their heads up. Beatriz was still driving, unscathed. Huber examined his body just to make sure he wasn't Swiss cheese.

"Everyone all right?" Beatriz asked, scanning their faces in the rearview mirror.

One by one, they all confirmed they were unhurt.

Huber noticed Carlos look at Jessie. "Do you still have the tablet? Is it safe?"

She nodded. "*Sí. Está aquí.*" She rapped her stomach with her knuckles, producing a metallic sound.

"*Maravilloso . . . mi amor, maravilloso.*"

The old man looked at Hannah and then Huber, his eyes relaxing as he slumped into his seat. "What an adventure . . . you know, I see your grandfather at times . . . we travel together in dreams . . . slaying giants, rescuing maidens, and finding gold."

Huber smiled at the thought and, for the first time in two days, allowed himself to relax.

● ● ●

No one spoke as the van traveled toward Compostela. After his ordeal over the last two days, exhaustion overtook Huber, and he slept most of the way. The sun woke him up just as it started to rise in the east. About a half hour later, they arrived at the pier.

Beatriz pointed to a large, white sailboat that was docked at pier number twenty-three. Several Native American men were rigging the sails and moving around on the deck.

"There it is," Pincho said. "We will load the treasure upon that craft and we will all sail for America."

"How did those guys get inside the castle?" Huber asked.

"Halcón, Hawk, Carlos, and myself arranged the plan of stealing back the real tablet, rescuing Malia, and delivering the Dead Man's Treasure back to the mountains. Hawk was able to enlist the help of a Zuni elder to forge the fake tablet. We were lucky things turned out as well as they did."

"So we're headed back in that?" Hannah pointed to the ship.

"*Sí.* There are enough provisions upon the vessel to last

us for our two-week journey to Virginia. From there, you
will be taken back home along with the treasure. I will
see Malia to her parents in New Mexico and help them
protect Cíbola's location. I fear the Brotherhood won't lag
far behind."

"What about us?" Alejandro asked.

"You and Yesenia will stay with my parents for now."

Huber noticed Hannah's downcast face at the comment. He tried to hide his own disappointment that he
wouldn't be seeing Yesenia anymore.

"My old man doesn't like me crossin' the sea all by
myself. Why can't we fly?" Scott said with trepidation.
Huber remembered Scott had confided in him that he
was deathly afraid of deep water.

"It is too dangerous to fly home from here," Pincho
admonished him. "The Brotherhood will be swarming
the airports searching for us."

"Let us come with you to New Mexico," Huber
implored.

"Yeah, we can help," Hannah said.

"You've played your part and done so very well. The
Dead Man's Treasure will be returned to its rightful place
and you shall be returned to your homes in one piece.
You've accomplished what you set out to do. Your part in
this fight ends here." Pincho then turned to Carlos. "As
does yours, old friend. You will go with my mother and
father. They will look after you as well while in hiding."

"No . . ." Carlos croaked. "A knight does not shirk

his duty in the greatest hour of need," he said with starry eyes.

"No, Don Carlos!" Pincho insisted. "It will be too dangerous. You won't get that lucky again."

The old man arose with renewed vigor and anger, no longer mindful of his wounds. "I will see this quest through! This is what I've been waiting for my entire life. I will see it through, I say! Not to mention that up to this point, everything has been accomplished using *my* resources. It is only right I accompany you on this mission. Do not deny me this!"

"But you are hurt, my friend." Pincho pointed to the gashes on Carlos's arm and head.

"This?" He touched his bandaged head. "A scratch! A mere graze from a dragon's tooth. Nothing that will stop a knight. A true knight-errant will never stop fighting even if his bowels are falling out of him!"

Huber scrunched his face at the thought.

Pincho faltered. "All right, your grace. Come along then and finish your quest."

"We're coming too then!" Jessie spoke up.

Huber brightened and dared to hope.

"*Así es*," Alejandro said. "Abuelo is in charge of us, so we *must* go! Don't make us stay here!"

"I wouldn't think of it," Carlos said. "We will need you on the journey, of that much I am sure."

"Fine," Pincho relented, "but should anything happen to any of you, I will not be responsible."

"You? Responsible?" Beatriz choked on her laughter. "That's fresh."

"Look!" David pointed to the hooded, masked man waiting on the dock by the boat.

It was Halcón. Standing next to him was Eagle Claw.

"Our friend has come to see us off."

One by one they piled out of the van and jogged up the deck toward the waiting sailboat. Huber had never been on a sailboat before. The idea of traveling over the ocean was exciting. The fact that Yesenia would also be on the boat didn't hurt either.

A man on the ship yelled they were ready to depart. Beatriz and David starting kissing everyone good-bye.

"Thanks for letting us sleep in the library," Huber said as Beatriz came to him.

"My pleasure. Should you ever make it back to Salamanca, know that you're always welcome to sleep in my break room." She smiled. "Take care of Paco. Keep him away from the bottle."

"I'll try," Huber said.

Huber watched as the old man and woman said a long good-bye to their son and waved their farewells before getting back into the van and driving away.

Afterward, the group approached the pier where the Falcon awaited them. Eagle Claw was now on deck getting things readied for their departure.

"*Gracias*, brave knight," Carlos said and gripped the Falcon's hand. His face was still shrouded beneath his hood and mask. "The plan went perfectly!"

Halcón nodded and whispered, "The tablet?"

"Returned to its proper owner," he said, motioning to Malia, holding a duffle bag.

The Falcon nodded approvingly. "Safe journeys then," he whispered.

Pincho shook hands with the man, then he and Carlos boarded the ship. Alejandro, Yesenia, and Hannah took their turn giving their thanks before stepping onto the gently rocking vessel. Scott did the same, then closed his eyes and took a breath as he boarded the vessel. Huber and Malia waited to shake hands with the Falcon last.

Huber gripped the Falcon's hand. This was the first time he'd seen the man in the daylight. Though his face was still disguised, the sun crested the horizon and Huber caught a glimpse of his left eye beneath the hood. Huber instantly froze. The man's eye was a bluish-white color.

"No . . ." he whispered. "It can't be."

The Falcon's lips turned to a tight grin before he gripped Huber's arm and pulled him in close. As he did, the Falcon's sleeve crept up his arm and Huber noticed a tattoo of a serpent. *"Hola, jóven,"* he snarled and tossed the boy aside. Just as quickly he snatched Malia and held her facing the craft, bringing a shiny blade to her throat.

"Halcón! What are you doing?" Malia gasped.

"What is the meaning of this, good sir?" Carlos bellowed from boat.

Eagle Claw and the Ute men instantly crowded to the side of the ship, tranquilizer darts ready to be fired toward the Falcon. The man held Malia in front of him as a shield.

"What are you doing?" the large, muscular Eagle Claw yelled out. "Release her!"

"It's him!" Huber yelled. "It's Salazar!"

Everyone on the boat stared at the man, unblinking and unbelieving.

"Juan Hernán? *¿Mi sobrino?*" Carlos said, confused. "But how?"

With his free hand, the Falcon removed his hood and tore away his masquerade, revealing his lined, scarred face. "With difficulty," he breathed.

"We watched you die," Huber said in shock.

"Salamander . . ." Scott mouthed. "No way."

They all looked as if they were seeing a ghost.

Using his free hand, Salazar stuck his hand into his pocket and retrieved something. It was a small gold coin, almost identical to Huber's. Only it was dented inward at the center. "This coin," he said, "is what saved me. I had placed it within my shirt pocket that afternoon in the mountains. The bullet struck me just where the coin protected. Fate saved my life. These men," he said, "drug me deep within *Tesoro de los Muertos* believing me dead and sealed me up inside. I nearly starved . . . wasting away to nothing . . . living in the dark while feasting on insects and mice. Then I heard it—the bell chimed. I counted to thirteen. Shortly afterward, I was blinded by light and then I saw *him* . . ."

"Who?" Carlos said.

"*El Rey Fausto.*"

"Fausto?" Huber repeated.

Salazar nodded. "*Sí . . . el rey de la cofradía* himself. Your supposed teacher! You see, years ago, I joined the Brotherhood, starting as a lowly foot soldier and working my way up to *capitán*. There was even talk at one time of me being made *comandante*—just below the rank of the Kings. However, that role was given to another. When I was denied my rightful place, I forsook the Brotherhood and was branded an outcast. I wandered for many years. However, there was one thing I knew which the Brotherhood did not—that there existed a map drawn by Pedro Salazar himself, leading to *Tesoro de los Muertos*. Of course, the Brotherhood had heard rumors of *Tesoro de los Muertos* and Coronado's men breaking away. They'd searched for many years, but none of them knew what I did. At last, desperation drove me to my uncle and I found out the location of the map."

"And then you tried to kill him! Murderer!" Jessie yelled out.

"Juan Hernán," Carlos said softly and shook his head. "It cannot be."

"*Sí,*" Salazar whispered and dropped his head for a moment. He continued on. "The treasure was to be shared only between myself and my long lost brother, Antonio.

However, one does not simply quit the Brotherhood. Unbeknownst to me, when I arrived to Colorado, the Brotherhood was already there. The day I was released from the mine was the first time I'd actually seen King Fausto in person. At first, I thought he'd come to rescue me and I was overjoyed to see him. In reality, he'd come to punish me and take the treasure for himself. Fausto and his men drug me from the mine and removed the Dead Man's Treasure. The small band of Ute men guarding the mine that day were no match for their numbers. Fausto brought me back here . . . tortured me for my treason and left me to rot in that awful dungeon for months. However, he allowed me to keep this coin which saved my life, so I could stare upon it, wishing that it had not."

"It's no less than you deserve," Huber said, glaring. "All of this is your fault."

Salazar nodded. *"Así es, jóven* . . . I suppose you are right."

Huber's chest began to rise. "You killed my grandpa!"

Salazar didn't stir, but he averted his gaze. "We all have regrets."

"What?" Hannah said beside herself. "What are you talking about, Huber?"

"He killed Grandpa Nick when he didn't give up the map!"

"You never . . ."

"I know. I didn't see the need to tell anyone."

Hannah was in shock, her eyes brimming with tears.

Huber continued to look upon the face that had haunted his dreams for so long, unable to believe his eyes.

Salazar continued, "While imprisoned, I heard the voice of a young girl in the cell next to mine. Her name was Malia. She told me where she'd come from. I was able to find out why the Brotherhood had taken her after piecing together conversations I'd overheard from the guards and Kings. *The Golden City . . . Cíbola . . . Dorado . . . the tablet . . . and the Golden Staff.* There would be no stopping them. One day, I was to be brought before the Three Kings for yet another inquisition."

Huber's feet were still sore from his own inquisition.

"But . . . they made the mistake of only having Susurro escort me back to my cell. I took him out and slipped away undetected through the secret entrance I'd learned of as *cápitan*. Since that day, as the Falcon, I have been trying to destroy the Brotherhood."

"And find the Golden Staff for yourself!" Hannah screeched. "You've been using us all along."

"You've been watching us since we arrived in the city, haven't you?" Huber asked. "I've seen you."

Salazar grinned ever so slightly. "When one is faced with death, starvation, and torture, he comes to think upon his life, *jóven* . . . upon his deeds . . . and what awaits him afterward. I know what awaits me. I promised myself that should I survive the Brotherhood's tortures and escape, I would devote my life to seeking revenge upon all those who wronged me and gather in all the riches I can. I'm the one who brought these men here to reclaim the Dead Man's Treasure! I engineered your capture and escape. You should be thanking me!"

"You used us as a diversion!"

"Perhaps. But you and the Ute have obtained what you sought, haven't you? Consider it a parting gift. We are now square. You all can go your way, I'll go mine."

"Let Malia go!"

"Imagine, *jóven!*" Salazar said, almost in trance. "A staff which will turn anything it touches into gold. Imagine living life to its fullest—as the most powerful and wealthy man in the world. *I will fill my cup!*"

"Juan Hernán," Carlos said softly from the ship. "There is no happiness in revenge and riches. It is not too late for you to change your ways . . . perhaps even help us."

"Yeah it is," Scott said. "Once a snake, always a snake."

Carlos ignored the comment. "I am sorry, Juan Hernán, whatever failings you have, you possess because of me. Do not punish the girl or anyone else for my shortcomings. Release the girl. Seek penance and forgiveness."

"I do not ask your forgiveness for what I've done," Salazar spat.

"You . . . killed . . . my . . . grandpa," Huber repeated slowly and deliberately.

For a split second, Salazar's face seemed contrite but instantly resumed its menacing gaze. "I cannot change what I have done, Yoober. Had your grandfather cooperated, he would not have suffered the fate he did. He chose his fate."

"Coward!" Hannah yelled and went to jump from the boat, but the men on the ship constrained her.

"Take *Tesoro de los Muertos*," Salazar went on. "Return it to the mountains. I no longer have any use for it. However, I *will* be taking Malia and the tablet with me."

As he finished his sentence, a speedboat pulled up alongside him on the other side of the dock. The man driving the boat had long hair, knotted in dreadlocks. He idled the speedboat to a purr. Huber instantly recognized the man he'd sat next to on the plane to Salamanca and encountered within La Cueva de Salamanca. It was Willow.

"Hey, dude," Willow said to Salazar. "I brought the boat like you said!" He noticed Huber on the other side of the pier.

"Willow?" Huber said unbelievingly.

"Hey, Huber! How's it going man? I hope you didn't forget the wisdom I shared with you." He laughed. "Sorry for the deception. This guy paid me a king's ransom to spy on you from the time you left the states. What can I say? I needed the cash."

Huber tried to control his anger, watching helplessly as Salazar stepped backward and dragged Malia with him into the waiting speedboat. Salazar called out as the boat slowly backed away into the water. "I advise you all to return home and all scores will be settled. Do not pursue me. Do not seek Cíbola. Should you get in my way, I will not hesitate to do what I must. You have the Dead Man's Treasure. Take it. Go home." Salazar then looked directly at Huber. "We are square," he said, then motioned for Willow to take off. The boat sped away through the water like a bullet with Malia inside. Huber couldn't stomach the thought that she'd escaped the Brotherhood just to be taken by Salazar.

Seething with rage, Huber and the others skulked along the sailboat, debating what to do. For several moments, no one said anything.

Pincho sauntered forward. "I cannot believe Juan Hernán is alive."

Carlos said nothing, appearing lost in his own thoughts.

Huber kicked a bucket, then plopped himself against the railing and slid to a sitting position, still attempting to process all that had happened.

"What do we do now?" Scott asked, turning to his friend. "Maybe we should just go home, dude. I mean, we did what we set out to do. If we go after that golden staff thingy, we're gonna half 'ta deal with the Brotherhood *and* Salazar both. Let 'em duke it out on their own. This ain't our fight."

Hannah also appeared dejected. "Maybe he's right, Huber. The Zuni probably don't need our help. I'm sure they'll rescue Malia. We barely escaped this place with our lives. That whole thing about the golden staff is probably just an old folktale anyway."

Huber stood and looked at them intently, "Say it's not a story. What if the golden staff actually exists? Think about what will happen if the Brotherhood or Salazar finds it!"

"How do *we* stop them?" Alejandro asked. "He has Malia and the tablet."

"We know they're headed for New Mexico. We'll find Malia's family and their tribe. Maybe they can help us. We can't just let them win!"

Carlos seemed to stir. He arose from his sitting position and out of his stupor. His eyes glazed over. "Yes, the boy is right! A true knight will never give up. Not while he has breath within him. He'll run where the brave dare not go! Fight against unbeatable odds! Raise the anchor! Unfurl the sails! Set course for the new world. The Grand Enchanter's goals will come to naught! The serpent's head will be crushed and evil shall be vanquished! The captives shall go free and our fair maiden will be rescued from the infidels!" The old man stomped around the ship, commanding its crew as if he were captain. Eagle Claw and the Ute men seemed to regard him with passing curiosity if not with a little annoyance.

Huber turned to Yesenia. "Think he'll be like this the whole trip?"

She nodded. "It's going to be a long couple of weeks."

Eagle Claw approached Huber and Hannah. "I

thank you for your efforts in reclaiming the Dead Man's Treasure." He glanced at the three hefty chests sitting on deck. "They will be returned to where they belong. However, it appears we must be more careful who we trust," he said, obviously referring to the Falcon. "We will help you and your friends in your quest. I will do all I can to help the Ute and Zuni form an alliance to defeat this evil."

Huber nodded his thanks and thought back to his earlier conversation with Grandpa Nick while imprisoned. "We'll do all we can to honor your father's sacrifice."

Eagle Claw gripped Huber's shoulder but didn't say anything. He then walked away, issuing commands to the crew members, only to be parroted by Carlos.

Somebody tapped Huber on the shoulder as the boat began to drift from the dock. It was Hannah. Her earlier exuberance seemed to be tempered. "Mom and Dad are going to expect us back. We can't just go off looking for Cíbola without telling them. I'm sure they're already worried sick that we haven't called them."

Huber hadn't thought about this. In all the turmoil and excitement, he'd almost forgotten all about home. "I don't know. We'll have to think of something."

At the conclusion of his statement, Hannah and Huber heard Jessie calling their names frantically. "Huber! Hannah!" She ran toward them, looking worried.

"What is it?" Huber asked.

Jessie's eyes widened as she handed him her cell

phone. Huber brought his free hand to his mouth. His face turned white as a sheet.

"What?" Hannah said.

Huber let the phone fall out of his hand and into his sister's. A picture message had been sent from a blocked number.

"It's from the Brotherhood." Jessie panted and covered her mouth with her hands.

Displayed on the screen was a picture of Huber and Hannah's parents, Robert and Ellen, next to Scott's father, Brad. They were each blindfolded and bound to chairs. The text read *Tal es el destino de todos que impiden la Cofradía.*

The twins and Scott looked upon each other anxiously as Jessie translated the words. "Such is the fate of all who cross the Brotherhood."

La aventura concluye con
HUBER HILL
&
THE GOLDEN STAFF OF CÍBOLA

Fall 2013

Acknowledgments

I **NEVER THOUGHT** I'D write more than one book. Here I am finishing up my second and working on the third. It wouldn't be happening if there weren't readers like you who actually enjoy what I write. Thank you from the bottom of my heart. You've allowed me to realize a dream and passion. I hope you continue to enjoy my stories in the future. I love hearing from you on social media or during book signings. Those interactions are the fuel that keeps me going.

MANY THANKS TO JULIEANN, my wife, who is my best friend and chief collaborator on all my projects. It's so nice to have someone who loves you whether you succeed or fall flat on your face. My son, Daniel, who is smashing the keys as I type. I hope you enjoy these books one day when you're older. Mahalo, Leinani, for your matchless gift. Thank you, Cindra (my mom), who always believes in me. To Jack, my big brother Kirk, Michiel, Madison,

Mallorie, Granny HaHa, as well as Jeanette, Ray, Bob, Cindy, and Justin—thank you! I'm also thankful to Dean Nielsen, who brainstorms with me and comes up with incredible concept art. Without family and friends, I'd be nothing.

I'M ALSO GRATEFUL FOR the inspiration and support from two outstanding authors, Obert Skye and Frank L. Cole.

THANK YOU, CEDAR FORT, for believing in me and the Huber Hill series. Angie Workman, Josh Johnson, Melissa Caldwell, Bryce and Lyle Mortimer—all amazing. Mark McKenna, who did a wonderful job on the cover just like the award winning first! I'm excited to see what you come up with for the third.

LAST, I SHOULD THANK Gordon B. Hinckley for his quote I read each time I get discouraged: "Cynics do not contribute, skeptics do not create, doubters do not achieve."

Discussion Questions

1. Have you ever wanted to travel abroad to study? If so, where would you want to go and why?

2. When Scott encounters a new culture, he feels out of place and offends his hosts. Why are new things sometimes uncomfortable to people? Why is it important to respect the culture and values of others even when they're different from our own?

3. During the bullfight at La Glorieta Stadium, Alejandro argues that bullfighting is a proud cultural tradition, while Yesenia sees it as cruelty to animals. What do you think? Why do people cling to cultural traditions?

4. At the University of Salamanca, Hannah is elated to stay the night in a centuries old library. If you could spend the night in any building outside your house, where would it be? Why?

5. Inside the Brotherhood's castle, Huber feels alone and that he's up against unbeatable odds. What kinds of difficult situations have you faced before? How did you get through them?

6. Toward the end of the novel, Fausto underestimates Don Carlos. Have you ever made wrongful assumptions about someone due to their age, appearance, or background?

About the Author

B.K. BOSTICK RESIDES AMONG the magnificent Rocky Mountains. In addition to writing, he has spent his career in education. He earned his bachelor's degree in psychology from the University of Utah and his masters in psychology from Utah State University. He has worked as a teacher, after school program coordinator, teacher mentor, and currently loves working for the Open High School of Utah. In his spare time, he enjoys eating Cheetos and watching old episodes of the *Twilight Zone*.

SALAMANCA
España

PLAZA DE LOS TOROS
LA GLORIETA

UNIVERSIDAD
DE SALAMANCA

RÍO TORMES